PLAYING *for* KEEPS

PLAYING *for* KEEPS

A NOVEL

RANEE` S. CLARK

Covenant Communications, Inc.

Cover image: *Football Background* © Andrew Rich, iStockphotography.com

Published by Covenant Communications, Inc.
American Fork, Utah

This is a work of fiction. The characters, names, incidents, places, and dialogue are either products of the author's imagination, and are not to be construed as real, or are used fictitiously.

Printed in the United States of America
First Printing: June 2015

21 20 19 18 17 16 15 10 9 8 7 6 5 4 3 2 1

ISBN-13: 978-1-62108-850-9

To my grandma Eva Savage, who always knew
something like this would happen.

Acknowledgments

First, to the guy who deserves to have his name on the front of the book next to mine: my brother, DJ Savage. He answered a million texts, had more than his fair share of brainstorming conversations, and helped me make Anthony into the most believable football player a romance novel could have. He and his friends on CougarBoard came up with so many great nicknames for Anthony, I had to use them all.

To my people, the writers who make me shine: my critique partner and writer BFF, Kaylee Baldwin. She stretches me, and I love her for it. Gina Denny, who didn't have her hands in this particular manuscript but whose voice is in my head anyway. Donna Weaver, Pauline Hansen, and Jillian Torassa, who all read for me, and my girls in the ANWA PM Writers chapter—you ladies are awesome.

To my siblings and cousins, who all offered up their names for this book: DJ, Jordan, Sean, Mat, Keesha, and Savanna (Rose) Savage; Nikki Savage Sanford; and Brian, David, and Eric Allred. Thank you, guys!

To the fantastic team at Covenant, especially my editor, Stacey. Here's to a bunch more!

To my amazing parents, Doug and Robyn Savage. Your support and excitement means the world to me. Love you!

To my boys, who still think it's awesome that their mom writes books—even if they are romance and don't have enough adventure.

Most of all, to my husband, Adam. You are my biggest cheerleader and my best support. Thank you for watching the boys and cooking dinners and buying me laptops, for being positive that my books are so good they'll make us millions. I would have never been able to write a guy like Anthony if there hadn't been a guy like you. You're the best.

Chapter One

THE FOOTBALL SAILED GRACEFULLY THROUGH the air, a perfect spiral if TyAnne Daws ever saw one. She grinned when it landed in her younger brother's outstretched arms. Walsh barely had to try. As long as he made it past his defender, a catch like that would equal a touchdown. She pushed a sweaty strand of brown hair behind her ear.

When he turned toward her, he smiled ruefully. "Nice pass, Ty."

"What's the face for?" She quirked an eyebrow, holding out her hand for the seventeen-year-old to toss the ball back.

"Like Kent is ever going to throw something as perfect as that. Practicing with you is hardly practice anymore. It's like dreaming." He jogged back to their makeshift line of scrimmage and pitched the ball to her.

"Well, I've thrown at you enough times; I should be this good by now."

"Try throwing some bad ones. Make me work." He lined up next to her again.

Sighing and shaking her head at his instructions, Ty rolled the football around in her hands. Since she lived only a few minutes from her parents' home in Orem, she could come and play football with Walsh whenever she wanted. She anticipated needing the stress release several times in the coming semester.

"Okay, what do you want to run this time?" she asked.

"Throw a long, out route, but this time not so easy to catch."

She counted off and drew her arm back, ready to throw. Walsh sprinted toward the fence on the other side of the yard before he cut outside. She made sure to toss it wide, forcing him to stretch for the ball. He landed on his stomach in the grass, but he caught it.

"I know you can throw better than that."

Ty turned to see her dad stepping onto the porch behind her. "Walsh told me to throw it badly." She rested against the rails of the porch while she waited for her brother to jog back.

"Wasted talent. You should have gone out for football."

Ty laughed. "Right, Dad." She held out her hand again for the ball Walsh tossed her. "What next?"

"A slant."

Dad waited for her to throw again before he said, "Your mom mentioned you added a football coaching class to your schedule."

Ty blushed and stared at Walsh instead of looking Dad in the eye. "Yeah. I thought it would be fun to learn some things. Not that I'm ever going to coach football for real but, you know, to beef up on what's going on."

"And meet Rocket Rogers?"

Ty winced when Walsh's throw jabbed her in the shoulder. The mention of the popular BYU quarterback distracted her, and now she had to chase the missed football across the grass. Oh, well. It gave her a minute to recover her composure, not that she could hide her obsession with Rocket from her dad. Or from anyone.

"Dad . . ." She took a deep breath but couldn't put into words what meeting Rocket would mean to her. She'd waited for so long.

He chuckled. "You're not fooling anyone, Ty. Only a few people know football better than you, and Rocket is one of them."

"Another slant," Walsh instructed.

She waited again and tossed it, this time short. Turning to her dad, she let her lips relax into a smile, giddy she'd landed a spot in Rocket's class. Come Friday, she would get to finally see him face-to-face.

"Well, it seemed like a good chance to meet him." He and Ty were both now seniors at BYU, and she didn't have much time left to meet him.

"Mind if I come?" Dad headed over to the grill and flipped the lid up.

Ty moved onto the porch to watch him. "Funny."

"Ty, head's up!" Walsh said.

She looked up in time to catch his pass. Without waiting for him to reset, she threw the ball long and high.

"Got a game plan for winning him over?" Dad asked.

"Dad!" She watched Walsh sprint and then dive, catching her pass on his fingertips before it rolled into his hands. She turned back to her dad.

He gave her a mock exasperated expression. "What? This is my one shot at having Rocket Rogers for a son-in-law. I don't want you to blow it."

"Thanks for the vote of confidence." She stepped back as the heat *whooshed* out of the grill.

"A few, well-chosen words and he'll fall for you like a rock."

"You know we're talking about the most popular guy on campus, if not the most popular football player in the nation right now."

"And?" One by one, Dad plopped down the hamburger patties, which hit the blackened grill with a sizzle.

Ty took a deep breath, relishing the mingled scent of charcoal and seasonings. "It's not going to be easy to get his attention. The guy who helped me get into the class said a bunch of girls are taking it this semester, not to mention all his other 'friends.'"

Dad shut the grill and rested his arm on top of Ty's head, a habit of his since Ty didn't even reach his shoulder. "Let me give you a piece of advice, Ty."

Ty bit her bottom lip to hold back a smile. "And what would that be, oh, master of dating?" She looked out over the lawn. Walsh hadn't gotten up from his last catch. He was lying in the grass on his back, tossing the football into the air.

"Rocket is a superb football player. He can probably smell fear a mile away." Dad pointed at her with his spatula. "Think about that."

She slipped her arm around his waist, heading inside with him to get more food. "Sure thing, Coach."

"That's my girl."

A brown-haired boy stepped outside, raising his hand for a high-five from Ty. "Yes! Ty's here."

"Hello, Kent." Ignoring his outstretched arm, she shook her head at Walsh's best friend.

"You free Friday night?" He leaned toward her.

Kent's attempts to date her were not new. Her love of football—and resulting football IQ—impressed most of Walsh's high school football team. "Well . . . um . . ."

Walsh vaulted the rail of the porch and landed next to the grill. "Dude." He scowled at Kent. "Gross. How many times are you going to ask her out before you get it? She's way too old for you."

"She's the awesomest girl I know. Someday she'll say yes." Kent darted around Walsh's attempt to tackle him. Average passing aside, Kent was a pretty good quarterback.

Walsh turned to Ty, who watched from the sliding glass door. "You've got to learn to tell people no, Ty. You can't go out with every guy that asks you because you're spineless."

She folded her arms and sighed. "I'm too old and set in my ways for you to change me now."

Walsh snorted with laughter and waltzed toward her. "Well, someday you're going to be the most overworked Relief Society president in the Church, and I won't be around to save you."

"Point taken." She reached up and tried to put him in a headlock, but since her brother had outgrown her by the time he was ten, it was a lost cause. He obligingly lowered his head to her level, but she shoved him away.

"What about after my mission?" Kent asked.

"I'm going to be married to Rocket by then." Laughing, she opened the door and headed inside.

"That would be awesome . . ." she heard Kent say before she closed the sliding door.

Yes, it would be. Anthony "Rocket" Rogers was the perfect package—good looks, exceptional talent, hard worker, smart, and like a brother to his teammates. Well, that's what the newspaper articles always said about him. Now that she had a chance to get to know him better, she meant to see for herself. She didn't think he would disappoint.

"What can I do to help?" she asked when her mom came into the kitchen.

Mom gestured toward the counter. "Help me haul all this out to the picnic table?"

"Sure." Ty gathered a few things and waited for Mom to fill her arms before following her out of the kitchen.

"Harly said you came to his class today. How was your first time volunteering with them?"

Ty grinned. Volunteering in his class would be the highlight of her week—well, next to seeing Rocket three times a week. "Perfect. They're all so adorable. Compared to my interning over at Provo High School, it was heaven."

Mom arched an eyebrow. "You prefer rowdy five-year-olds to imparting your love of history to high schoolers?"

"It's not the kids in the history class I'm struggling with; it's the teacher." Ty piled the food she had into one arm and opened the door. "She doesn't want to hear any of my ideas. I think she wants me around to do her grunt work."

Mom laughed. "Keep your chin up. It's still the first part of the year. Maybe the more she gets to know you, the more open she'll be to letting you give your input."

"I hope so."

After a great dinner at her parents' house, Ty thought she might have to roll herself out to her car. Dad made a mean burger, always cooking it just right, and she ate what seemed like a small mountain of Mom's famous potato salad.

"Stay and play more football with us," Kent begged, hopping up from the table despite having eaten enough food to fill a small elephant. "We'll call some of the other guys to come over."

"Even if I thought I could do more than shuffle after that meal, no. I have homework."

Probably hoping to butter her up, Walsh scooped up her paper plate and dropped it in the garbage with his. "Your classes just started Tuesday. You can't have homework already. We'll give you some time for your food to settle, then we're playing."

Ty shook her head. "I have a lot of credits this semester. If I get behind now, I'm toast."

"Ty. Homework or football. Is that really a choice?" Walsh planted his hands in front of her and leaned toward her.

"I think I'm going to take your advice and stand firm, Walsh. No." Smiling, Ty fled the table for her car. She moved a lot faster than she thought she could. "Bye!" she called over her shoulder to her laughing family and a disappointed Kent.

Cars crowded University Parkway and University Avenue on Ty's way back to her apartment. Her normal ten-minute drive lasted double that. She tried to distract herself by thinking about the book on the Civil Rights era she should start reading. She considered what she might write her big paper on for her historical-teaching methods class. Still, her mind kept finding a way back to coaching football and the realization she would meet her hero on Wednesday. After watching him from afar, it still seemed surreal.

By the time she got home, she had given up on trying to get Rocket out of her mind. She climbed the three flights of stairs to the small apartment on the top floor of her building at the corner of 400 North and 400 East. With a perfunctory wave to her two other roommates, both camped on the couch for an episode of *Grey's Anatomy*, she crossed the living room and headed down the short hallway to her room. After dropping her backpack near the door, she settled on her bed with her laptop.

She'd already given up any hope of doing what she should, planning for how to cram in all the homework she'd have with eighteen credits. Now that she was taking coaching football, her schedule could get tight. And what if . . . what if she managed to date Rocket? She tried to keep from smiling, but she couldn't. Yeah, then her homework schedule would definitely get tight.

Ty was one of *those* girls. The ones that followed Rocket Rogers religiously. The ones that waved *Marry Me Rocket Rogers* signs at all the football games. She watched BYU play every week, either from the stadium or parked in front of her parents' TV in Orem. She might have been different from some girls because she understood what Rocket did on the field but, considering she shoved three extra credits into her already full history education schedule to meet him, probably not.

Before she fell too deep into dreamland, she opened a web browser and pulled up YouTube, opening her subscribed list. Rocket's channel popped up at the top. She clicked on it and scrolled to some of the older videos, the ones from his high school years.

Almost without thought, she chose a video from his senior year, when his team won the state championship. They clinched it in the first quarter (no one came within twenty points of them that year), but there was a spectacular play right before the half that Ty loved to watch.

The offensive line worked hard to keep the defense away, but when Rocket couldn't find an open receiver after several seconds, the line crumbled and three defenders got through. They almost had him down, but he rolled sideways over the back of one defender and landed on his feet, running twenty-five yards for a touchdown. Grinning to herself, she resisted the urge to watch several more videos and reached instead for her books, determined to accomplish *something* productive that night. But instead of going over her historical-teaching methods homework, she picked up the coaching football syllabus she got from the teaching assistant the day before. *Complete a game plan, 5–7 pages.*

Ty's mind didn't start churning out football possibilities. It turned to something Dad said earlier. *Got a game plan for winning Rocket over?*

A game plan.

Without thinking—since she'd stop herself if she did—Ty flipped open the coaching football textbook and searched for a section on game plans.

A successful game plan includes three elements:

* An analysis of the team's strengths and weaknesses.
* Offensive and defensive plays the team executes well, including plays that display the team's talent and versatility.
* An analysis of the opposing team's offense and defense, including weaknesses and strengths.

She read the example before opening a blank document and filling it with ideas. She was laughing to herself when her roommate's voice interrupted.

"Hey, Ty?"

Ty pulled her screen down, biting her lip as she turned toward Rosie. "Um, yeah?"

One of her perfectly plucked eyebrows slid up at Ty's reaction. She wished she could freeze Rosie's cynical-yet-fabulous expression for herself. Rocket dated girls like her all the time. In fact, Rosie liked to brag about the fact she'd gone on two dates with Rocket the year before.

"Kevin and Cameron are here. You know, our home teachers," Rosie said. She dropped her voice. "Our very hot home teachers."

"I didn't know they were coming." Ty scooted off the bed to follow Rosie.

"They brought back-to-school cookies that look awful," Rosie whispered. "Looks like we might need to have them over to teach them how to cook. Or just to feed them."

Her effortless ability to find a way to invite hot guys to their apartment gave Ty an idea. *Game Plan Key: Weakness—Looking and flirting like the girls Rocket normally dates.*

"Rosie?" Ty reached out, snagged her roommate's arm, and pulled her back into the room. "Will you do me a favor?"

"Like what?"

"So . . . I got into one of Rocket's classes." She didn't mention which. It still embarrassed her that she'd signed up for coaching football.

Rosie's jaw dropped. "You're joking! How lucky is that?"

"Not exactly lucky." Ty smiled conspiratorially, though she knew it would never captivate the way Rosie's did. "I know a guy in the class, and he said there were empty seats on Wednesday. So I added it to my schedule."

"I never knew you had something like that in you." Rosie smirked, nodding with appreciation.

"Anyway, I could use your help getting his attention. He likes girls like you." Ty motioned to her own outfit. Jeans and a BYU football T-shirt. Of course, she had gone over to her parents' house to play catch with Walsh, but still, her wardrobe didn't get much more complicated.

A contemplative smile spread across Rosie's face. "Of course. Using my tricks would be like vindication that he didn't call me after that last date. You know, like proving to him I've got what it takes to get his attention." Her bottom lip slipped out in a pout, but she reeled it in. "Yeah. It'll be fun."

Seeing the wheels turning so quickly in Rosie's mind worried Ty. She offered her own smile and headed out to the living room. What had she gotten herself into?

The two guys, both already making themselves comfortable, looked up when Ty and Rosie came in.

"Hey, Ty." Cameron held out the plate of cookies. Ty thought they might be chocolate chip. The lumpy, overdone circles on the plate made it hard to tell.

"Hey, Cameron." She waved away the cookies. Since Ty had two beautiful roommates who knew how to flirt, their home teachers had gone above and beyond all summer, dropping by all the time and scheduling multiple appointments a month, even when the girls reminded them they'd already given the lesson.

"You sure?" He leaned toward her over the arm of the couch he sat on next to Kayla.

"I just got back from my parents' house for dinner. My stomach can't hold any more."

He nodded and pulled the plate back, handing the cookies to Kayla. Pressing her lips together, Kayla hopped up and took them to the kitchen.

The other home teacher, Kevin, shifted forward in the recliner he sat in. "So, what do you think of BYU's defense? We're going to be tough to beat, right?"

Though Rosie kept her face neutral, she crossed her arms. "No. Absolutely not, Kevin. No football talk. Ty's the only one that can follow."

"Ah, come on, Rosie." Cameron reached his arm across the couch and tugged Rosie closer into a one-armed hug she didn't oppose.

Rosie giggled, mollified by his cozy position with her. "Nope. Gospel topics only."

"Gospel topics only?" He lowered his head in feigned disappointment.

"Maybe after the lesson we can discuss . . . other things." Rosie snuggled under his arm. If Ty had thought to bring her laptop out, she would have taken notes. Rosie was gold.

He rubbed his hands together, still keeping his arm around Rosie. "Then we should get right to it."

Any other time Ty would have felt left behind as Rosie and Kayla flirted their way through a lesson with no mention of football, or any other sport for that matter. Tonight she soaked up every move they made—the way Rosie leaned into Cameron, how Kayla faced Kevin the entire lesson, the sheer volume of enthusiastic nods, appreciative sighs, and compliments.

When the guys left with invitations for dinner the next night, both Kayla and Rosie stood at the door while Kevin and Cameron descended the steps and waved before getting into Kevin's car. Once the car disappeared down the street, Rosie shut the door and turned to Ty.

"And *that* is how it's done."

* * *

Anthony Rogers resisted the urge to drop his head onto his desk and laugh. There were even more girls in his coaching football class today than the first day. How many girls were going to coach football? Brian, the teaching assistant and Anthony's mentor, had told him maybe one or two took the class each semester. There were at least eight, all of whom had tried to engage him in conversation about football and proving their interest in this class boiled down to one thing: him. And now another one—a shockingly short girl with deep brown hair—stood in the doorway. She scanned the room with innocent-looking, pale blue eyes. Her gaze stopped on Anthony and the empty seat in front of him. He'd been resting his long legs on the chair, pretty much preventing anyone but the boldest from taking it.

The girl hadn't been there on Wednesday. He would've remembered her. She was cute. She didn't look high-maintenance like some of the other girls. Like the one wearing a draped pink shirt, high-heels, and dark skinny jeans. She'd moved to the seat next to him mere seconds after he walked in, and he thought she might have put the tip of her heel through the shoe of another girl to do it.

But the girl in the doorway? Kudos to her jeans and BYU T-shirt. He couldn't help but wonder if it was one of those shirts they'd passed out at the last game that had his number on the back.

He smiled and pulled his legs off the chair, all but inviting her to take the seat. (Just to see the back of her shirt, of course.) An adorable scarlet color swept up her cheeks before she darted in his direction. She dropped into the chair, sitting sideways, but not looking at him either. Anthony waited. She'd turn. They all did. In fact, all the girls in the room were looking at him right now. Either that or glaring at the girl sitting in front of him.

She didn't disappoint. "Hi."

"Hey, I'm Rocket."

Her eyes widened, and for the first time, Anthony felt stupid for his normally successful pick-up line. Why was that? Girls ate that line up.

Then she smiled again; the bewildered expression disappeared. "I'm Ty—Anne," she added the last as an afterthought. "Um, but Ty to most people."

"Ty? That's kind of a boy's name, isn't it?"

"Well, if you knew my dad, it would make sense." She pulled out a notebook and opened it.

"Wanted a boy?"

She laughed. "Yeah. That and . . . a football player."

Anthony grinned. All the girls said that—well, not that their dad wanted them to be a football player—but they made a football connection somehow, like that was all it took to get his attention. It surprised many he liked to talk about other things. Chances were this girl was no different.

She sucked in a deep breath and plastered a smile on her face. "He named me after Ty Detmer."

He'd never heard *that* before. "You're joking."

"Nope. Not joking."

"That is—awesome."

She beamed. "Thanks."

He liked her style. The other guys would too. She was definitely worth the few minutes it would take to get to know her. "So a bunch of people are coming to my house tonight. Want to come?"

She mumbled something that sounded like, "That was easy."
"What?"
She blinked and then grinned. "I'd love to."

Chapter Two

"THAT'S THE BEST YOU'VE GOT?" Rosie ran a hand across her forehead.

"What's wrong with this outfit? It's the fourth one you've rejected."

Rosie sighed, sounding long-suffering. Ty resisted rolling her eyes. Perhaps recruiting her knowledgeable roommate to help her get Rocket's attention was a bad idea. Rosie was taking this "mission" too seriously. But Ty needed her. She knew things necessary for survival in this blitz on Rocket's heart. *Game Plan Key: Show versatility.*

"Apparently you don't know the type of girls you'll be up against tonight," Rosie said in a tone too serious for the subject of clothes and a party.

Girls like you, Ty thought, running her gaze over Rosie's outfit. Skinny jeans, fancy shirt, frilly flats, a scarf—and she planned on staying home tonight. Ty thought about the other girls in the class earlier that day—all of them dressed up for Rocket, and she was in a plain Jane T-shirt and jeans. And tennis shoes, of all things.

"Pretty ones." Ty tried to keep the sarcasm from her voice. At least most of it.

Rosie barked out a harsh laugh. "Yeah. Gorgeous ones."

Ty needed to take a stand. "I'm sticking with this. I don't want to look like I'm trying too hard. Outfits like the ones those girls wear will look stupid on me anyway." Besides, her sunny yellow Bermuda shorts made her happy. Paired with a white T-shirt and a pale blue cardigan, she thought she looked pretty chic. Right down to the T-strap sandals Rosie had insisted she wear.

Rosie tossed a skirt onto the bed. "Fine." She sat in the chair by Ty's desk. "Remember the safe topics?"

"Anything football." Ty ticked the first off her finger.

"Yes. Amazingly, you're safe there. Compliment him, either his playing or his looks or whatever. He's that type of guy."

Ty folded her arms. Rosie had been on two dates with Rocket, but Ty knew way more about him than Rosie did. Considering the number of football games Ty had seen him play, she should. And all that stalking on Facebook? Every article written about him in every newspaper ever? She couldn't count the number of times she'd fallen for him all over again because of pictures he posted with kids at BYU football camps, face-splitting grins on their faces. It had to add up to something. *Game Plan Key: Study game film of the opposing team. Check.*

"He's not that shallow." Sure, it was a possibility that things like the photo ops at the camps were all for show—ways to make him into a golden boy—but she didn't think so. Kids didn't grin like that just because an adult told them to. Ty was betting it all that Rocket was more than the hot jock Rosie wanted to make him out to be.

"You talked to him for five minutes in class," Rosie pointed out. One corner of Rosie's lips tilted up in a smirk Ty knew could turn a few heads.

Yeah, this would be easier if she could pull off expressions like that. She wanted to run into the bathroom and try it out. Not that she wanted to *be* like Rosie—for now she needed to seem like Rocket's type: confident, gorgeous, flirty, charming. Once she had his attention, she'd give him the one-two with her real personality. The football knowledge would blow him away. She was perfect for him.

Ty decided not to argue with Rosie. She wouldn't understand how you could tell a lot by the things a guy did on the football field. Like how smart he must be to see every hole or execute plays so well. How hard he must work to throw such beautiful passes. How a guy as good as him had every right to walk around like he owned the field, but then didn't. How he ended every play with a pat on the shoulder, a high-five, or a grin for somebody.

"Don't hover over him," Rosie went on.

"Obviously."

"There should be plenty of other football players there to flirt with," Rosie said. She hadn't seemed to hear the sarcasm dripping from Ty's voice. "They'll love that you sound like you know what you're talking about with them."

"I do know what I'm talking about." Ty stood. If she didn't get out of this apartment soon, she might decide to stay home. She should have expected Rosie's take-charge approach might come with more "take charge" than Ty bargained for. "I'll see you later."

A gleam lit Rosie's eyes. "I want a full report."

"Done." Ty waved over her shoulder and headed out the door. She decided to walk the few blocks between her apartment and Rocket's. Behind 400 North, houses became more prevalent than apartment buildings. She slipped out the paper he'd written his address on. He probably rented one of the nearby houses with some of his teammates.

She shoved the paper back in and grinned. She had thought actual hang-out time with him, outside of class, would take a few weeks. Now she was about to enter his house after "knowing" him one day.

"I'm going to marry Anthony Rogers," she said to herself and quickened her step. Rosie wouldn't approve of her rushing to get to the party—"Nobody shows up to a party like that on time."—but who cared? She was going to a party at *Rocket Roger's house*. "Anthony," she corrected herself. If she wanted to come off as different from the other star-struck fans, she should start with addressing him by his real name, prove she knew he was a person and not just some nameless uniform that could throw a great pass.

As she suspected, the address turned out to be a house. On the doorstep, she paused to smooth her shorts and shirt and adjust her cardigan. This was it. All those years of watching him and waiting for the chance to meet him came down to this. The next step. Becoming his friend. Then—his girlfriend. *I can do this.* She knocked.

The door opened. "Hey." The guy who answered swung the door open wide and grinned. His short, dark hair curled around the nape of his neck and ears. Behind him she caught sight of a small living room crammed with people.

But she forgot all about them as soon as she recognized the guy who answered. "David Savage? Number twenty-one?" she asked, feeling a bit dizzy. Rocket's favorite receiver. "I've wanted to tell you, nice catch in the bowl game last year. You know the one . . . ?" She tilted over an imaginary out-of-bounds line, snagged an imaginary ball, and hugged it close to her chest keeping one foot in the air.

His face lit up as he ushered her inside. He was built like a typical receiver, muscular but not too beefy. She'd seen his long legs carry him down the field in a flash.

"You must be DTR's new girl—the one named after Detmer." He made a path for them through the party-goers, his hand on her shoulder as he guided her through.

"DTR?" she repeated. She tried to appear casual even though the fact that Rocket had talked about her sent her heart racing. Shifting her weight back and forth in an attempt to contain her excitement, she looked around the room and hoped to catch sight of Anthony.

David looked mischievous. "Rocket, er, Anthony. Some girl last year had a sign that said, 'Let's have a DTR,' and it stood for Dreamy Tony Rogers instead of Define the Relationship. It sort of stuck with some of the guys."

"Does anyone call him by his first name?" she asked. Though she was anxious to see Rocket, she couldn't pass up a chance to glean as much information as she could—espcially from David. He'd played football with Anthony since middle school, and everything she ever read said he was Anthony's best friend. *Game Plan Key: Know your opponent's offense.*

David frowned. "Uh . . . maybe Mama Rogers? I mean, his mom." He didn't even seem sure of that.

Mama Rogers? DTR? This was starting to get complicated. "So what, his girlfriend even calls him Rocket? Or DTR?"

David's eyebrows spiked. "Girlfriend? As in singular? No." He laughed and ducked his head.

Ty wondered what his reaction meant. *No girlfriend? Good. Girlfriends plural?* She sighed inwardly and set her jaw. She made another, closer inspection of the room. More than a fair share of girls crowded it. Well, she hadn't thought Rocket would hand his heart over, even if he had invited her over after talking to her for five minutes. She'd known from the start winning his heart would be tough. No need to get discouraged already. She remembered Rosie's advice to flirt with the other guys on the team.

"So what do they call you then? Dreamy Davey?"

David slung an arm around her shoulder. He had to hunch to do it since he was so tall. "I give you permission for that one. But Beast is fine. Or Davey. Or if you want to forget about DTR, I'll let you be my girlfriend, and you can call me anything you want."

Not a bad backup plan. Ty grinned. "I'll let you know how it works out." She looked around for Rocket again.

David sighed but didn't seem offended. Plenty of other girls to console him mingled in the room. "Story of my life," he moaned. "DTR's castoffs."

"I bet there are a lot of those."

David laughed. By this point, they'd reached the inner-sanctum of the house: a kitchen stuffed full of more bags of potato chips than Ty'd ever seen in her life—and she had three younger brothers!

"Hey, Dreamy!" David shouted across the room. "Detmer's here." He pointed down at Ty's head, which was probably invisible to Anthony at that point, considering the wall of taller people between them. Story of Ty's life.

She looked up. "Detmer?"

"Why not?"

Having the Beast christen her with her own nickname was definitely something to cross off the bucket list. She shrugged her approval.

She waited for Anthony to move away from the leggy brunette he'd been chatting with. Her skirt was definitely not honor-code-passable. He looked up but didn't put any space between him and the beautiful girl he was standing shoulder to shoulder with. She tilted her head toward Anthony and followed his gaze. If Anthony turned back to her right now, they'd almost be kissing. Ty cursed her shortness. He'd never have an "accident" like that with her.

He straightened and started to move away, but the girl ran her fingers down his arm and gripped it. She slid toward him and tilted her head back. The inviting gesture impressed Ty. She almost couldn't blame Anthony if he wanted to stay.

Luckily for Ty, he made the effort to break away. He grinned as he approached. While David's smiles and sparkling eyes were charming, Anthony's strong, lightly scruffy, model-like face dazzled the jealous thoughts right out of Ty's head. She wanted to sift her fingers through his short, sandy blond hair. She probably couldn't reach.

"Hey." He bent close so she could hear his greeting over the buzz of conversation around them. It was quite a ways from his height of six-three to the top of her five-one. Her head cleared his elbow by mere inches.

Was it a good or bad thing he hadn't used the new nickname? "Hey."

He nudged some room for them to rest against the arch separating the kitchen and the living room. "Glad you came."

Ty's heart thumped steadily quicker. She stood in Anthony's house, his face as close to her as it had been to the brunette's a few minutes before. A million warnings ran through her mind. She couldn't blow this. She had to take advantage of this chance or all that time preparing would be in vain. She just needed a few dates, and if it didn't work out after she put her best effort into it, so be it.

She brushed her hands over her shorts, trying to wipe the sweat off without attracting notice, and blurted out one of the witty lines Rosie suggested, "What girl in her right mind would turn down an invitation from Rocket Rogers?"

"Who indeed?" His gaze darted away, scanning the room before coming back to Ty's face. She tried not to let his brief lapse bother her. Then he wiggled his eyebrows. "'Cause this is the easy part, right?"

Ty cringed. He'd heard her say that? Well, she wouldn't catch Anthony Rogers by acting like a blushing wallflower. He liked leggy girls who sported mini-skirts. Resisting the urge to roll up her Bermuda shorts, she leaned back against the arch, trying to appear relaxed. "Exactly," she said. "*Keeping* you is the tricky part."

Anthony tilted his head. "Up for the challenge?"

"Couldn't be much harder than you breaking Luke Staley's most-touchdowns-scored-in-a-season record this year." The stat rolled off her tongue a lot easier than Rosie's premade line.

A slow grin spread across Anthony's face. "Come on, Detmer. There're a few guys who need to know you." He put his hand at the non-friend, sweet spot at the base of her back and guided her to the living room, where he planted her in front of the largest person Ty had ever encountered.

"Ty, meet Leprechaun."

Ty choked over the nickname. "Does anyone here have real names?"

The Leprechaun laughed, causing minor vibrations throughout the room. "Sean O'Callaghan. Center."

"I know who you are. Why do they call you Leprechaun?"

Sean slapped her on the shoulder. She looked down to make sure her feet hadn't sunk into the floor under the pressure. "Well, partly because of the last name and partly because no one can get to my gold." He jerked his thumb toward Anthony and settled on the couch, patting the cushion next to him.

Win the friends, win the guy. With a glance at Anthony, she dropped into the seat. "True."

A girl already sitting on the couch scooted over to make room, leaning back against the couch, folding her arms, and glaring at Ty.

"Good luck getting a date with one of these guys," the girl said under her breath.

The jealousy wafting off her was stifling. Ty nodded, hoping she looked understanding. "I know. There're a lot of girls here." A peek behind her showed a couple more moving toward the couch, including the mini-skirt girl from the kitchen.

"Yeah." The girl next to Ty laughed without humor and looked away.

Ty turned back to Anthony, trying not to laugh or appear intimidated. He held her gaze, like he was waiting for her to crack. Finally he grinned and shoved his hands in his pocket, looking around before he asked Sean, "You seen Deej?"

Ty knotted up her fingers to keep from fanning her face. This house was the who's who of the football team. "Deej? Is that the best nickname you guys have for DJ Kaiser?"

David the Beast, who sat on the arm of the couch next to Sean the Leprechaun, rolled his eyes to the ceiling and tapped his chin. "Well, he goes by Emperor."

"And Roll," Sean added.

Ty laughed. "Roll?"

"You know, like the bread? Kaiser roll," Anthony said.

"Yeah." She shook her head. "Sounds like he's giving you a run for your money in the nickname department."

"No one will ever catch up to DTR," David said.

"That's the truth, and I'm not just talking nicknames." Anthony leaned over and punched his teammate in the arm.

"Wait, wait." Ty waved her hand, trying to look serious. "Are we talking his rushing stats or girlfriend stats?"

"Ohhhhh!" Sean rumbled the couch with his laughter. The girls around them joined too late, sounding awkward.

"Bam!" David pointed at Anthony and high-fived Ty. "Don't turn your back, Dreamy. This one's too good to be true."

Ty beamed at Anthony. Anthony shoved David off the couch. She grinned wider and swallowed her triumph.

* * *

Both Beast and Leprechaun had kept Ty in their sights all night, and the crowd around her had grown by the minute. Anthony tried to keep down the irritation as they all piled outside after the back-up quarterback challenged Ty to a football-throwing contest. She'd seemed so comfortable with them—and didn't seem to worry about whether he came out or not.

They all laughed now as they headed back to the couch, and Anthony couldn't tell if she'd won or lost. It bothered him how badly he wanted to know.

It seemed like Anthony was the only one of his teammates who could stay away from her. All of them waited to regale Ty with some glorious play and wait for her feedback—because she'd seen them all. He didn't know how it was possible, but she wasn't lying about it either. He wouldn't put it past some girl to spend hours going over football tapes in an effort to ensnare Rocket, but she obviously loved football. He saw it in the way she reenacted her favorite plays right there in the living room, garnering cheers from the guys and mocking laughs from the girls. Her face shone. He kept catching himself staring at her. She kept catching him too.

Too good to be true. Anthony glared from his post, propped against the doorway between the kitchen and living room. He had to admit she talked football better than any other girl he'd come across. He wouldn't mind going out with her and getting some of that one-on-one praise for some of *his* best plays. It would definitely be a step up from the girls that watched a few games and then floundered the minute the conversation went past, "You scored three touchdowns that last game. That's so amazing!"

He drained the last of his root beer. He'd been careful not to hover like the others. That wasn't Rocket's style. He'd dropped by, recaptured Ty's attention, and waited for her to follow him around the room like the other girls. But she didn't. She didn't seem to notice he was missing. Yeah, she was good.

He smirked. *But Rocket's better. Been doing this a lot longer; I guarantee it.* So he rested against the wall for a moment longer. He wouldn't go over there and let her win this battle of wills.

His phone vibrated, distracting him. He pulled it out and saw a text from his brother-in-law, Joe.

Gotta work out of town this weekend. Take the boys to church for me?

He typed his answer quickly, thoughts of Ty and the party fading for the moment. *Definitely. Think I can get Nikki to come with us?* It'd been a long time since his sister had gone to church, and he'd do pretty much anything to get her back there.

You're welcome to try, but you know what her answer will be. Don't push her.

Yeah, yeah. Your ward meats at the crack of dawn, right?

Something like that. Thanks.

Another shot of laughter from Ty interrupted Anthony as he typed, *No problem*. He pushed send and looked up. She was laughing—hard—at something David had said . . . again. He'd better go reel her in before she decided awesome-in-his-own-right Beast was awesome enough for her. He couldn't resist her with all that football knowledge and innocent laugh and sparkling eyes and—Anthony stopped himself with a shake of his head. He wouldn't let her take over his thoughts, even if she did seem perfect.

"Hey, Ty?" He sauntered toward the couch. She looked up. His ego said, *Uh-huh. That's right.* He needed proof that this girl, despite her uncanny knowledge and resulting popularity with his friends, was like all the others, someone who figured she knew all about him.

"Yeah?"

He had her in the palm of his hand. She tilted toward him, her face flushed. He should take the win, but the competitive side of him wanted a couple extra touchdowns. A sure victory. A clear show no girl would get the best of him.

"You want to take a walk with me?" he asked with his swoon-inducing, crooked smile. He bent so his lips brushed against her ear. She tilted her head, and her hair grazed his face. Soft. And it smelled good. He ignored it. "So we can spend some time alone?" he said.

Ty stared at him, blinking. It took her several seconds to regain composure, and Anthony reassured himself he still had it.

"Oh, yeah. Of course." She hopped up.

A collective groan rumbled through the players around her. Seriously? Ignoring the disappointed expressions, Anthony took Ty by the elbow, guiding her through the maze of people and trying not to laugh at the jealous looks she garnered from the girls, especially from Sophie Pope. She probably thought her latest leg-revealing skirt would be enough to keep him next to her all night.

"Which way?" he asked when they reached the sidewalk.

Ty looked at her watch. "It's getting pretty late. We might as well walk in the direction of my apartment." She pointed north.

He led the way, enjoying the slow pace they set in the comfortable warmth of the September night. Anthony waited a few minutes before he broke the silence. "Well, Miss Popularity, how did you like the party?"

She smiled at him, eyes wide and glowing. He wondered if she'd practiced that expression or if it was part of the innocence that hovered right below the surface of her personality. He tried not to second-guess his analysis of her. Plenty of girls knew how to bat their eyes to reel a guy in. He didn't mind the attention. He just had to remember it was probably an act, and there was no point in him getting in too deep with her.

"It was fun. Thanks for inviting me, Anthony. Really."

Anthony thought he preferred girls calling him Rocket—petting his ego, recognizing the place he worked so hard to build for himself—but he liked that she called him by his first name. That surprised him. And she sounded so genuine, like she wanted to actually get to know *him* and not just the football star everyone else saw.

He chuckled. "Don't worry. I'm sure the guys will beg me to invite you back. They like it when the girls can talk shop with them."

She nodded then took a deep breath before she answered. "What about you? Don't you like it when the girls talk shop?" she asked.

"Sure." He shrugged. "I've never met one who read defense better than the Beast."

She opened her mouth then closed it again, staring at the sidewalk for several seconds before she spoke again. "It probably gets old when girls only talk about football just to get a date with you or something." Pink spread across her cheeks, and she only held his gaze for a moment before she turned away and he caught a slight cringe.

"I like talking about football. If I didn't love it so much, I wouldn't be where I am, but most girls don't talk about it like you do." It surprised him to hear that come out of his mouth. Admitting that she might have some leverage with him. It was probably that innocent act of hers—tricking him into thinking there was more to her than just another girl who wanted to date the star quarterback.

She rolled her eyes and waved her hand at him. "My dad makes me play quarterback—of course—when he's teaching my little brother, Walsh, plays. And I've been to all his games and a lot of his practices. Sometimes his coach asks *me* advice." She winked at Anthony.

He stopped in the middle of the sidewalk. "Walsh?" he repeated. "No. Seriously. You're kidding this time." He reached out and grabbed her elbow, turning her back toward him.

Laughing, she let his fingers slide down her arm and walked on. Anthony stumbled a little. He couldn't remember the last time his touch hadn't stopped a girl in her tracks. She'd hesitated though. *Right?* He hurried to catch up, trying to shake the feeling he might have lost a few yards with her.

He mentally slapped himself. A little bit of playing hard to get wasn't anything he couldn't handle. He smiled. His sister would like Ty. Nikki got a kick out of any girl who didn't fall all over Anthony.

"If you knew my dad, you wouldn't question it," she said.

Anthony walked closer to her now. He hoped the nearness would unsettle her, give him the upper hand. "So how many brothers do you have, and are all of them named after BYU quarterbacks?"

"Three and no." She paused for effect and looked up at him with a twinkle in her eye. It was such a strange combination of confidence and innocence. He thought he might be smitten. That was the only word to describe her startling effect on him. Not a big deal, though.

"My littlest brother is named Harline," she said.

He burst into laughter. He knew he could like a guy who named his son after a receiver who made a winning play against Utah. He could definitely like a girl raised by a guy like that.

"Well, don't keep me in suspense. What's the other one's name?" he asked.

"Steve Young Sarkisian Daws."

Anthony laughed louder. "No!" He gasped for breath. "You're pulling a fast one on me. No one names their kid something like that."

She grinned from ear to ear. "Dad couldn't choose which great Steve to go with, so he chose both."

"And your mom let him?"

"Do you think she would've married a guy like my dad—a guy who named his *daughter* after a quarterback—if she didn't love football as much as him?" Ty studied him as she said it, and he knew what she was insinuating. A girl like her was perfect for him.

Honestly? She was probably right, but Anthony couldn't admit that yet. He wouldn't mind spending some time with her . . . for now. Nothing serious though. She intrigued him. He'd be careful not to let her suck him in.

He cleared his throat. "Probably not. Where do you live anyway?"

She pointed farther down the block. "Right up there. If you want to head back, I can walk the rest of the way myself," she offered. She bit her lip and looked away. Did she feel bad for her implied "I'm the girl for you" statement?

"What kind of stories would you tell about Rocket if I let you do that? You'd ruin my rep." He bumped her shoulder.

"I'm hoping to tell all kinds of stories to ruin your rep." She bumped him back and stayed close.

Somehow the challenge made Anthony like her even more. *Betchya I can make you fall for me.*

And his ego answered, *Betchya I won't.* A voice in the back of his mind whispered, *You already are,* but he pushed it aside. He knew what he was doing.

They talked football the rest of the way to her apartment, and Anthony enjoyed it. Two faces stared out a window on the third floor when they got there. He covered a snort of laughter with a cough.

Ty looked up and froze. He waved. The two girls waved back, looking both sheepish and delighted. Ty covered her face in her hands. "Oh, I can't believe them," she moaned and then took a deep breath before facing him. "Well, um, thanks. I'll see you in class Monday." She turned toward the building.

Where did her bravado go? The challenge? Two overexcited roommates and she wanted to hoist up a white flag. That disappointed him. He expected more.

Just to clinch it, he grabbed her arm and pulled her close. From there, he saw the exact diamond shade of her eyes, full of surprise—genuine surprise. He weaved his fingers into the soft, brown curls resting against her neck and bent his head toward her. Her eyes widened. Still smiling, he kissed her. Instead of fireworks, they heard delighted squeals from the third-floor audience.

The noise faded into the background when he realized what he'd done. Kissed her. And he liked it. When he pulled his face back and let out his breath, he couldn't draw another one. He started to move in to kiss her again. And maybe again and again.

But Ty, her eyes still closed, didn't notice. She sank from her tiptoes back to the balls of her feet and rocked backward, out of the reach of his lips.

"Wow," she whispered.

The little voice in the back of his head said, *Tell me about it.* He jerked his hand back, hoping he didn't yank out any hair in his haste. "See you later, Detmer," he grunted and disappeared before he did something even more stupid, like hold her hand and walk her up to her apartment.

Chapter Three

ANTHONY PULLED UP IN FRONT of Nikki's house and stifled a yawn. Nine o'clock seemed too early for church, but he'd promised Joe he'd make sure Porter and Eli went. Anthony pushed his door open and got out, surveying the two houses that sat side by side, both with meticulously manicured lawns and flower beds. Nikki's doing. If Anthony had been left in charge of his parents' house while they served their mission, he'd be lucky to get the lawn mowed once a month.

As he made his way up the sidewalk to the house on the right, his gaze found the flowerbeds on either side of the covered porch. Beautiful carnations, even for September. Nikki had a knack for that. He laughed darkly. Nikki had a knack for making everything perfect. But *knack* wasn't quite the word—as the perfectly spaced carnations attested. Seven of them on each side, patterned purple-white-purple-white. He sighed.

He hurried up the steps and tapped on the door. His older nephew, three-year-old Porter, opened the door. "Rocky!" Since Porter couldn't pronounce either Anthony's given name or nickname, they'd settled on Rocky—well, really, Porter had settled on it.

Anthony hoisted him up, holding him upside down by his middle. Porter laughed and shouted with glee. Nikki came around the corner from the kitchen. Anthony swiftly spun Porter so his head faced up and turned to his sister—feeling bad for the glint of anxiety that crossed her expression.

"Hey, Nik."

Nikki reached up and smoothed Porter's hair then Anthony's, though with his short cut, it was unlikely anything was out of place. "What did Joe have to do to convince you to get up this early?"

Anthony put Porter down and retucked his Sunday shirt, guilty feelings full-blown now. "He didn't have to do anything. He just had to ask. When does he get back?"

"Tonight, thank heavens."

Anthony looked over the living room, noting the piles of clothes and open plastic totes. Trying not to be obvious, he counted the piles. "You okay?" he asked, turning back to her.

Nikki rolled her eyes. "I'm fine." She followed his gaze to the living room. "They needed to be sorted. I've been putting Eli's stuff away willy-nilly as he grows out of it."

Anthony burst into laughter. "I doubt that."

She glared at him. "Well, for me, okay."

"There are seven piles."

"It's habit by now." She avoided his stare and headed back toward the kitchen.

"Nikki—"

"I'm fine," she called over her shoulder. "Let me be a mom. Moms sort things. Ask ours, Bum Face."

He hesitated then chuckled and followed her. When they were kids, their mom had caught Nikki calling him "butt head" and washed her mouth out with soap. The next time he annoyed her, she called him Bum Face, and everyone had laughed so hard it stuck. What would Ty think if she knew this far less glamorous nickname?

He also wondered what Ty would think of Nikki. So far he'd never met a girl who understood his sister and didn't treat her like she was crazy. Not that he'd introduced her to many. Only one since he got home from his mission.

Nikki was wiping up Eli when Anthony reached the kitchen. He started to give it a cursory inspection and stopped himself. If Nikki said she was fine, he'd give her the benefit of the doubt.

"Hey, E." He held out his fist to bump it with the fourteen-month-old. Eli slapped at it. "We'll work on it, buddy."

"You realize Eli can't go to nursery, right? You'll have to take him to priesthood, so you might as well leave him here."

"Nope. Eli doesn't want to be left behind, do you?" Anthony undid the high chair belt and lifted the chubby toddler out.

"No, no, no," Eli chanted back.

"See?" Anthony turned to face Nikki, who grinned at them.

"I swear that's the only word he knows."

"Rocky?" Porter asked from the doorway of the kitchen. "Is it time to go to Primary yet?"

Anthony glanced at his watch. "Yep. We better get moving." With Eli still in his arms, he headed back for the living room. He hadn't noticed it before, but a brown diaper bag with baby-blue polka dots rested next to the door. Way manly. If Beast could see him now.

Anthony threw the diaper bag strap over his shoulder while Nikki watched from across the room, her arms folded, anxiety creeping into her expression. "You sure you're going to be okay?"

"I've done it before—"

"With Mom." Nikki approached him and adjusted Eli's already centered tie.

Anthony grabbed her hand and held it. "Maybe you should come with us, if you'd feel better."

"Stop, Anthony. You know I can't."

"Nik . . ." He swallowed. "Don't you think things would be better if you came to church again?"

"Going to church isn't going to take this away and make me normal again."

Normal. Like back when Anthony was in middle school and his sister didn't have to count everything in sevens and didn't plan on medications and counseling and her mom living next door so she could have a family and a life.

"Maybe not," he conceded, "but it could help."

Nikki clenched her jaw, maybe to keep it from trembling, but Anthony never felt guilty about this, just sad. "It's not like I don't have enough *faith*, Anthony."

"I know." He tugged at her hand. "We'll sit in the foyer. I'm a big guy. People are scared of me."

A tiny smile appeared on her lips. "Awe and fear are two different things. You attract people like bees to honey. Thank you, but I'll skip facing the whole ward wanting to get a good look at my brother."

"Okay. The mother's lounge."

She shoved against his shoulder. "Not today, Bum Face. Go. You're going to be late."

He waited, just to see, but she started looking anxious again, so he opened the door. "Come on, Porter. Let's go to Primary."

* * *

Monday morning Ty was still thinking about Anthony's kiss. While she spent some of the last three days replaying the unexpected moment his lips touched hers, mostly she moaned, "I'm such a loser."

She set aside her water bottle and scooted her books to the side so she could lay her head on the table in the library. This distraction wasn't helping on the homework front. "Wow," she said into the tabletop, "I said *wow*."

She tried to reassure herself the way her roommates did. "You kissed Rocket Rogers," Rosie had said when Ty related to them why Anthony disappeared without so much as a good night. "I think *wow* is an acceptable way to react."

Clearly Anthony didn't, Ty argued with herself. *I'm such a loser.* She hadn't proven herself any different from the girls at the party. A hanger-on waiting for a little attention from the big star.

"Hey there, Detmer."

David Savage's voice startled her as he slid into the seat across from her. Her hand flew outward and sent her water bottle rolling across the table. The lid flipped open, but his quick hands grabbed it before any spilled.

"Nice." She took a breath, ventured a smile, and asked, "Would you mind if I had a redo? You can walk back in, and I'll pretend to be the cool girl from the party."

David grinned. "Are you saying all that stuff you spouted Friday night was an act?"

Ty's heart stopped and stuttered before starting again. *Um, yeah. Parts of it.* "I do know football," she finally said to David's knowing expression.

"Of course you do. You can't fake an in-depth conversation like that." He settled back in his chair. "Knowledge like that gives you a fighting chance with him."

Ty gulped. "*Fighting* chance?"

One corner of David's mouth slipped up. "Of getting a few weeks of Dreamy's attention."

She tried to summon back the girl that wrapped half the football team around her finger. "As opposed to a few days?" After the way she reacted to his kiss—not to mention her crazy, spying roommates—she would've felt lucky if he talked to her again.

David nodded. "Exactly."

She traced the edge of one of her books. "I'm not like the other girls, you know." Sure, some of the confidence she channeled Friday night made her seem like one of them, but she only needed that long enough to reel Anthony in.

"I'm aware." David chuckled. "Which makes me wonder why you'd waste your time on Dreamy when you could have a hunk like me?"

"Waste my time? You must not know him as well as I thought you did."

David leaned across the table, a thoughtful expression replacing the amused one. "And what makes you think that? I've been playing football with him a long time."

"I know that." She smirked at him.

David pulled a notebook from his bag. "So what makes you different?"

"I've watched him since before BYU." She stared at her tray, wondering how not to sound like a stalker. She appreciated Anthony for more than his quick feet and good looks. *That* made her different, right?

David waited for her to continue.

"My freshman year of high school I watched him play against Riverton. It was his last game of the regular season, and he was about to break the school record for rushing yards, but he—"

"Let Jordan Vans run the ball all night because some scouts were there to see him," David finished, impressed.

She cleared her throat and laughed. "Yeah . . . so even when he's playing football he's more than a football player."

"You're too good for him, you know," he said.

Her laugh came out more natural now. "You're only saying that because you want me to go after you instead."

He shrugged. "Can you blame a guy for trying?"

* * *

When Anthony arrived at his coaching football class on Monday, Ty already sat in the chair she had the week before, her petite figure bent over the desk, nose buried in a book, unaware of the world—or the fact that Rocket walked into the room. It unnerved him she didn't even notice when he dropped into his seat behind her. He thought the breathy "Wow" that almost undid him Friday night proved he'd kicked the challenge up a notch and she'd bowed in defeat.

But maybe *wow* meant, "Wow, I thought kissing Rocket would be something, and yet it felt like kissing my brother." He found that possibility unlikely.

The whole thing didn't do much to improve his mood. He couldn't quite shake the feeling Nikki wasn't as okay as she said. He couldn't think of anything that had happened that might set her back—she'd handled their parents leaving for their mission well, better than anyone expected, and had been doing fine the fourteen months they'd been gone. He'd hoped, despite his reservations, seeing Ty would help him out of his weekend funk.

He flipped open his notebook and tried to go over his notes. Surely the sound of him turning pages would alert her.

But no. She was oblivious.

"Hi, Rocket," the girl who'd worn high-heels—and wore a different, sparkly pair today—ran her hand along his arm.

"Oh. Hey." He eyed Ty. What had captured her attention so totally? He bet she was reading a romance novel or something, imagining him in the role of the hero. Of course she was. Either that or ignoring him on purpose, trying to play it cool or something. He craned his neck to see what kept her so engrossed.

It was a history book. *A history book?*

"Hi, Anthony."

She caught him half-standing in his chair and bent toward her. Who'd have thought *that* would get her attention?

"Hey, Ty." He grinned and stretched his arms high over his head before plopping back down in his seat. The *yeah-right* smile on her face said he wasn't fooling her. Out of the corner of his eye, he glanced at High-Heel Girl to see if she'd caught his awkward failure. She was glaring at Ty. He stifled a laugh.

"How's it going?" he asked.

She shrugged, nodded at the book, and smiled. "Not too bad. You?" She turned around in her chair so she faced him.

She didn't seem fluttery . . . Well, she'd had three days to get over something as momentous as kissing him. "Great. Great. Looking forward to the game this weekend. One of my buddies from high school is a running back at Utah State, and I can't help but love it when we beat them."

Her face lit up. "It's going to be great, right?" she gushed. "That new receiver they have—what's his name? The one we lost to them—"

She scowled at such disloyalty, which made Anthony bite back a laugh. "Anyway, they're saying he's good. And if our secondary can't step it up, the Aggies are going to eat our lunch on the long bombs." She bit her lip and offered a half-hearted shrug. "I'm rambling. Sorry. Like you don't already know all that."

He'd overheard some of her commentary on the last couple games at the party Friday night, but hearing her talk like a pro up-close and personal like this? It had him picturing himself calling her up after the game to see what she thought. He'd never even consider a post-game rundown with girls like Sophie Pope or High-Heel Girl.

"They're fast on the perimeter too." He leaned forward, getting into the conversation, and then caught himself and sat back against his chair.

She didn't notice. She had giddy written all over her face. "I can't wait to see what you do against their defense on the run. They only allowed about eighty yards on the ground per game last year."

Anthony liked this conversation way too much. Before he knew it, he'd be asking her out to discuss offensive strategies and getting in over his head with a girl he already liked more than he should. He better reign it in. "You doubt the great Rocket Rogers?" He eyed her, mockingly offended.

She played right into his hand. "Never." She held up her phone. "Do you mind if I take a picture with you? My brothers don't believe that I know Rocket."

Two things about that sentence bothered Anthony. One, she said *know* instead of something amazing like *kissed* or *am in love with*. Two, she called him Rocket, which he found he didn't like the sound of off her lips. But of course, he *was* Rocket Rogers, and nothing as small as Ty Daws had ever posed a problem to him before, so he shook it off.

"Sure," he said.

She stood up to move next to him, barely having to crouch to rest her shoulder against his. Like the unexpected feeling when they kissed, he realized her touch affected him more than he was ready for. And she smelled like . . . well, he played football. He didn't know girly scents, but it smelled soapy and maybe—flowery?

He needed to get a handle on this. Get back on top, start calling the shots. On the field he'd never let another player shake him up. He hadn't ever let a girl do it either—well, not for a while anyway.

As she was about to snap the picture, he pressed his lips against her cheek. Instead of looking at the camera, he closed his eyes and half-smiled.

The proximity tempted him to reach over and tilt her chin toward him. Kiss her again like he meant to Friday night. That careless part of him started pointing out things like, *Why not?* And, *She's right about being perfect for you.*

When she showed him the picture, he had to chuckle. Ty had turned toward him, her eyes wide and mouth half open.

Against his better judgment—and to distract himself from those lips—he said, "This is great. Send it to me."

She laughed with him, though her fingers looked like they might be trembling. They slid across the touch screen for a moment before she hesitated. She ran a hand over her hair and bit her lip. "I don't have your number." Then she forced a smile, and a mask of confidence swept away the endearing embarrassment. "You'll have to give it to me." Her tone sounded teasing. Like another challenge. The whole thing struck Anthony as backward. He kissed her, but she was nervous about asking for his phone number.

He hadn't thought about this part. He had the numbers of dozens of girls in his phone. But when it came to girls who had his number . . . there were less of them than there were times he'd been sacked since his freshman year at BYU—twelve. One of them never called anymore. Anthony wouldn't answer if she did.

"You know what?" Ty's voice broke through his thoughts. "I'm definitely Facebooking this—you can't stop me. You could steal it from there." She looked at her phone again, still smiling.

She was smoothing things over for him. It didn't hurt her feelings that he wavered before giving up his precious phone number. It seemed so . . . nice. Genuine. Not conniving. Not manipulative. How many other girls would pass up the opportunity to have his number? Ty didn't even seem fazed by his refusal, just concerned for him. So thoughtful.

"Sure," he said. "Let me see that." He held out his hand for the phone.

She started to hand it over then pulled back, supposedly out of his reach. "You're not going to delete the picture, are you?" She wrinkled her eyebrows together.

Anthony laughed. "No. If you get it printed, I'll even autograph it for you." He grabbed the phone, added his number to her contacts, and sent the picture to himself.

She blew out a breath of pent-up laughter, rolling her eyes to the ceiling. "That was totally fan-girl, huh?"

To his surprise, he realized the tension mounting in his shoulders since Sunday had loosened. He liked her tone. It sounded real. "Yeah, but in a cute way."

That tell-tale blush crept up her face, and her small, pink, tempting lips curved.

"Thanks," she said, so quietly he had to resist the urge to lean out of his chair to hear it.

He handed the phone back, and their fingers brushed. For some reason, it affected Anthony more than even kissing her did—not that he wouldn't like to try that again.

Maybe tonight. A few dates, some good football conversations—maybe even holding her hand a little bit. None of it had to mean anything. People did it all the time. As long as he didn't let her *really* get to him. "Ty?"

She looked up, but Brian, the TA, interrupted, starting class. She waited though, her eyes on his expectantly.

Dude, Rocket, this is not good.

So he smiled and turned his gaze to the front of the room.

Chapter Four

When Ty saw Anthony later that afternoon in the parking lot by the Richards Building, she almost ducked behind a car. It was too much of a coincidence. He'd think she was stalking him, and for once, she hadn't been. She stared forward and quickened her pace, hoping he wouldn't notice her.

But how could he not? He was coming up the sidewalk from the indoor practice field and would walk right past her. Unless she hid behind a car. Which sounded like a good idea about now.

"Ty?"

Too late. She looked up and braced herself. "Oh. Hey."

He stopped, and she realized she couldn't keep walking on without looking rude. Right? It would be rude, not a well-played, hard-to-get maneuver? She stopped too.

"Where are you off to?"

"Provo High School." She pointed. "I have an internship there."

"Doing what?"

"Right now? Grading papers and doing other menial labor for the teacher."

He laughed. "Mind if I walk you?"

"Really? I mean, sure." She resisted the urge to slap her forehead. Would the nonsense ever stop flying out of her mouth? At this rate, despite Anthony's quick invitation to hang out with her, she'd never end up on a real date with him. She surged forward. Out of the corner of her eye, she saw him smiling. Well, at least he wasn't running the other way.

"So what class are you interning for?" He broke the silence.

"Western Civilizations. It's an AP class."

"History?"

"Yep. That's my major—secondary ed, history."

"Sounds . . ."

"Boring?" Her nervousness started to disappear as they settled into the same familiarity they'd enjoyed when he'd walked her home Friday night.

"That's not what I was going to say." He chuckled.

"But it's what you were thinking." They paused at University Avenue, waiting for a chance to cross. She turned to gaze at him. "History is just stories."

"Lame, poorly told stories." One corner of his mouth turned up, and his eyes danced as he teased her.

"Really fun, inspiring stories."

He smirked and narrowed his eyes at her in a playful challenge. "Prove it."

She worried her lip as she racked her brain for a history story to impress him and then grinned when she remembered the paper she'd written in high school for her American history class. "Do you know who won the first bowl game?" she asked. "Michigan—New Year's Day in 1902. They beat Stanford so bad—49 to 0—that Stanford conceded the game with eight minutes left to play."

His smirk fell away to reveal an impressed smile. "Okay, I'll give you that. That's pretty interesting but not very inspiring."

She laughed. "True."

They'd reached the school too fast, and Ty couldn't dawdle. She had to hurry inside and be responsible. "I have to go," she said reluctantly. "Thanks for walking with me."

"It was fun . . ." He glanced around and opened his mouth, but nothing came out for several seconds. "So . . . so, I'll see you around." He waved and hurried back up the sidewalk without a backward glance.

Disappointed and wondering what he hadn't said, Ty opened the front door and checked in with the secretary before heading to Mrs. Frazier's room.

The middle-aged woman looked up from her desk as Ty entered. "Ty. Perfect." She picked up a stack of papers, and Ty's heart fell. Another day of grading.

"Mrs. Frazier, I found this great activity online last night—"

"Ty, I have seven periods full—chock full—of juniors and seniors. I don't have time to plan new activities." Mrs. Frazier shoved the papers toward Ty, her heavily hair-sprayed, thin brown hair shifting a little to one side. She grinned as the stack of papers settled in Ty's arms. "The nice thing about history, dear, is it doesn't change."

"But historians are discovering new evidence and forming new theories all the time." The bell rang, and more than twenty juniors poured into the room, drowning out her argument. Mrs. Frazier continued to smile expectantly at her, so she took the papers and found a spot at a table in the back of the room. Pulling out some silly stickers she'd found at a teacher supply store—complete with historical figures to match their positive messages—she went to work.

* * *

Though Anthony knew he could handle himself around Ty (probably) and saw nothing wrong with a meaningless two-or-three-date relationship with her, he decided, at the last second, not to ask Ty out after he walked her to her internship. Instead, he called Sophie Pope and took her out. Falling for Sophie didn't worry him. The thought had never crossed his mind to take Sophie over to meet Nikki and the boys. She was safe.

This obsession with Ty is nothing serious . . . He told himself to stop thinking of her and pay attention to the beautiful girl sitting across from him in the restaurant. Sophie had long, dark hair that lay attractively over her shoulders, almost the same color as Ty's, except Ty's was softer.

Shut up, he reminded himself.

"So big game this week . . ." Sophie said.

For some reason, Sophie's trademark short skirt bothered him tonight. Sure she had great legs. He liked that about her, but he couldn't picture Ty—

Stop.

Anthony was tired of arguing with himself. He thought going out with Sophie would keep his mind off how much time he'd spent the last three days convincing himself he was in control of the situation with Ty. Maybe he should've asked Ty out. Then he wouldn't be sitting here comparing her to Sophie. If he'd taken Ty out, he could get her out of his system.

"Um, Rocket?"

Anthony looked up and remembered Sophie. "Yeah?"

She smiled, a slow, flirtatious smile that Ty never got quite right. Sophie pointed to some people standing by the table. How long had they been there? "These people want to know if they can take a picture with you." She seemed delighted at the attention he garnered. He bit back annoyance—at her mostly.

"Oh, sure." He knelt and draped his arms around the shoulders of two little boys, with their dad on one side and their mom on the other while Sophie snapped the picture. What would Ty think of how often people stopped him for pictures, autographs, or handshakes?

He sighed. If he couldn't control his thoughts, he'd end up calling Sophie Ty. As he sat again after telling the family good-bye, he promised himself he'd focus on this date.

"Thinking about football?" Sophie reached across the table and ran a finger over the top of his hand.

"Uh, yeah." That wasn't a lie. Thinking about Ty was basically the same as thinking about football.

Because he was obsessed with both?

"Worried about the game?"

He managed not to extract his hand from underneath Sophie's. "Sure."

She tapped his hand with her fingers. "Don't worry, Rocket. You're going to do great."

Her answer disappointed him. Ty would've said something like, *Their defense is a lot bigger than we're used to. Better tell Leprechaun to play as tough as he can, or you can count on at least one more sack.*

And the worst part was, before Ty, he never cared if the girls he dated understood football or not. It had been enough for them to declare him the greatest, best-looking player ever. Why did Ty have to know about the history of bowl games or the strengths of the USU defense and be so irresistible? He'd been happy dating girls he knew he'd never fall for.

"Thanks," he mumbled. Sophie pulled her hand back and fingered a strand of her hair, twisting it with a disappointed frown, which made Anthony feel bad. He tried a charming smile. "Just a little worried. You know, nervous about the game."

Her frown disappeared, replaced by a smile. "No need. You're Rocket Rogers, after all."

He nodded. "Yes, I am."

Sophie abandoned the opposite side of the booth and slipped in next to Anthony, scooting over so she rested in the crook of his arm. "So do you mind forgetting about football for a couple hours?"

"No problem." Maybe if he did, he could forget about Ty too.

* * *

He'd managed to get through dinner without any disasters. Now they sat in his car outside Sophie's apartment. The best remedy to clear Ty out of his head would be to kiss Sophie, right?

He put a hand on her neck and drew them closer together. She tilted her head, waiting. He closed his eyes; his lips hovered over hers. Her breath tickled his chin. He tried not to let the hint of marinara bother him.

Kiss her.

It wasn't like he'd never kissed Sophie before. She was pretty good at it. Better yet, she wouldn't expect anything special from him because he ended the night with a farewell peck.

He needed to kiss Sophie and make his kiss with Ty meaningless—make her just another girl.

So why couldn't he do it?

"Rocket?" Sophie whispered.

"Mmmm." He attempted to buy time.

"Something wrong?" She nuzzled his cheek.

"Mmmm."

She didn't notice the complete lack of answer.

This was the stupidest thing that had ever happened to him. Was it Ty's football knowledge? The fact that he could carry on a conversation with her about his true love? No. He had plenty of guys to talk football with. He didn't need Ty for that, right? Sure, he enjoyed listening to a girl say intelligent things about the game, but was that something to fall apart over?

Was it because she acted different from the other girls? An anomaly he needed to figure out? Ty Daws was just a girl.

A girl who could probably run a triple option—in a kiss. That image wasn't helping.

He couldn't kiss Sophie. No matter how hard he tried. He had to figure out this thing with Ty first. He opened his eyes. Sophie had opened her eyes too, looking worried.

"Rocket?"

He darted in, dropped his lips on her cheek, and pulled away. "I'll call you."

She froze for several awkward seconds. Anthony cringed, thinking about what she'd say to people. Still staring at Anthony, Sophie pushed the door open and tumbled out of his car. On her way across the street, she kept looking back at Anthony.

He banged his head on the steering wheel. On second thought, he was never speaking to Ty again.

* * *

When Anthony got home, he slammed the door. David looked up from a playbook. His gaze jumped to the clock then back to Anthony.

"Is the time on your cell phone wrong?"

Anthony glared. "No."

"It's eight o'clock."

"I know how to tell time."

"You left like an hour ago. I've spent longer waiting for a table." David put down the playbook and rubbed the back of his neck. "Are you sick?"

Anthony dropped onto the couch. Tipping his head back, he pinched the bridge of his nose. "It wasn't working out."

David bent forward, resting his elbows on his knees. "Since when has that stopped you?"

Anthony clenched his jaw. The whole night gave him a headache. Why didn't he go straight to his room?

Because he needed advice from his best friend.

"Are you hurt?" David pressed. He sized Anthony up, no doubt looking for some injury.

Anthony sat up and stared at David. Time to get his confession over with. "I'm only telling you this because you're my best friend."

David swallowed hard, and the blood drained from his face. "What's up?"

If the situation hadn't been so serious, Anthony would have laughed at David's reaction. Dropping his head into his hands, Anthony said in a strained voice, "The whole date was a disaster."

"I'm sure whatever it is—huh?"

"Beast! I messed things up big time with Sophie." Now Anthony threw his hands up and sank back into the couch, staring forlornly at the ceiling.

"Dreamy . . . seriously? You had me all worked up over Sophie Pope?"

"It gets worse."

David froze. "How bad is it?"

"When I dropped Sophie off, I was in the Red Zone, fourth and inches. I fumbled, threw an interception, whatever. I couldn't kiss her. I choked. Big time."

David tossed a pillow at his friend as he heaved a massive sigh of relief. "I could've had a heart attack over here. You had me thinking honor code violation or something."

How could David not get it? They were talking about Anthony's reputation with the ladies. He sat up. "Did you hear me?" he asked. "My lips were so close I could almost taste the lasagna she had for dinner, and I ended up kissing her cheek. I'm *Rocket Rogers*. I kissed her cheek!"

"There's something wrong with you." David picked the playbook back up.

"I know." Anthony buried his head in his hands again, relieved David understood.

David shook his head. "What happened?" He flipped the page.

"Ty. Ty happened."

David wiggled his eyebrows. "You couldn't kiss Sophie 'cause of Ty?"

"Couldn't stop comparing Sophie to her all night. What's going on with me?"

"Well, I'm guessing you probably didn't go over to Ty's after your date."

Anthony sucked in a quick breath. "Of course not. I've been trying to forget her. Why would I go over to her apartment?"

"And *that's* what's wrong with you. You're trying to forget the best thing that's ever happened to us—"

"Us?"

"If you were any kind of a friend, you'd end it with her quick so I can have a run at her," David said.

Anthony wagged a finger at him. "No, no, no. There's just something about her. Once I figure it out, I can put her behind me."

"Maybe it's that she knows football better than His Majesty?" David tipped his head toward DJ's room.

Anthony didn't even crack a smile. "More than that." But what? For example, her passion over something as mundane as history had him interested. She seemed like the type of person he could be good friends with, someone he wanted to hang out with and not just a way to get a date for Friday night.

"I can think of a number of things." David rubbed at his cheek and eyed Anthony before speaking again. "Ty is one in a million, Dreamy. I think she wants to know you for real, not just score a few dates or end up with a superstar or something. You should give her a chance."

Anthony closed his eyes, trying to ignore the fact that David had a crush on Ty too.

So that was what he was calling this now. A crush?

A crush. That was simple. Not too serious. A harmless infatuation that would go away after a few dates.

The slight vibration in the floor warned Anthony that Sean was joining them. "What's wrong with Rocket?" he asked David. "Is he sick?" The same worry Anthony heard in David's voice earlier now tainted Sean's.

"Yeah." David snorted. "Love sick."

Not love. Seconds after the words left David's mouth, Anthony leapt off the couch and pinned him to the floor, rubbing his face in the carpet. Sean laughed so hard Anthony worried the walls might come down.

"Don't. Say. That. Word," he threatened.

David grinned and didn't fight back.

Chapter Five

TY SLID OFF THE COUCH, leaning closer to the TV. "Oh, come on. Come *on*!"

The defensive linemen came in too fast. Anthony darted back and forth before scooting through a couple defenders, ending up at the bottom of a pile after gaining only two yards.

"What's with the offensive line today? He doesn't have enough time," she said.

"He's had to scramble the last four plays," Walsh agreed.

"He's getting tired," Dad said.

Ty stood up and plopped back on the couch. BYU was up by ten with four minutes left in the fourth quarter, so she wasn't really worried they might lose the game. The defense had played awesome, thank heavens. It was just, now she knew Anthony, had talked to him, had *kissed* him, she felt his pain more. This had to frustrate him. He had fewer rushing yards than any of his games this year, and though he had no turnovers, there had been a couple close calls.

"Settle down," Mom said from her seat next to Dad. "Everyone has bad games once in a while, and we're winning. Quit whining."

"No way." Walsh crammed half a bag of chips into his mouth at once, scattering crumbs across his lap and the cushions. "Rocket doesn't have bad games." When Mom scowled at him for his mess, he swept his hand over the crumbs and sent them flying to the carpet.

"You're cleaning that up." She pointed at him. Walsh shrugged.

"Considering what he had to put up with on the line today, Anthony's having a great game," Ty defended him with more vigor than she meant.

Walsh, Mom, and Dad all turned to stare at Ty. She sank back in her seat.

"Ty loves Rocket! Ty loves Rocket!" Twelve-year-old Stevie sang from behind her.

Walsh snorted with laughter. "Tell us something we don't know, Stevie."

Ty tossed a pillow at Walsh and turned back to the game. Despite having convinced herself that BYU would win, she still sighed with relief when they scored another touchdown after running a minute and a half off the clock.

* * *

After the game ended, she wanted to text Anthony and tell him good job, but she didn't. He kissed her because he was Rocket Rogers, not because he couldn't resist Ty.

She snuck another peek at the picture on her phone, the three-thousandth time that day. *But I'm reeling him in*, she promised herself. So instead of calling him, like she would have loved to do, she followed her mom into the kitchen with the empty bowls and cups from the snacks.

"You were awfully defensive about Rocket today." Mom popped a carrot into her mouth—the only leftovers, probably because the carrots spent the second half of the game sitting on the kitchen counter instead of the coffee table in the family room.

Ty dumped the cups from her hands into the sink. "Oh, Mom, stop it. I'm always defensive." She smiled for her mom though. Mom understood everything about Ty's obsession with Anthony. Ty pulled her phone from her pocket. "Look at this." The kiss on the cheek was nothing. Ty knew that. But the picture made her insides swirl every time she looked at it. She had to share it with someone. Well, with more than just everyone on Facebook.

Mom squealed like Ty's roommates had and grabbed for the phone. "Oh, Ty!" Then her face softened, and she tilted her head. "Oh . . ."

Dad walked in. "What's going on?" he asked, leaning over Mom's shoulder.

Confused, Ty frowned at her mom. "What, Mom?"

"He looks . . . almost . . . besotted." Mom handed the phone back.

"Besotted?" The butterflies took flight in Ty's stomach. She kind of thought that too, but besotted? Anthony? "Mom. Really."

"Of course he is!" Dad swiped the phone. "What guy could resist Ty? She's one in a million."

Ty laughed and shook her head. "Thanks, Dad. But we're just friends. He's got a girl-a-week reputation."

Mom tapped her chin and shrugged. "He looks like you might mean more than just his girl of the week."

Maybe? *Don't go there. Not yet.* "Don't get my hopes up. He's kissed a lot of girls—and not on the cheek." *Game Plan Key: Know your opponent's offense.*

Walsh's voice interrupted. "You guys looking at the replay of that last touchdown? That throw was pristine. I just want to catch one pass from Rocket in my life." He nudged Ty and looked over her shoulder at the phone. "Oh." He rolled his eyes. "That again. Thought you told me he kissed you on the lips."

Ty swatted at her brother, but he ducked out of the way. "Walsh!" she hissed. She tried to cover her embarrassment with false indifference. "Unfortunately I didn't get a picture of that."

"Let me see!" Stevie saved her from any more comments by clamoring into the room with five-year-old Harline behind him. Biting back a smile, Ty displayed the phone to them.

"Ewww!" they both echoed. Ty, her parents, and Walsh laughed.

Harline skipped around the kitchen. "K-I-S-S-I-N-G!" he sang at the top of his lungs, echoing a song Stevie had been tormenting Ty with earlier.

"Harly, do you know what you're spelling?" Walsh asked.

Harline paused. "Mississippi?" He took off again, continuing to spell *kissing* for their enjoyment, while Stevie added his chant, "My sister knows Rocket. My sister knows Rocket."

Ty looked at her mom and pushed away the fluttery feeling. Yes. She knew Anthony. But that was all—for now anyway.

* * *

After the exhausting game, Anthony thought he'd fall asleep on the bus ride home. David had started snoring as soon as the bus rolled away from the stadium, but Anthony had tried for the last forty-five minutes and didn't seem anywhere near sleep. His mind wouldn't stop going, hopping back and forth between concern for his sister and thoughts about Ty Daws. Instead of analyzing what the latter meant—it'd been over a year since any one girl had occupied his thoughts this much—he reached for his phone and called Nikki, despite the fact that it was almost midnight.

Because he was worried, he counted the rings. He tried to keep his sigh inward when she answered after the seventh. "Hey, nice game," she said.

"Should've come. You know I can get you good tickets, right? And it was a beautiful day." He kept his voice soft so he wouldn't wake up the sleeping players around him. Although, Anthony could have a dance party in his seat and Sean's chainsaw-like snoring from in front of him would probably cover the sound.

"You know I like the view better here. And can you imagine me wrestling Eli for a three-hour game . . . and the long drive to Logan?"

"Excuses, excuses."

"Joe will bring Porter sometime."

Maybe he worried too much. Nikki sounded fine. "I'm a pretty good football player."

"So they say. To tell you the truth, I'm not seeing it."

"Thanks. I can always count on you to keep me humble."

She laughed. Deep. A good laugh. A little more of his tension crumbled away. "You? Humble? That'd be the day, Bum Face."

He almost said, *Hey, Nik. There's this girl. You'd like her, I know it. I think I'd let her get away with calling me Bum Face too.* But that made the whole thing sound a lot more serious than it was. More than a crush. Like he wanted Nikki to meet her. Instead he said, "What's up with you?"

She paused. Sighed. "I knew this was more than a friendly chat."

As hard as he tried to keep it down, and even knowing most of his frustration wasn't about Nikki, it broke out in his next words. "Is it such a bad thing to care about you?"

Another pause. "Joe's home. You know that, right? Is this about the clothes? Seriously, Anthony, they're just clothes. Just piles of baby clothes."

"You counted the rings before you answered."

She replied too fast. "Sheesh, you're as bad as me. I'm fine. Be my little brother, okay. I like it better when you're not trying to be Mom."

He blew out a long breath. "Okay. Fine."

"You did good today. Better than usual."

He grinned. She was placating him. "Now I know something's wrong. I don't think you watched the right game. Are you sure you weren't watching an old game?"

"Hmmm. I wondered why the Utah State players were wearing green. Uh, oh. I think I might have woken up Eli. Better go."

"Okay, later, Nik."

She said a distracted good-bye, and Anthony hung up the phone, sure he felt better.

* * *

For Ty, Saturday mornings meant sleeping in as long as she wanted. Especially since she didn't live at home and didn't have her mom coming in every thirty minutes after eight a.m., giving her a guilt trip about wasting the day away. Some Saturdays, like this one, after a week full of late nights doing homework, she could languish in bed until after noon and not feel guilty.

So when she got a text just before ten, it felt way too early to be up. After the beeping woke her, she reached across her nightstand and picked it up, squinting at the text from a number she didn't recognize.

Our ward has a service project today. Helping out with a family ward's Primary activity. Want to come?

She furrowed her eyebrows. *Who is this?*

David, of course.

How did you get my number?

Stole it from Dreamy's phone. Well, want to come?

Did she want the chance to see Anthony again this week? Yes. Did she want to come off like she was crashing a ward service project to see him? No.

Does Anthony know you're inviting me?

Is that really important?

So, no, Anthony didn't know. She heaved a sigh. Who was she kidding? Of course she wanted to go.

Where should I meet you?

:) 395 East 600 North at 10:30. See you there.

Having only thirty minutes to make herself presentable, Ty busted out of bed, hurried down the still-quiet hallway of her apartment, and got into the shower. She was short on time, so she braided her hair while it was still wet and made up for it by wearing a pair of jeans she'd always thought made her seem taller and the best working T-shirt she owned, a red, Mountain View High School Bruins T-shirt instead of her usual BYU tee.

The chapel where the Primary activity would be was close enough for Ty to walk to—or jog, considering she was a few minutes late already. Not that she minded, since she hoped to blend in with the other students and avoid awkward questions about what she was doing there when she didn't go to their ward.

Since the day was warm, everyone was mingling on the lawn when Ty arrived. She spotted Anthony and his roommates easily. Even though a bunch of kids and adults surrounded them, they towered above everyone. She started across the lawn.

"Hey there, Detmer."

Ty turned halfway around, expecting to see David standing behind her. Instead she locked gazes with an unfamiliar kid only a few inches taller than she. His brown hair stuck up in all the wrong places, especially the mass in the middle that looked like an attempt at a faux-hawk. He was dressed exactly like Anthony. Exactly. Right down to the khaki shorts and white T-shirt. Strange.

Ty managed a polite smile. "Uh, hi."

"Remember me? I'm Dylan. From the party? At Rocket's?"

Something about the way he said Anthony's nickname made Ty want to cringe. It sounded so . . . fake. "Uh, there were a lot of people there."

Her answer didn't deter Dylan. "I agreed with you that they should be playing Kaiser more."

"Oh." Nothing came to mind. Not even vague recognition. A million people came to that party. "Um . . . yeah . . ."

He beamed. "I knew you'd remember. I'm hard to forget."

She tucked a strand of hair behind her ear. "Yeah."

"Do you want to sit by me?" He motioned to an unused patch of grass.

She hated to turn him down, but she had a plan. She needed to stick to it. "Well—" She looked around.

David appeared at her side and rescued her. "Detmer promised to sit by me."

Dylan scowled at David, who smirked. Without another word, Dylan turned and dropped onto the grass with his back to them—and everyone else.

"Sorry," Ty said, but he wouldn't look at her. She followed David but kept glancing back at Dylan. She wouldn't have wanted Anthony to get any ideas about her and this guy if she'd sat with him, but she didn't want to be heartless either. Dylan knew enough about her to remember a nickname. That should flatter Ty, shouldn't it?

David led Ty toward Anthony, Sean, and DJ. He pushed his way through the crowd to stand next to Anthony. "You're welcome, by the way," David said to her.

"For what?" Anthony asked.

"Some kid's trying to steal my girl." David jerked his thumb over his shoulder.

Ty and Anthony looked in the direction David had indicated. Dylan had turned around, and the second he saw Anthony surveying him, his glare disappeared. He grinned and waved enthusiastically.

Anthony turned to David. "*Your* girl?"

David shrugged then winked at Ty. "I called dibs."

Did Ty imagine the possessive way Anthony had spoken? The swirly butterflies that had resided in her stomach since he kissed her on the cheek in class took flight again and seemed to flutter around her heart.

"Back to your corners, guys." She playfully put her hands on both their chests. "You don't seriously call dibs on girls, do you?" She didn't wait for the answer. They might, and she didn't want to embarrass them. "My head's big enough. Any more talk like this, and I might not fit into the church to help out."

Anthony hung his arm over Ty's shoulder—maybe a little possessively, she hoped. "Yeah, but considering the size of Beast's melon, you're safe," he said.

"*My* melon?" David's eyes widened. "You're the one who fell apart because—" A fake smile appeared on David's face. When Ty glanced back up at Anthony, she almost keeled over from the peripheral effect of the nasty glare Anthony gave David. Anthony seemed ready to pummel David for whatever he'd almost said, which for some reason, made Ty want to rescue *Anthony*. Like the day before, watching the game, she didn't like seeing him vulnerable.

She jumped in to show she had no clue what David almost said and that it didn't matter. "Because he lost that beanie last year? The one he's had since high school and was good luck?" She patted Anthony's arm, her fingers tingling. She focused on her words, ignoring the thoughts trying to push through. Like if Anthony would ever hold her hand. Or take her out on a date. "Remember, you broke the most-yards-in-a-game record that day?"

The dirty look slid away. Anthony chuckled and nodded. "Some beanie, huh? How did you know about that?"

It had seemed like such a good idea when it first came to her. Now she looked like an eager beaver. "Uh . . ." She fidgeted with the hem of her shirt. "The announcers went on and on about it the whole second half."

"Oh." Anthony nodded. Did he seem maybe a little impressed? "So I didn't realize you were in our ward."

Heat flooded her face. "Oh. Um. I'm not. David invited me to come over and help out."

The good news was Anthony didn't move his arm from around her shoulder. The bad news was he threw David an irritated scowl. "I see. Well, pretty good game last night?"

Though she knew her cheeks were bright red, she still laughed. "You did what you could," she teased. Then she remembered she should flirt. Show Anthony she needed him. She replaced her goofy, "cute" smile with the you-know-you-want-me version Rosie taught her. It worked for Rosie, well, for a few days. "I thought since I proved my football value to you, you'd call me after the game." She added a tiny pout at the end, for good measure.

Anthony moved his arm away from her but stayed right next to her, their shoulders brushing. He grinned. That smile was reward enough for Ty. She could sit and stare at it all day long. There was something amazing about it. More than confidence. More than amusement. Sometimes when she saw him smile, she glimpsed real joy, like when the camera caught him at just the right moment after a good play. He had worked so hard to get to the top of his game. Her heart flipped every time that smile graced his face, and her own smile wavered.

"Oh yeah?" He angled his body so they stood even closer. "It was pretty late."

What with the rapid pace of her heart and the wobbliness in her knees, she worried she might faint any second. Truth was, it impressed her that he and the other guys had shown up when they couldn't have gotten to bed earlier than two in the morning. Coming to participate in a service project after only a few hours of sleep? It went a long way toward proving her theory that he was more than just a star football player.

Warmth slid down her, stretching over her, and she wished she could keep it from overheating her face. "Sounds like you didn't want to hear a lecture about running too much." It came out in a voice barely above a whisper instead of like a confident statement.

His smile turned triumphant. "I won't disappoint you next time," he promised. A voice interrupted their moment, shouting something about getting started.

Ty didn't want to look toward the direction of the voice. She wanted to stare at Anthony for a while, even though he grinned wider and wider the longer she did.

"I'll hold you to that," she whispered, turning her attention to the front of the group.

A blonde with her hair pulled back into a ponytail was introducing herself as the Primary president and thanking them all for coming. "We'll start out with a song—something simple I'm sure you all know, 'I Am a Child of God'—and a prayer. Then my counselors and I will divide you all up for the stations."

Ty couldn't help another peek at Anthony, who caught her watching him. She blushed again and turned back to the steps, where the Primary president led the opening song. But when Anthony started singing, Ty's voice stopped in her throat. He had a clear, confident tenor, the kind that pierced her chest. The kind that made her heart stop. She thought she knew everything about Anthony Rogers. How did she not know he could sing? She turned to him and gaped.

Anthony must have felt her gaze. He turned his head enough to peer at her then rotated to look her in the eye. "What?"

She shook her head, still lost in the spell his voice had cast over her but afraid it might fade away if he didn't keep singing. She didn't think about anything Rosie told her to say. She didn't think about how she was supposed to act in front of Anthony. "Don't stop singing."

A confused expression crossed Anthony's face along with a cloudy smile. "Okay." The sound of his normal voice—though she still heard the music in it now and wondered how she missed it before—snapped Ty back to the present. There was no stopping the rush of heat to her face. She pressed her lips together and turned toward the Primary president, refusing to look at Anthony until someone came to assign them to a station for the activity.

She managed to work alongside him at the "I Want to Be a Missionary Now" station without embarrassing herself any further, but that probably had more to do with the fact that the kids kept them too busy to talk. With always at least three or four kids snuggling in her lap while Anthony talked about missions, it became less and less of a shock each time he sang "I Hope They Call Me on a Mission" with the kids, though from the amused expression on his face whenever he caught her eye, she figured she must still be staring at him all doe-eyed.

By the time the last of the sticky-faced kids had left the church, she was glad David had invited her. She'd had a blast with Anthony and the kids—even managing not to laugh when a little boy named Damien left a couple crucial letters out of his name when he made his missionary name tag. Anthony had to turn around while Ty told Damien the name tag looked great and added the *i* and *e* back in when he wasn't looking.

* * *

Rosie was up when Ty got there at almost one o'clock. Grinning, she collapsed onto the couch where Rosie was eating cereal and watching *How I Met Your Mother* reruns.

"Where have you been?" Rosie asked.

"At a service project with Anthony's ward."

Rosie's tired eyes grew larger in an instant. "He invited you to come help?"

Ty shrugged. "David did, but I spent the whole time with Anthony."

"Good for you!" Rosie patted her shoulder.

"Um, thanks?" But as condescending as Rosie sounded, Ty couldn't keep from grinning stupidly.

Rosie waved her fingers in front of Ty's face. "What's with the smile?"

Ty rolled her head to face Rosie. "He can sing."

"He can sing?"

Turning her gaze to the ceiling, Ty sighed. "Yeah, like an angel."

"Um. Okay."

"He's even more perfect than I thought. Man, Rosie, you should've heard his voice. It was . . . it was . . ." Ty clasped her hands over her heart. "I don't know."

"Angelic?" Rosie said sarcastically.

"Yeah."

When Ty didn't continue for several seconds, Rosie cleared her throat. "Um, anything else?"

Again Ty lolled her head to the side. "Huh?"

Rosie whacked Ty with her spoon. "Sheesh. You're useless. He can sing that well?" Rosie squeezed her eyes shut and shook her head. "Don't answer that. You'll go off again. So, it seemed like he was having a good time?"

Ty thought about how proud Anthony had been of the *Elder Best-Quarterback-in-the-World* tag she'd made him, and how he'd worn it even while they cleaned up after the activity. "Yeah. I think so."

"Good." Rosie nodded officially. "We'll have him wrapped around your finger in no time."

Ty sighed, still wanting to revel in the memory of his voice. "Sure."

"This is going great." Rosie clapped her hands and grabbed Ty's, shaking them in her excitement.

Ty grinned and let Rosie babble. Her enthusiasm complimented the warm feeling still lingering in Ty's chest. She didn't mind the rambling, though the words sort of rolled over her without sinking in. Something about stepping up her flirting and making Rocket aware of Ty's feelings without being too obvious. Ty softly hummed the tune of the closing song, trying to recapture the exact tone of his voice in her memory.

Anthony Rogers was almost perfect. She'd better enjoy this while it lasted.

Chapter Six

As she headed out for her usual Sunday evening with her family, Ty was glad she donned her soft, comfortable, dark blue BYU sweats and a white football T-shirt—until she saw Anthony jogging toward her from down the street, wearing the same sweats.

She pinched the bridge of her nose. Any chance he'd see this as flattering? She dropped her hand and plastered a smile on her face. Between this and the goofy way she acted about his singing, she'd never see him darkening this side of the sidewalk again.

"Hey." She waved and when he got closer said, "You should've called, and we could've worn the same thing."

Anthony laughed. His eyes darted down her figure. He seemed pleased. *Don't get your hopes up*, she cautioned herself.

"You make them look a lot better than I do," he said.

Her eyebrows shot up. She jammed them down. "Well, thanks."

"I came to invite you to the weekly Sunday dinner at Coach's house." Anthony put his hands in the pockets of the sweats.

He wasn't nervous, was he? Then it hit her what he'd asked. Her mouth dropped open, and she drew a breath. He wanted *her* to come to Sunday dinner at the coach's house? Except . . . she'd promised the boys she would come home for sure today. She and Stevie beat Walsh and Harly in a contentious game of Go Fish on Friday night, and Walsh and Harly had demanded a rematch.

It would do Anthony good to hear her tell him no, a voice said, but Ty didn't know if she could believe that voice. It sounded an awful lot like Rosie's, and she'd only gone on two dates with Anthony. Anthony didn't remember her. Which didn't surprise Ty.

"Oh," she managed to answer. "I would . . ." Was she really going to say no? "But I promised my brothers I'd be there for dinner tonight."

Anthony jerked his head back and stared at her. "You must like those brothers a lot." He forced a laugh.

Thinking about Walsh, Stevie, and Harline brought a smile to Ty's face. "Well, I happen to think they're pretty cool."

He shrugged at her. She hoped it was just disappointment now crossing his face and not something worse. "Tell them I said hi," he said.

"I'm not sure if I should. They might tell everyone they know that Rocket knows them."

"I'll hope you'll give me the chance." The corner of his mouth lifted.

"They'd die of excitement," she said.

He was walking backwards, probably eager to get away. *Stupid, stupid, Ty.* Those boys deserved an absolute pounding for taking away her chance to eat Sunday dinner with Anthony at his coach's house. Why didn't she say yes? She'd seen her brothers the day before. She resisted the urge to run after Anthony and take it all back. That would be worse.

"See you tomorrow." He waved.

He waited long enough for her to wave back before he turned and jogged back down the street. Ty spent the drive to her parents' house cursing her decision. They would've understood. Especially for Rocket.

"I'm home," she called when she got to the house. The smell of her mom's chicken noodle soup wafted from the kitchen, so Ty headed that direction. Both her parents stood next to the counter, laboring over the meal—her dad with his hands in a big bowl of roll dough and her mom cutting the homemade pasta into thin strips.

"Hey, Ty." Her dad swung a large arm over her shoulder, tucking her into a one-armed hug, strings of sticky dough dangling from his fingers.

"Hey, Dad," she said, her voice muffled.

Mom turned, wiping her hands off on a dish towel. "Well?" she asked, eager. "How are things going with Anthony?"

"Pretty good, but"—Ty held out two calming hands—"remember: we're just friends."

Dad wiggled his eyebrows. "For now."

"Yeah, he could lose interest any minute."

Harly ran into the room. "Did you talk to Rocket today?" Stevie ambled in behind him, trying to appear calm. Ty laughed at the excitement in his eyes.

"I did. I told him I was coming here, and he said to tell you guys hi."

Harly and Stevie froze. "For real?" Stevie asked. When Ty nodded, he pumped his fist in the air. "Rocket said hi to *me*!"

"Me too!" Harline scowled at Stevie before he began running around the kitchen shouting "Rocket" at the top of his lungs.

"You think he might ever come here?" Walsh asked from the doorway.

Stevie threw his football into the air and caught it with his knees. "That would be *totally* awesome!"

Ty surveyed the members of her family and realized how much she hoped Anthony might come over. Really hoped. More than ever before. "You never know. Maybe."

Whoops filled the kitchen. Ty had half a mind to record her brothers' reactions to show Anthony later. She looked over at her mom, who held up two hands, fingers crossed. Ty nodded and mirrored her actions with a wink that made her seem more confident than she was.

After dinner, Ty lingered. Here, without all the talk of what to do to reel Anthony in, she could pretend like it might last longer than a couple weeks. Rosie always seemed desperate, as though every interaction between Ty and Anthony might be the last, and Rosie would be a failure if the relationship didn't end up getting serious.

Once she and Mom cleared the table, Ty offered to clean the kitchen while Mom and Dad played a card game with the younger two boys.

"Just a warm up though," Walsh said as he followed Ty into the kitchen. "We still have that rematch."

"Yeah, yeah. Better make it good. It's the whole reason I turned down going to dinner with Anthony at his coach's house." Ty opened the dishwasher and started filling it with the dishes from the sink.

"You're kidding, right? He invited you to dinner, and you turned him down?"

"It seemed like a good play at the time."

Walsh rested against the counter and folded his arms. "Why?"

She could count on him not to pull punches. "Rosie is always pointing out how I shouldn't push too hard, and I shouldn't look too needy. I don't want to scare him off."

Walsh narrowed his eyes. "And you think turning him down for dates is a good thing? Girls are so crazy."

"This is a big deal, Walsh. Getting to know him like this? Not just reading about him on the Internet but actually figuring out what's real about him and what's just hype? It's once in a lifetime. I have to take advantage of it, but I can't screw it up either. It's a fine line to walk." She sighed and resumed loading the dishwasher, concentrating on lining up the plates by size, mostly so she wouldn't have to consider whatever skeptical face her brother was making.

"You make it sound like you think it's temporary."

"Isn't it?"

He snorted. Ty thought she heard him mutter "crazy" under his breath. He walked around her toward the sink and gathered up a pile of silverware before answering. "It would tick you off if I said something like that about football. Like, we have no chance for taking state this year, so I'm going to live in the moment during the games and try not to lose too badly."

"This isn't a football game." Heat rose up her face as she thought about the game plan document on her laptop. She bent over to stick more silverware in the basket, straightening after a few seconds of silence, when she was sure her face had returned to its normal color. "He's so . . . much more than even I expected. I'm scared I'm going to ruin what chance I have."

"You know, you're right. This isn't a football game. It's a lot more important. So it seems like it'd be a lot more important to be yourself. My sister has always told me I'm supposed to focus on things turning out how I want them to."

Ty stared at him and bit her lips together. *Game Plan Key: Design plays that utilize the team's talent.* Well. Maybe he was right.

* * *

Anthony arrived five minutes early for coaching football on Monday. High-Heel Girl and a couple others waved as he walked in. He nodded but paused next to the table at the front of the room to chat with Brian instead of indulging in some flirting. He didn't feel like it today.

"Good afternoon, Mr. Rocket." Brian handed him a corrected quiz from the Friday before. "Good weekend?"

The razing he got at dinner the night before came to mind. The dozen or so guys there couldn't believe Rocket got turned down. They wouldn't have known if David had kept his mouth shut. Anthony wondered about his best friend's priorities lately.

"I've had better," he said with a sigh.

Brian looked up from the stack of quizzes he was still grading. "What do you have to lament about?" He put down his pen and stared at Anthony.

"What, Rocket can't have a bad day?" Anthony scowled. He shouldn't care so much about what the guys said last night. With any other girl, he wouldn't care. But with Ty, he did care, and that worried him. Why had she turned him down? She acted interested in him at the party, let him kiss her, flirted, and was even awed by him at the service project. She confused him in a way that made him need to know more.

Had she really turned him down to go see her *brothers*?

He wanted to like her all the more for it. It reminded him of the relationship he had with Nikki. And if he'd found a girl comparable to Nikki—well, that was pretty scary too.

But he couldn't help wondering if it was part of her play-it-cool act. Another tactic. Something any other girl might try.

"You're too good at football and have too many dates to have anything to complain about." Brian pointed a stern finger in Anthony's face and broke him out of his thoughts. He went back to grading.

Anthony glanced toward the door. "Oh, really? Weren't you as good at football and had just as many dates in your day—"

"In my day?" Brian snorted. "Two years ago hardly qualifies as 'in my day.'"

"And I still recall seeing you down a time or two."

"I wasn't as good at football as you. Nowhere near your skills with the girls."

"You're only saying that 'cause you're afraid Angie will hear about it somehow." Anthony chuckled and wondered what was taking Ty so long to get to class.

Brian looked up again as Anthony chanced another peek at the door. "Waiting for someone?" Brian asked.

Anthony shrugged. "Like who?"

"Like . . . what do they call her? Detmer? Beast told me she's got you all messed up." Brian's shoulders shook with silent laughter.

Why couldn't David keep his mouth shut about Ty? He'd have Anthony married off to her if Anthony didn't watch him. "Rocket doesn't get messed up over girls."

Brian's voice took on a serious tone. "I recall you getting pretty messed up over—"

"That's different. That was before I knew better."

Brian set down his pen then rested back in his chair the same way Coach did when he was about to get all wise. "So, what? Is that what all this dating has been about? Making sure something like that doesn't happen again?" His raised eyebrows and challenging expression showed Anthony what he thought about that tactic.

Anthony stood. Through the doorway he could see Ty speed-walking up the hall. "No," he said, but he knew his defense was pointless. "It took me longer to find out that Keesha was like all the other girls. I have my process streamlined now."

Brian shook his head and picked his pen back up. "No more than two or three dates and you have them all figured out?"

"Yep." He turned to walk to his usual seat in the middle of the room so Ty didn't think he was waiting for her.

"How long before you know with Detmer?" Brian asked. Anthony shrugged and settled in his seat. Brian looked at him long enough to make Anthony pull out his phone and fiddle with it to break his stare.

"Sounds like if you don't, David will go after her," Brian said.

"Good for him," Anthony grunted, still intent on his phone.

Ty slipped into the seat next to him a few seconds later. "Hey, Anthony." She flicked at one of her earrings and stared down the hallway she'd left.

Anthony smiled, probably for the first time since Sunday night. She sat there like it was the natural thing to do. Like a friend, instead of like some girl desperate for his attention. Is that what he liked so much about her? How easy it was to be around her? Nothing more than a female version of David. Not so much pressure on him.

Except he couldn't stop thinking about her romantically. "Hey. What's up?"

She frowned, turned away from the door, and faced Anthony. "This'll sound stupid, but I thought someone followed me from my apartment up to class."

"I bet it's spies from TCU, waiting for the perfect opportunity to kidnap you and ruin my game this weekend," Anthony teased.

She beamed, lighting up her eyes and infusing a glow in her cheeks. Anthony thought he might grab her face and kiss it over and over. He was unapologetic about how much he liked to kiss girls and, right now, especially Ty.

Resting her chin in her hands and leaning forward, she asked with a quiet, hopeful voice, "You'd play bad if I went missing?"

Part of Anthony would like nothing better than to reassure the girl in front of him that yes, he would have a bad day, but the other part—the part that had a reputation to think of—overrode it. Maybe she had charmed him, but he needed to keep things light. If he didn't remember that, in the end, she'd disappoint him. Like Keesha had.

He swept a charming smile across his lips. In that instant Ty's sweet, wishful look dissolved. The expression left in its wake made Anthony hate what he was about to say, even though it came easy. "Of course I would." He kept trying to make Ty out to be just like all the girls he'd dated in the last year, and if that was true, why did he feel bad for his usual act?

She plastered on her own poised expression, but now Anthony saw right through it. "Good to know. I'll try to avoid getting kidnapped."

"Phew." Anthony wiped a hand mockingly across his forehead.

She opened her notebook, turning the pages and finding the next empty one. "So, how was dinner?"

"Awful," Anthony answered. "All the guys were disappointed you didn't come." He exhaled, glad for the change of subject. Things could've gotten awkward.

She looked up again, meeting his gaze with a strange mixture of emotion in her eyes: half the hope from before swirled with her own brand of fake charm. "*All* the guys?"

A chance to redeem himself. He swept in to take it. "Maybe one more than the rest."

"Next time I'll ditch my pesky brothers then."

He laughed. "I'm touched."

"You shouldn't be." She leaned on the back of her chair, giving him her full attention. "They bugged me about you all night. It was terrible. I should've gone with you."

Despite the fact that he'd been grinning since she showed up to class, it felt more natural now than ever. It made him think of Nikki again. He liked that Ty had a thing for her brothers. He liked that he understood it. "Glad you learned your lesson."

She pressed her lips together. He wondered why she tried to hold back her smile. He liked it. A lot. That much he'd admit.

"Me too," she said.

* * *

For Ty, the best part of coaching football was that Brian assigned a project for which they would need partners. And though the details were fuzzy, Ty remembered being brave enough to ask Anthony if they could work together. He'd accepted. So the rest of Ty's day had blurred by in a daydream sort of way.

In one sentence and with one contemplative look, Rosie blew all of Ty's blissful haziness away. "There's something not right about this whole thing."

Ty looked up from the math refusing to hold her concentration and frowned. "What? What do you mean?" She rested her head against the couch, waiting for Rosie's latest analysis.

Rosie held out her hands and spoke in a this-should-be-totally-obvious tone. "He's *kissed* you."

"Yeah. He's kissed a lot of girls. Including you," Ty pointed out with a twinge of jealousy. Why, she didn't know. Rosie never got this far with Anthony, although from the tilt of her head and the condescension in her expression, Rosie didn't think Ty had gotten too far either—partners or not.

"He hasn't asked you on a date. It's been about a week since this operation began, and he *kissed* you"—Ty rolled her eyes at the drawn out way Rosie kept saying *kissed*—"but he hasn't asked you on a date yet." Rosie tapped a finger against her temple. "Does that sound strange to you, or is it just me?"

Ty thought about Walsh's suggestion to focus on the good. "Maybe it's better. He's getting to know me, so it could mean he thinks I'm different than the rest of them."

Rosie pointed her gaze at the ceiling. "No one's different enough."

"Maybe I'll be the first." Ty decided to ignore whatever else Rosie wanted to delve into and try to get some homework done. She wondered if this whole thing was Rosie's vicarious second chance with Anthony, the opportunity to learn from the mistakes she'd made and make Ty a success. The idea bothered her. At what point would Rosie step in and claim what she'd rightfully won?

A knock on the front door interrupted, and Ty got up to answer it.

Dylan, the kid from the service project (and apparently the party at Anthony's), stood outside. "Hey there, Detmer."

"Oh." Ty scrunched her nose at the way he used her nickname again. Like they were already BFFs. "Hello."

He nudged his way inside. "What's up?"

Ty stood by the door, holding it open. "How do you know where I live?"

"Saw you walk in after class. I just live down there." He shrugged and waved in no particular direction.

Ty still held the door open. His vague answer made the hairs on her arms stand on end. "What do you need?" She shared a glance with Rosie, whose slanted brows suggested she felt the same about this intrusion as Ty did. It didn't surprise Ty that Rosie could sniff past Dylan's try-too-hard exterior to the sort of creepy center. To most, he must appear normal. Messily styled brown hair, although Ty noticed he'd combed it off to the side, the same way Anthony had worn his today. How would Dylan even know that? He wore stylish jeans and a snappy button-up shirt. But something—his pushiness, maybe?—made Ty want to shiver.

Be kind to everyone. Her mom's voice filtered into her brain. Mom had said those words every day when she dropped them off for school and now whenever Ty left the house after a visit.

"Are any of your football friends dropping by tonight?" Dylan asked. He bent over the couch to peer out the window, like Anthony or David might walk up the steps any minute. When no one appeared, he dropped onto the couch.

Ty felt an inkling of what Anthony must feel whenever a new girl started flirting with him—being used for his popularity. Shame touched her cheeks, flushing them with heat. *I'm different. Especially now.* She thought of the warm feeling that erupted in her chest when Anthony told her it'd ruin his game if something happened to her. Nothing distracted Anthony from football. And he didn't mean it when he said Ty would, but he said it anyway. *I'm different*. She looked at Rosie. Her roommate slid her shoulders upward in a confused shrug.

"Not that I know of." Ty knew her answer came thirty seconds later than anyone expected.

Dylan leaned back, spreading his arms out over the top of the couch. "I see. You guys busy? Want to watch a movie?"

Ty shut the door in defeat. "I have homework."

Dylan glanced at the math book sitting on the couch next to him. "Great. I'll watch while you work." His thin lips opened in a smile.

Be kind to everyone. Ty sighed and plopped down, crowding the arm of the couch to keep as far away as possible. "Okay."

* * *

By the end of the opening credits, Dylan's fingers had brushed up and down Ty's back. She'd gotten up to get drinks and use the bathroom to put distance between them, but she couldn't deter Dylan. He'd held her hand when he walked to the door. And if she hadn't pushed his shoulders back before shutting the door, he would've kissed her. He didn't seem able to read body language, and Ty didn't know if she had it in her to tell him she wasn't interested. He'd put some effort into putting himself out there. Creepy effort, yes, but all things considered, maybe his social skills were just lacking.

Ty felt bad for him. How could she add to that? So the next day when she saw David and DJ sitting at a table for lunch in the Wilkinson Center, she had an idea. While Dylan didn't exactly like David, he admired football players in general. Maybe if one of them let him down easy for her, it wouldn't be so bad.

"Hey." She collapsed into the chair. "I need your guys' help." After the words tumbled out, she gulped, realizing how forward she sounded. Again the comparison between her and Dylan jumped at her. He'd acted like one night at a party made them instant friends, and now she was doing the same thing. But David's grin eased her conscience.

"Saw the light, did you?" he asked. "You're dumping Anthony for me. No need to explain. I understand you couldn't stay away."

The tension cramping most of Ty's muscles relaxed. "First of all, I can't dump a guy I'm not dating. Second, no. I won't date you. That might hinder my efforts to date the guy I'm not yet dating."

DJ laughed. "That's not the best way to ask for a favor."

"True." Ty turned to David. "I'll put on my sweet face, but no flirting."

"Then I'm not promising anything." He folded his arms and waited, his eyes dancing.

"You remember that kid Dylan from the service project?" she asked.

David angled himself toward her, resting his elbows on the table and watching her over his joined hands. "The one that got all prickly when I wouldn't let you sit with him?"

"Yeah, him. He showed up at my apartment last night. And invited himself to watch a movie then got kind of touchy-feely." She waited, hoping for a magic solution from them.

"Guy's got guts," DJ muttered.

David elbowed him; then his easy expression turned guarded. He shifted again so he sat back in his chair, for all intents looking uninterested, except for his fingers softly drumming the table. "Speaking of that guy you're trying to date, how come you're asking us and not him?"

Ty hadn't thought to. The task seemed beneath him, not to mention presumptuous. They hadn't reached a point in their relationship—if you could call it that—where she felt comfortable bothering him with other guys that showed her unwanted attention.

"Oh. Well, I saw you guys first," she admitted. Looking away, she ran a finger along the edge of the table. "And I can't say I'd feel comfortable asking him . . . yet." She added the last with a hopeful glance at them.

David studied her, not answering for what felt like several hours; all the while, Ty fidgeted in her seat and tried not to make eye contact. Every time she peeked at DJ, he seemed confused about David's reaction.

At last he shrugged. "Okay, sure. We can talk to him."

"Really?" Ty sagged with relief and couldn't stop from smiling. "You would?" She knew she should wonder at how easily Anthony's friends accepted her. Her expert level of football knowledge helped, but something about hanging out with them felt natural. Like when she was with Anthony. When she could forget about not messing up, things felt so right.

"Sure." An impish smile took over David's expression. "You're our girl now, Ty, whether you like it or not."

"'Our girl?'" She raised her eyebrows. "Like I'm the property of the team?"

"Until someone snags you for his own." David laughed. "And if Dreamy doesn't soon, I'm taking over."

Ty blushed but answered, "Why would you want another one of Anthony's cast-offs?"

David laughed before taking a large forkful out of what looked like a small pail of macaroni and cheese. "This time it would be worth it."

"TCU is going to force you guys to run on Saturday. Your stats aren't going to be good, Beast. How do you feel about that?" Ty took out her math homework, hoping they'd go with the change of subject.

A grin overtook David's mouth, revealing a row of food-stuffed teeth. "In case you've missed the last fifty or so games I've played in, I know how to put one foot in front of the other."

"Mmm-hmm. So you say."

DJ laughed. "We need to figure out how to keep her around."

David eyed her. "I've got a few ideas."

Ty shook her head and turned to her own lunch. She agreed, but for now, she was just glad they'd promised to take care of her Dylan problem. One step at a time.

Chapter Seven

"You know, I'm starting to get a little jealous of Beast," Anthony said as he and Ty gathered up their books Wednesday after class.

Her breath caught. "I didn't think Rocket Rogers got jealous of anyone."

"Well, it rarely happens, but I blame it on you. You've hung out with Beast twice now, an honor you've never bestowed on me." Anthony had intended the observation to be lighthearted, but he realized his negative thoughts on sharing a crush with David had probably shown through. He thought he'd managed to wrangle his feelings for Ty into the friends category. Maybe he'd have to try harder.

She took a deep breath and brushed his upper arm. He drew a sharp intake of his own. If he was going to be just friends with her, they needed to avoid physical contact of any kind. He might quit caring how serious it could get with her, the girl who *seemed* different, but he knew couldn't be. They were all the same around here. He'd worry about finding a wife when he left Provo and his football fame behind.

"Don't worry about Beast." She pulled her hand back and clenched it against her side. "He's just doing a favor for me."

Anthony rolled his gaze upward and struggled not to care. "Are you trying to make me more jealous?" His lightness came off a little too false.

"No! He's just . . . he said he'd talk to that Dylan kid for me. No big deal." Her eyes widened with a sort of fear. What was she afraid of?

He tried laughing it off. She deserved someone like David. He could give her the kind of relationship she probably wanted. Too bad Anthony wasn't that generous. "Who's Dylan?"

She shrugged. "Some football groupie with a crush on me. I think he thinks I can get him closer to you guys." She swept her books into her bag and turned to leave the classroom.

Anthony followed, hoisting his own bag onto his shoulder. So she was going to David with her problems? "Is he bothering you?"

Ty eyed him over her shoulder, flashing a goofy grin. "Dylan or David?

Some of Anthony's irritation melted away. "Either one."

She shrugged and leaned into him, burning his shoulder with her presence. When she wasn't trying too hard, they fit together. "Not yet." She winked.

He should ask her out. Get the one or two (or three or four, maybe) dates over with. To prove his theory right, of course. "Want to do lunch?" he asked. "You know, to plan out our playbooks."

She nodded. "Of course." Then her expression fell again. "Oh . . . no, you're going to think I'm trying to get out of going out—of hanging out with you."

Anthony's mouth tried to twitch into a smile despite the disappointment welling up, again. Her concern was endearing. Even so, this time he wasn't telling David about this; although, considering how much she'd been seeing him, Ty might tell him herself.

"Your brothers?" Anthony guessed. The way she kept turning him down had to make her at least a little different, right? He couldn't decide if this observation made him happy or not.

She stopped in the middle of the hallway and gripped Anthony's arm. It seemed natural, but it still sent a zing through him. "Here's the thing. I use my lunch break on Wednesdays to help with math centers in my little brother Harly's kindergarten class."

"Math centers?"

"Yeah. You remember in elementary school, rotating around to different stations to do different activities? Well, I hang out at one of the stations and help them do math stuff. I'm headed over now. But"—she took a mighty breath—"well, you could . . . come. If you wanted." She whipped her hand away from his arm and rushed on. "I mean, you might cause a minor riot showing up like that, so it's a risk. And I understand if—"

"I'll come."

Her gaze snapped to his, her eyes softening. "You want to?"

"I do want to." And he really did. He started down the hall, leading the way out of the building and toward his car.

Technically he hadn't taken her on a date yet, so he was still ahead of the game, though his objectives had gotten a bit fuzzy. Prove to Ty her charms had no affect?

Then again, he hadn't taken her on a date yet, and he was still interested. Oh boy.

* * *

Ty was right about the minor riot. As soon as they saw Anthony, a dozen kids started yelling and rushing him. Their teacher, Mr. Franklin, couldn't recover his voice quickly enough to call order. So Ty took control, which made Anthony smile.

"I hope you don't mind, Mr. Franklin. I thought the kids would enjoy meeting him." She tried to seem contrite, but Anthony had watched the pleased-with-herself expression growing since they left campus. He didn't know what to think. A bunch of rowdy kindergartners wasn't the type of date he would've planned. Her offering him up as a fun person to meet should be proof she saw only Rocket and not Anthony, but that didn't seem right.

Mr. Franklin, still staring at Anthony, shook his head. "No! Absolutely not. No problem at all. What a treat. Thanks for coming, Rock—Mr.—er—"

"Anthony is fine, sir."

Ty broke in with a straight face. "He also answers to Dreamy or DTR, among a few hundred other nicknames."

Anthony elbowed her, softly of course, overcoming the urge to add "Bum Face" to that list. It seemed natural to tell her.

Her joke helped Mr. Franklin relax and laugh. "I'll stick with Anthony."

"Rocket?" A little boy with the exact same shade of chocolate-brown hair as Ty tugged on Anthony's shirt. One quick, unnecessary comparison to Ty's face and he knew this must be Harline.

"Yeah, Harly?" Anthony crouched and smirked at the surprised, yet enchanted, face of the little boy's older sister.

"You know my name?"

"Of course I do. I'm friends with your sister, aren't I?"

"Rocket knows my name!" Harly shouted, and the riot ensued again.

"Harly! Harline Daws!" Ty shouted to regain his attention. "Didn't you want to ask Anthony something?"

Harly raised an eyebrow at her. The expression was so similar to Ty's that Anthony nearly started laughing. "Anthony?" Harly repeated, confused.

Ty rolled her eyes and reluctantly called Anthony by his nickname. "Rocket. His name is Anthony, Harly."

Anthony didn't think this information would stick with Harly for long, but he grinned at Ty for trying. None of the other girls cared this much about calling him Anthony. A point in her favor maybe?

She rewarded him with a bewitching smile. He gave her a little slack and didn't try to talk himself out of falling for her. A little bit.

"Right. So, Rocket?" Harly turned his attention to Anthony. "Are you going to play football with us?"

Ty answered first. "We came to help with math centers." Harly dropped his chin, and Ty reached for his hand. Daring a peek at Anthony, she bent over and whispered, "Maybe Anthony will come over sometime to play with you and Walsh and Stevie."

Anthony knew she was trying to help, but it caused a round of angry protests as the rest of the class demanded Rocket come to their house to play football with them too. Ty frowned at Anthony and mouthed, "Sorry."

Anthony laughed. Mr. Franklin came to the rescue. "It's not every day Rocket Rogers visits, so if it's all right with him, we'll skip math centers and head outside today."

It was a good thing Anthony had no problem with this plan because the entire room filled with resounding *yays*.

* * *

Ty played quarterback for the other team—and she was as good as Anthony suspected. After stopping up another one of his team's runs, she rubbed the top of her brother's head. "Maybe next time you'll choose your own sister over Rocket."

To which Harly shouted, "Never!"

Anthony agreed with Ty though. Her team was winning. Anthony had been sacked more in the last thirty minutes than in his whole life. It didn't help that his own team was usually part of the pile that ended up on top of him.

It was also possible Anthony was having more fun in this game than any other. Except maybe that game his senior year of high school when his coach turned him and David loose to do whatever they wanted. The thing was, girls had always finagled a way to make football the common factor between them, but none of them had ever thought to have a backyard game with him.

Anthony tore his gaze away from Ty and turned his attention to the huddle. "Okay, we're going to blitz, guys. Do you know what that means?"

To no one's surprise, Harly's hand popped up. "When they snap the ball, everyone goes for Ty."

Anthony gave him a high five. "Exactly." Anthony lined up behind the smallest defensive line he'd ever had the pleasure of playing with. They faced off with Ty and a center that might rival the Leprechaun, though not in size. Despite her petite frame, the little blonde girl had fiercely protected her quarterback.

As Anthony suspected—and secretly hoped—his players didn't wait for Ty to finish her count before they rushed in. Laughing, Ty backed away from hungry players, admonishing the little girl to be soft when she sent a boy twice her size to the ground.

Anthony threaded through the miniature line to Ty. She tried to dance away, but he was too quick. He swept her over his shoulder and headed for his end zone.

"What?!" Ty squealed, trying to wiggle free, but she was light and easier to hold than most footballs. And truthfully, he liked holding her. A lot. "Anthony. Anthony! Anthony Rogers, put me down. This isn't fair."

He laughed. Cheers followed them as he headed down the field, especially when he slid Ty off his shoulder in the end zone. "Safety," he called triumphantly.

She tried not to smile at him. Her lips pressed together, and her eyes danced defiantly. "Not fair. I was down way back there. Forward progress."

"You're going to argue football rules with *me*? Do you know who I am?"

She tilted her head to one side. "Um, some guy who thinks he might be good at football."

Laughter rushed out of him. A picture of her hanging out with Nikki and knocking him down a notch or two flashed across his mind. "Yeah. I know a little bit. Quit whining. It's only two points for us. What's the score now? Thirty-five to nine?"

"I always knew I was a better football player than you." She raised one shoulder in a half-shrug that somehow slung her closer to him. He lowered his face toward her, surprised at how natural the movement was and how quickly he found himself a breath away from her lips. Just another kiss. Not a big deal.

Surprise shot through her eyes, acting like a magnet. She wasn't triumphant. With a soft sigh, she lowered her eyelids, but not before he caught a look of contentment, a look he knew was mirrored in his own eyes.

His lips had barely brushed hers when a dozen kindergartners reached them, all of them shouting and jumping around. It forced him to open his eyes. She shrugged again, looking disappointed before she chased the expression away with a smile.

"Better luck next time," she whispered before breaking away.

He burst into laughter, turning to follow her, certain, for the first time, there would be a next time. He'd make sure. Maybe it would take a few more dates than he thought to cross Ty off his list.

Chapter Eight

Ty decided on the way home she wouldn't tell Rosie about the kiss. Rosie would think something was wrong about Anthony not finishing it, despite the rowdy kindergartners clamoring for a victory lap. She wouldn't realize how great the mere touch of his lips was, how it was almost better than their actual kiss. Ty knew she hadn't misread Anthony. Last time he'd kissed her as a challenge. Today he *wanted* to kiss her.

So before she pushed open the door of her apartment, she tried to wipe the dreamy smile affixed to her lips. "Anthony went to Harly's class with me today," she announced.

Rosie looked up from the kitchen table, where wires and three laptops surrounded her and an unfamiliar boy.

"What's going on?" Ty asked.

Rosie walked over, grabbed Ty by the arm, and dragged her forward. "This is Wayne. He's in my computer class. Well, he's the TA."

"What are you doing?" Ty saw Anthony's Facebook profile on the middle computer. "Rosie?" She turned to her roommate. The bliss she'd carried from lunchtime through the rest of the day floated away, leaving her confused.

"You said there had to be some girl who was different from the others," Rosie said. Ty nodded, surprised her roommate remembered that. "Wayne is going to figure out if there ever was and who she is."

"Why?" Ty faltered. She'd made it, hadn't she? Gotten Anthony's attention. Gotten him to hang out. His behavior today told her he no longer considered her a passing, two-date fling. Was Rosie trying to get her a ring? From Rocket Rogers? The thought alone almost made Ty double over with laughter.

She wouldn't mind a good couple months with Anthony, but Ty had to stay realistic.

"If we know how she's different from all the other girls, then we can make you different." Rosie smiled brightly.

I'm already different. But she bent forward anyway to inspect Wayne's setup. "How are you going to figure it out?"

Ty thought that a guy who owned this many laptops should look nerdier, but, except for his lankiness, he looked normal. Cute even, in a rumpled sort of way.

He scrubbed his hand over his short, blond hair. "I'm searching Rocket's Facebook account for girls who posted stuff to his wall. We'll filter them out with a variety of measures."

A *ding* interrupted his explanation. Wayne's fingers flew over the keyboard in the middle. Pictures flashed across all three screens. "I have the top five girls Rocket has interacted with." He punched another key. "Number one, Keesha May." Pictures rolled up, filling the middle laptop screen. Pictures of a dark-haired girl and Anthony. Smiling. He looked at the girl with an expression Ty had only ever seen him use on the football field. She'd never come across these in all the years she'd followed Anthony. He'd posted so few pictures of his private life. Mostly she'd seen football stuff—pictures of his state championship team, the day he signed his letter of intent to play for BYU. And since they'd become Facebook friends a few days before, she hadn't thought to check out his private past. It never occurred to her. She knew him personally now. What would she have thought if she'd known about this girl all along?

Ty's throat started to close. In that moment she knew she'd never be *that* kind of different. Anthony had never smiled at her like that. Ty entertained him for now. She was novel.

He had loved that girl.

Then Rosie read the last post between them, from over a year before. Something Anthony posted on Keesha's wall.

"*I can't wait for tonight. I have a huge surprise for you.*" Rosie scrunched her nose and leaned over Wayne's shoulder, her face close to his. Did Rosie notice the bright pink tint to Wayne's ears at her nearness? "Wonder what that meant," she asked.

Ty struggled to find her voice. That was the last post. They broke up that night, she suspected. She also had a guess for what the huge surprise was. He almost married this girl. And whatever stopped it was worse than a bad breakup.

"Stop," she said in a strangled voice. "This isn't okay."

Rosie straightened, eyeing Ty with a determined expression. Wayne had the decency to grimace and turn away.

"What? If you want to be that girl"—Rosie pointed at the screen—"then we have to play a little bit dirty. It's on Facebook, Ty. He put it out there in the first place, and there's nothing wrong with us taking a look and using it for our advantage."

Ty caught the word *our*. She shook her head. "Seriously, Rosie. Stop." She turned and headed for her bedroom. She didn't know how, but she had to get those pictures out of her head.

* * *

The next morning Ty called Walsh on her way to class. Her thoughts the night before had churned around Anthony and the way he'd looked at that girl in the pictures. She needed to clear her head. Maybe Walsh could help.

"Three computers to stalk him on Facebook? Don't you do that fine with one?" Walsh had asked after she told him the story.

"Thanks," she said dryly.

"He dated that girl a long time ago."

"Yeah. He dated her for eight months but hasn't dated anyone seriously since." Ty studied the sidewalk in front of her as she confessed this.

"How do you know that?"

"Heard Rosie and Wayne talking after I went to my room."

"I think you're overreacting."

Ty wanted to scream. Why did he always have to see life so simply? Was it a boy thing? It made the night she spent analyzing it seem pretty stupid. "The Rosie-stalking thing or the serious-girlfriend thing?"

"Both."

"Walsh, help me out here. Why hasn't he asked me out on a real date yet? Because of her?"

Walsh sighed his long-suffering, why-do-I-put-up-with-this-girly-stuff sigh. "What happened to being yourself and focusing on the positive?"

"I found out I have to compete with a girl who made him smile the same way football does. She was a big deal."

An uncomfortably familiar voice interrupted. "Hey, Detmer."

Ty started and turned. Dylan had fallen into step right beside her. *Right* beside her. His shoulder brushed against hers. *Be. Kind. To. Everyone.* The mantra sounded like it came through clenched teeth.

"Hey." She pressed her lips together and eyed him.

"Ty?" Walsh asked.

"Um, just a minute." She stared expectantly at Dylan, trying not to snap. "Can I help you?"

"Thought I'd walk with you to class." He grinned.

She hesitated, hoping he'd get that she wanted to go back to her conversation. In her experience, he'd never picked up on those signals, so she gave up. "I have to go, Walsh. I'll talk to you later."

"What's up?" he asked. Curiosity dripped off his voice.

"Later."

"Okay. Well, quit analyzing everything."

"Okay," she promised before hanging up, but fat chance of that. She surveyed the sidewalk as she pocketed her phone. "So you must live pretty close?" she asked him.

He shrugged. "Yeah. Who was on the phone? Rocket?"

Why was he so vague about where he lived? "Uh, no. My brother."

"Oh." He shrugged off a look of disappointment. "Mind if I walk with you?"

Did she have a choice? *Ty, not nice.* She noticed he didn't carry a backpack. "Are you going to class?" She avoided the original question, knowing it wouldn't matter anyway.

He smiled. "No. Just headed up to campus."

Ty couldn't help narrowing her eyes. "Oh." Was he being purposefully vague? A surprising chill ran up Ty's spine. She couldn't explain the icky feeling that always oozed over her around Dylan.

He looked around. "That's funny. I expected you to be walking with Beast or maybe Rocket."

"Yeah?" Ty increased her pace. The sooner she got up to campus and to class, the sooner she could wiggle out of Dylan's company.

"Yeah. When I talked to Beast a couple days ago, it sounded like he keeps pretty close tabs on you."

Ty made a mental note to ask about David's conversation with Dylan and the possibility David might not have been "forceful" enough. "He's just a friend."

Dylan swept an arm across Ty's shoulder and winked at her. "That's good to hear."

Ty faked tripping so she could duck out of his embrace. "Oh?" She jogged ahead of him.

"In a hurry?" Dylan asked.

"I've got class."

"So." Dylan matched her stride. "Since you're not dating any of the football players—right?"

Well . . . not technically. Yet. "No."

"Then we should go out. Tonight? I'll pick you up at seven."

Was that even a question? He didn't leave her any way out of it. Well, what could one date hurt? "O-kay," she agreed.

Dylan grinned, but it fell flat, not reaching his eyes or any part of his expression. "Perfect."

* * *

Being in Dylan's car reminded Ty of the time she'd played hide-and-go-seek with her brothers and gotten stuck in what she thought would be the perfect hiding place: the too-skinny laundry chute. The bucket seats in his older-model Camry sat way too close together, so she rested against the window to get as far away as she could. It wasn't enough. Dylan's hand kept slipping off the gearshift and on to her knee. Thank heavens for stop-and-go traffic and a manual transmission. The assaults were short in duration.

"You're going to love this restaurant. Every girl I know does."

Ty knew her answering smile looked nightmarish. She'd tried too hard since he picked her up. He liked her too much, and she had less than no interest in him. His touch made her want to scrub her knees off. His slick smile nauseated her. His total obliviousness worried her. Did he not notice she cringed every time they came in contact? Next time she'd ask Anthony to chat with Dylan. Maybe he could intimidate Dylan more than David had managed to. A genuine smile crept onto her face when she thought about telling Anthony that.

"There's that smile all the guys love." Dylan's fingers brushed across Ty's cheek. She jerked back, knocking her head against the window. Her reaction didn't bother Dylan. He didn't even notice. "Let's see what we can do to keep it there." His hand dropped to her knee, and he squeezed. A red light ahead forced his hand back to the gearshift. Ty breathed a sigh of relief.

Someone needed to tell him about body language and being too touchy-feely. Ty folded her arms in case he got ideas about holding her hand between stops. Already this date seemed to have lasted several hours.

"I bet it's fun hanging out with the football players all the time," Dylan said.

"Um, sure." It wasn't the first time Ty got the feeling Dylan only liked her because she knew Anthony and some of the other guys on the team. How did he expect that connection to pay off for him? Or did having Anthony's attention make her more attractive to other guys?

"You know, once they had a mind reader come for a party. It was like a vacation for him." Dylan laughed, hitting his hand against the steering wheel.

Ty forced a short laugh before defending them. "You have to be pretty smart to play at the college level, you know."

"Sure, sure." Dylan chortled. "I heard the coach tried to get them all brain transplants but the brains rejected them."

Ty blinked, shook her head, and watched Dylan laugh as though he'd told the funniest joke he could imagine. He held his stomach with his free hand—Ty was at least grateful for that—and he seemed to be having trouble breathing. She bit her lip to keep from telling him exactly what Anthony and David had to know before they even stepped on the field.

Dylan looked over at her, his laughter calming when he noticed her lack of amusement. "Okay, okay. So that's the wrong way to make you smile. How about this?"

He told an insensitive, obnoxious joke that made Ty gape. He laughed at her obvious shock, as if it delighted him. How could he imagine a joke like that would amuse her?

"You know, Dylan," she said, "I think you should take me home. I don't see this working out."

Dylan rolled his eyes. "Oh, come on, Detmer. Lighten up."

She wondered if he knew her real name. "I'm serious." She folded her arms tighter. "It's obvious we don't have the same interests. I don't like you like that, and you know I've been hanging out with Anthony a lot. Please pull over." She prided herself on her determination.

Just like that Dylan's entire demeanor changed. He narrowed his eyes and focused on traffic. "The date's not over," he snapped.

"This isn't going to work out between us. Sorry." Ty tried to make her pronouncement sound less . . . rude.

He clenched the steering wheel, his knuckles white. "I'll take you home after we finish our date."

The low, menacing way he said it scared Ty into silence. She wished they weren't miles away from her apartment. She'd jump ship at the next light. Maybe she could call Walsh or Rosie or even Anthony to come and get her. She looked at Dylan and wondered what he'd do. Stop the car. Come after her. She knitted her fingers together.

"Fine," she whispered. She tried to stay calm. Told herself Dylan was a guy with a crush. Her response to his "jokes" must've hurt his feelings, and he reacted with anger, scary anger.

He smiled, as though Ty had flicked a switch, and his good mood returned. "Just wait. You'll have a great time."

Be kind to everyone. Now her mother's words sounded like a warning. Ty stared out the window as buildings whisked by. After several awkward, silent minutes, he pulled into the Olive Garden. Why did he drive all the way to American Fork to take her there?

"Wait here," he said after he stopped. He got out and ran around to open the door for her.

Ty wouldn't jump ship on this date without backup. Big, intimidating backup. She used the few seconds to text Anthony. *Save me.*

Dylan pulled open her door. She stuffed the phone into her pocket and scrambled out. As they walked toward the door of the restaurant, Dylan rested his hand on her back. Knowing walking quicker wouldn't keep him at bay, Ty allowed it. She moved stiffly and wished her posture would convey how uncomfortable he made her. But considering no matter how stand-offish her attitude had been, he didn't notice, so she didn't get her hopes up.

A handful of patrons stood in the entrance of the restaurant waiting for tables. That was a relief. If there'd been more people, she would've had to stand closer to Dylan. Funny how she wouldn't have minded that dilemma if her date had been Anthony.

She didn't make an effort at conversation, answering shortly when Dylan did. It didn't stop him from trying. Ty thought about the phone in her pocket, willing it to buzz with good news from Anthony.

What was the worst that could happen? She tried to reassure herself. The next hour or so with Dylan would be uncomfortable. She'd eat fast and insist Dylan take her home so she could finish homework. She had a lot, and she would be up late anyway. And if he wanted to stay and watch movies again? She took a deep breath. She could go back to her bedroom. He couldn't follow her there. If he did, she'd be within her rights to punch him in the face.

Anthony didn't answer until the hostess sat Ty and Dylan at a table. *I'm that hard to resist, huh?*

Ty sighed with relief and propped up her menu in front of her. Hiding behind it, she texted back, *I'm serious. At AF Olive Garden with Dylan. Please—*

Dylan knocked down her menu-wall as she typed in the *e*. "It's not nice to text on a date, Detmer." His fingers wrapped around her phone.

Though he smiled, his eyes glinted with hardness. Ty clutched her phone, yanking it back toward her. She wouldn't give up her lifeline, her chance for rescue. "You're right. Sorry." She tapped the send button as she slid it into her pocket. It buzzed seconds later. Ty didn't risk a peek, but she hoped Anthony was on his way. Dylan would take the phone away if she looked, and then where would she be? She pulled her menu toward her, careful not to raise it off the table and infringe on Dylan's ability to see her face. She stared hopefully at the doorway.

"Know what you want?" Dylan asked.

Ty swept her gaze away from the doorway and looked at him. "Uh, no. Not yet." She tried to concentrate on the delicious looking meals in front of her.

The waitress appeared too soon. Ty knew that even if Anthony had answered, *I'm on my way*, she was still several minutes from rescue.

"You kids ready to order?" Their waitress, a short, middle-aged woman with a shock of stylish gray hair sweeping across her forehead, smiled at them.

As dismal as Dylan had made this date, Ty didn't want to leave him with a bill for a meal she didn't plan on eating. "I'm going to need a few more—"

"We're ready." Dylan flashed a smile at her. "I know what you want." He turned to the waitress, who ran a confused gaze over Ty before turning back to Dylan.

"I can come back in a minute," she offered, her voice giving away how awkward she must feel.

"No need," Dylan insisted. "We'll both have the Lasagna *Rollata al Forno*. It's her favorite." He nodded toward Ty.

The waitress turned to Ty, probably waiting for her to give her attentive date a look of adoration. She managed to whisper, "That's fine." She stared at Dylan, breathing shallowly to avoid overreacting to this latest assault on her privacy. Worse than his hand on her knee or on her back, how could he know what she always ordered at Olive Garden? What kind of guy sat across from her?

The waitress pursed her overly red lips and snapped her notebook closed. "Anything to drink?" She didn't bother looking at Ty.

"Just water." Dylan did turn to Ty.

She nodded her agreement.

Without another word, the waitress slid away, glancing back at their table.

"How do you know my favorite dish?" Ty asked when the waitress walked out of earshot.

"Facebook." Dylan rested back against the booth, studying Ty with an oddly calm intensity.

"But we're not friends." The words slipped out before Ty could stop them.

He laughed. Again, the fact that her actions didn't put him off troubled Ty. "Facebook isn't private. It's the Internet."

Pictures of Anthony and the girl, Keesha, assaulted Ty's memory. "Right," she said in a strangled voice. She closed her eyes. Did Anthony see her this way? Another girl hanging on desperately? She thought about his expression before he kissed her and even his genuine laughter when she said, *Better luck next time*.

She knew body language . . . didn't she? Ty's fingers burned with the urge to pull her phone from her pocket and check it. Maybe Anthony didn't answer in the affirmative. She just needed to see the screen.

She opened her eyes to meet Dylan's gaze. As she suspected, he still studied her calmly, no hint that he recognized something might bother his date. She felt compelled to respond, just to fill the silence with something, but she couldn't form a proper response that didn't involve accusing him of stalking her. *Stalking* seemed so strong, but how could it be anything but?

"No, it's not private. Guess I don't remember posting about it." She rested her elbow on the table and maneuvered her other hand to her pocket.

"It took some digging."

She almost had the phone out, but looked up at Dylan. "Oh?"

He'd answered so nonchalantly, as though it should flatter her he took the time to find that out. And was it? Was she overreacting?

"A girl like you is worth it."

She pushed the phone the rest of the way out and stared down without really seeing, her thoughts swirling around the unsettling conversation. It wasn't that bad, she reminded herself. Technically she did some digging of her own the other day. Not that she started it, but she'd looked at Anthony's profile a lot in the past too. That didn't make her a crazed stalker. So Dylan perused her Facebook page. He had a crush.

Her justifications didn't make her feel better. They didn't ease the creepy feeling she got around him.

Dylan reached across the table and gripped her arm so hard it surprised her. "Still distracted by your phone? Hand it over." He motioned with his other hand to give it to him. She wouldn't. She hadn't seen Anthony's message, but she wouldn't give up the phone.

She shook her head and quickly shoved it back in her pocket. "Thought it might be from my mom. I'm sorry. It won't happen again." She gave Dylan a wobbly smile and hoped Anthony showed up soon.

* * *

"Who is she?" Nikki asked when Anthony slid his phone into his pocket and pushed himself up off the floor where he'd been playing Candy Land with Porter.

Anthony ignored his sister and looked over at David, who sat on the couch with Eli in his lap. Having grown up together, David was like another brother to Nikki.

"Let's go," Anthony said.

David handed Eli over to Nikki and stood, frowning at Anthony. "What's up?"

"Ty texted me. She's on a date with Dylan and needs me to rescue her." A grin started to spread across his face—thoughts about finishing what they started during their kindergarten football game filling his head—until David frowned.

"With Dylan?" David clarified.

"Who's Ty?" Nikki broke in, and Anthony looked over to see she had followed them to the door. She looked from Anthony to David. "Is she that girl you were telling me about?"

Anthony slugged David in the arm. "Can't keep your mouth shut, can you?"

"What's wrong with telling Nikki?" David protested. "You were going to tell her, right?"

Nikki rolled her eyes. "He doesn't tell me about girls anymore."

Anthony was grateful she didn't say *since Keesha*. "What's the point?" he said, swinging open the door.

Nikki grabbed his arm before he left. "Don't, Anthony. Don't write her off before you know. David says she's pretty special—"

"Oh, does he?" Anthony said, glaring at his best friend.

"Don't write her off yet," Nikki finished and let go.

Anthony leaned over and gave her a hug. "I'm not promising anything, but I'm going to get her off a date with another guy, so that's something. Thanks for dinner."

"'Night." She stood at the door and watched them walk down the sidewalk to Anthony's car.

"Why'd you make that face earlier?" Anthony asked when they got in.

"I talked to Dylan and told him she wasn't interested. How'd she end up on a date with him?"

Anthony shrugged. "Well, however it happened, she wants out now. Who am I to say no?"

"Too true."

* * *

When they strode into the restaurant, Anthony saw Ty right away. He narrowed his eyes at her stiff posture, the way she sat as far back in her seat as she could. What was going on? She turned her head his way, her face pale but hopeful. When they locked eyes, her cheeks flooded with color. He rubbed a hand over his jaw, clenching it as the playfulness of this errand disappeared. She looked scared.

"Hey, Rocket!" A voice and a hand on his arm interrupted. "Can you sign this for me?"

Anthony paused and looked at a little boy holding out a kid's menu and one of his crayons. He forced a smile and scribbled his name before hurrying toward Ty.

His gaze found Dylan just as he noticed them.

"Rocket!" Dylan laughed, sounding excited to see him. He only nodded at David.

Ty jumped up. "Anthony," she sighed his name, and he could hear the relief in it. "Thanks, Dylan, but I'll get a ride back with Anthony and David." She darted between them, planting herself behind one of Anthony's shoulders.

Her reaction, coupled with David telling him he'd already warned Dylan off once, rang warning bells in Anthony's mind. He widened his stance and folded his arms over his not inconsequential chest. He resisted the urge to push Ty farther behind him.

Dylan's face reddened, and Anthony noticed his fists clenched against his sides. "We don't even have our food yet, Detmer."

Anthony stiffened at the nickname. He didn't want this kid using it in a way that suggested they were friends when she obviously didn't want to be anywhere near him.

"What does she owe you for the food?" Anthony asked, jamming a hand into his pocket.

Dylan waved his hands at Anthony, but the angry glint in his eyes didn't leave. "No, no, no. Don't worry about it, Rocket."

Anthony put both his hands on the table and leaned over. "Let me give you a tip, pal—"

"Dylan." His eyes gleamed as he gazed up at Anthony without fear. Instead, admiration shone in them.

"Unless Ty invites you on a date personally, I'd consider this relationship a failure."

"Well—"

"Stay away," David added, "or regret it."

They both turned without waiting for an answer. Anthony curled his arm around Ty's back. She shuddered and relaxed against him. He tightened his grip. Why was she so scared?

"Thanks, Anthony," she whispered. The trust she placed in him with just those simple words sent a burst of pride through him. She needed him, and not just in some game-playing, flattering-his-ego way either. She *trusted* him.

He smiled for the first time since seeing her in the restaurant. "Anytime."

* * *

Dropping Ty off at her apartment was harder than it should have been. Anthony could only kid himself with this friend stuff for so long. Thinking about Dylan's reaction and Ty's fear at the restaurant made him grind his teeth and almost sent his hand over the middle console to grip hers. And the hardest part was deciding if he needed to reassure her she was safe or reassure himself. The force of his protectiveness surprised him.

He didn't talk on the way back to the house, and David let him stew. The glimpses Anthony took of David showed the situation preoccupied him just as much. He pushed away another bout of jealousy. David could worry about Ty—as a friend.

Anthony parked the car in front of their house but paused when he got out, propping his arms on the roof of the car. "That was weird," he said.

David nodded, shutting his door behind him. "I thought Dylan was just some kid with a crush, but considering what Ty said . . ."

Anthony shut his own door and remembered the relieved expression on Ty's face when they came to the table, the way she jumped out of the booth, and the stuff she told them Dylan had said. "He scared her." Anthony almost growled the words.

David nodded solemnly. "Seriously." He followed Anthony toward the stairs. "What are we going to do?"

"Make sure he stays away."

Chapter Nine

When Ty got upstairs after Anthony dropped her off, Rosie and Kayla looked far too casual sitting on the couch together. She rolled her eyes. They'd spied on her again. She dropped into a chair, too amazed at how well the night turned out—considering how it started—to care.

"So Rocket dropped you off," Rosie said.

Ty knew her grin looked silly. She knew Rosie wouldn't approve. But how could she get rid of it? Anthony had charged in and saved her from Dylan. Just because she texted him. Just because she asked. "Yep."

"I thought you were on a date with . . ." Kayla snapped her fingers, trying to come up with a name.

"Dylan." Ty's heart thumped hard, not in a good way, when she said his name, but then she remembered the way Anthony leaned over the table and got in Dylan's face, the slight five-o'clock shadow lending to his intimidating, not to mention attractive, glare. And all for her. He did it for her. The silly grin slipped back on her face. "Anthony rescued me."

"As in, he finally asked you out?" Rosie tilted forward and squeezed a pillow. "It took longer than I thought, but you guys have been hanging out a lot, so that's something."

Trust Rosie to do her best to try to kill a mood with her cool calculations. "No," Ty said. "Dylan was being scary, so I texted Anthony, and he and David came and got me."

"Scary?" Kayla asked. "Like how?"

"Rocket and . . . David?" Rosie said over her. Clearly Dylan's behavior didn't bother her; she wanted to analyze Anthony's latest moves. "So not like a date, more like two friends—or brothers—coming to get you off a bad date?"

And *voilá*—mission accomplished for Rosie. Mood killed. Ty sat up and scowled. "Yeah. So?"

Rosie slumped back against the couch. "So? He's treating you like a cute little sister, protective. And he still hasn't asked you on a date."

Ty hated admitting she agonized over the same thing. Anthony dated girls all the time. On the one hand, this made her different from the ones that had been left in the dust already. On the other, he still hadn't asked her out.

She looked away from Rosie. "Maybe it's a good thing." She hoped.

Rosie rolled her eyes to the ceiling and shook her head. "A good thing?"

Two minutes ago Ty had been basking in the bliss of Anthony's knight-in-shining-armor act. Now Rosie thought it was nothing. He'd never swooped in for Rosie, had he? They never hung out. She never got to be his friend. What did she know? Why had Ty asked her to help?

"Yeah," she blurted, "maybe this means he won't 'get me out of his system' after a couple dates and move on." The moment the words rushed past her lips, she clapped a hand over her mouth.

Rosie didn't react. That made Ty feel worse. "I agree. He'll probably get you out of his system before that. Without ever taking you out."

"I didn't mean that the way it sounded."

Rosie ignored Ty's attempted apology. "When are you going to see him again?" She was already back to business.

Ty shifted in her seat. "Uh . . . in class?"

"You didn't make any plans tonight?"

She studied her hands. In Rosie's opinion, she was failing at this. "No," she said.

Rosie closed her eyes. "We need to work on getting him to ask you out."

Ty liked the way things had settled between her and Anthony. Would Rosie insist she put on another act? Step up her "flirt"? She sighed. "How do we do that?"

Rosie pushed Kayla away and patted the couch next to her. Kayla rolled her eyes and headed out of the room. "Come here. I'm going to teach you a few good moves. That's what athletes like, right? Plays. Planned moves to achieve a goal."

Ty hauled herself out of the chair, taking her time, but she granted Rosie a smile for her analogy. "Yeah. That's what this whole thing's about. Right? My game plan." Heat rushed into her cheeks. She hoped Rosie didn't press her about it. She didn't want Rosie to know she had one down on paper. Rosie would like that too much.

"Don't worry, Ty, we're going to fix this before the whole thing falls apart. We won't fail. Not this time."

Ty asked for this—and maybe she needed it. She sat on the couch and prepared to absorb another round of knowledge Rosie thought she lacked.

* * *

"I think you're going to find these papers very interesting, Ty," Mrs. Frazier said when Ty came into her classroom the next morning. She tapped them with her French-tipped nails and looked far too excited to pass them off to someone else.

"Great." Ty reached over and picked them up, taking a deep breath before she dove into yet another effort to get Mrs. Frazier to let her do more than slave over grading papers. Considering how much homework she had, she didn't need to waste an hour and a half doing busy work. "I wondered if we could talk about some things that might help me get more experience in actual teaching."

Mrs. Frazier grunted. "Believe me, dear, that *is* actual teaching." She waved at the papers in Ty's hand.

Ty laughed halfheartedly. "Oh, I know, but I had another idea for an activity . . ."

The look on Mrs. Frazier's face diminished Ty's enthusiasm to share it. "What is it this time?"

Knowing she wouldn't get another chance, Ty rushed on despite her wariness. "Since we've been studying how ancient civilizations developed, I thought it would be interesting to have them write messages to each other using only small pictures so they could see the importance of the development of written language."

Mrs. Frazier began shaking her head before Ty even finished the first sentence. "I'm sorry. We have a lot of objectives to cross off the list this year, and that doesn't accomplish anything."

Ty held back a sigh of frustration with difficulty. If it hadn't been for the interesting activities her high school history teacher had come up with, Ty would've never found her love for the subject. "It would get the kids excited," she said quietly.

Mrs. Frazier had already turned back to the history textbook in front of her. "I'm sorry. Not this time."

Ty nodded and took her place in the back of the room, discouraged that yet another day would go by without showing them how interesting history could be.

* * *

After school that afternoon, Ty had settled down at her apartment to read what promised to be a snore-inducing, thirty-page article for her biology class when a sharp rap on the door interrupted her. Rosie and Kayla were both out, so she turned, knees on the couch, and peeked out the window, trying to get a glimpse of whoever had knocked. She smiled with relief when she noticed the visitor's head almost reached the top of the doorframe. Not Dylan. After their "date," she was worried she'd run into him again, but maybe Anthony's warning would keep him away.

She took a deep breath. Rosie had spent a couple hours the night before making Ty practice useless things like how to suggest a date without sounding like it. She'd have to try to use one of the strategies. She yanked open the door as Anthony raised his hand to knock again.

"Hi." She beamed. Even if Anthony only saw her as a little sister or friend, she'd always be grateful he showed up to haul her out of that restaurant. She stood back so he could come in.

"Hey. I'm kidnapping you. Hopefully this will preempt any excuse you have to get out of going out with me. Visiting sick children in a hospital? Reading to the elderly? Give it your best shot."

Ty forced herself not to bounce around on the balls of her feet. She didn't even have to ask him if he'd seen the scary movie playing at the dollar theater downtown. Thank heavens, since she didn't want to go, but Rosie thought seeing a movie was a good "buddy" activity and a scary one presented the perfect chance to sneak in cuddle time.

But Anthony had asked her out without further prodding. "Just some boring article for a class I hate. I can read it later," she said. It would mean she'd be up until the wee hours of the morning again, but whatever.

Anthony rubbed his hands together in a mischievous way and stepped back out onto the landing. "Awesome. I don't beat out brothers, but I rank above boring homework. I'll take it."

She elbowed him playfully as she followed him out. "You only rank below *promises* to my brothers, not below the actual hooligans themselves."

He grinned. Shivers split up and down Ty's spine, drenching her entire body in something she'd never felt before. Except perhaps the time Anthony ran in a game-winning twenty-yard touchdown in the last seconds of a Utah-BYU game.

She forced herself to look away despite the fact that she wanted to stare at Anthony's face. "How about I take *you* out? You know, as a thank you for saving me last night."

Anthony's answering smile lacked feeling. "That was nothing." He cleared his throat. "What happened last night? How did you end up there with him?"

Embarrassed, Ty watched a young couple with a stroller walking on the sidewalk across the street. "He didn't give me a chance to say no. I thought it would be harmless."

"And it wasn't?" He flexed his fingers and then clenched them into a fist.

She didn't want to make more of a big deal over it than she already had. "It turned out pretty great, right?" Hoping to move off the subject, she leaned into his shoulder. She always felt giddy when he accepted this familiarity between them. "So I know a great place. It's out of the way"—Anthony's eyebrows rose—"and has awesome food."

"You had me at 'out of the way.'"

The blood rushed through her veins. She gathered up enough breath to speak. "Let me drive so you can close your eyes. In case this doesn't work out. I don't want you telling everyone about my secret spot."

Anthony tossed her his keys, which surprised Ty. She expected they'd drive her car. She eyed the sleek sports car before opening the driver's side door. "Okay," she said, hoping he didn't hear the nervousness in her voice. It'd be just like her to blow it with him by wrecking his car. "No peeking."

He settled into his own seat, buckled his safety belt, and closed his eyes. "Yes, ma'am."

* * *

The drive seemed long, so a lot of the conversation consisted of Anthony asking if they were there yet and how much longer it would take, to which Ty threatened to turn the car around or make him walk the rest of the way. The easy way she handled him made Anthony forget he was chasing a girl instead of the other way around. He'd dated charming girls before, girls that knew how to talk and flirt with him, but not like Ty. Though sometimes it seemed like she planned her actions or words to please him, most of the time he sensed an ease about her that he didn't expect. Sitting in a car with his eyes closed and teasing her was the most comfortable he'd been with a girl in a while.

When they halted, he tried to peek. "No looking." Ty covered his eyes with her hand. He almost reached up to grab it, but she pulled away too soon. What had happened to him? Something about last night changed everything. Perhaps the feeling of being the one to protect her?

So maybe he'd give Ty more of a chance than he gave any of the others. Follow Nikki's advice and not write Ty off yet. See what she was about and maybe figure out what it was about her that he liked so much.

A moment later his car door opened. She took his hand, pulling him out. He wound his fingers through hers, smiling to himself at her small hands. What a perfect excuse to hold her hand without it meaning too much.

"This way," she said in a breathy voice. His smile widened. He liked to hear how he affected her. It comforted him. Reminded him that even if he let himself fall for her—only a little bit—he still had some measure of control.

They walked down the sidewalk, Anthony trusting Ty not to let him fall on his face. When they stopped, she said, "Okay. Open up."

The familiar scrolled writing in the window stopped his heart; then it fell through to his feet. "I've been here before," he said. What an understatement. It got worse when a figure paused before opening the door. Long brown hair pulled off her face, the way she always wore it when she went to work. Six months of pregnancy had changed her slim figure and plumped her cheeks. Her eyes widened. She froze.

"*May's* Family Food," Ty whispered. "I'm such an idiot."

Anthony turned to ask how she knew about Keesha, but Ty blurted, "I think I left my phone in the car. Do you mind if we go back?" Anthony glanced sideways, noticed Keesha still motionless with the door half open.

"Of course." He followed Ty back down the sidewalk. Once they turned the corner, Ty let go of his hand and marched ahead, only pausing when she got to the car.

"I'm so sorry, Anthony. So sorry. I can't believe I didn't make the connection. I'm a disaster." She put one hand against her face, hiding the strangely loveable distress.

Why was he fighting a smile? She was right. This was a disaster. "How do you know about Keesha?" he asked.

She threw up her hands. "Because I stalked you on Facebook. Well, not really me—Rosie, but I let her. So I'm just as bad." She paced in front of the car. "I'm like the female version of Dylan."

"Except much more attractive." But Ty didn't seem to hear him.

"I've watched all your football games, even high school ones. Technically only your junior and senior year though—and the ones on YouTube. A few times. And I took coaching football because you're in it. I'm not going to be a football coach! I'm going to teach history to high schoolers."

Anthony laughed, not just at her rambling monologue, but at the frantic way she waved her hands and avoided his gaze. He didn't know why her confession didn't scare him. Because the part about her watching since high school meant she wasn't a band-wagon fan? That couldn't be it.

"I'm the reason most of those girls took the class—"

She charged on without hearing him. "And to top it off, I brought you to a restaurant your ex-girlfriend's family owns—"

He couldn't help himself. Maybe it was because he didn't want to go into the whole Keesha issue. Or maybe because she looked so hurt and upset he needed to fix it, like he had last night. He put his hands on either side of her face and pulled her toward him, stopping her speech by planting his lips on top of hers.

* * *

Ty held very still. She was afraid if she moved she might wake up from her dream. She didn't want that to happen. Anthony Rogers was kissing her. Even her need to take a deep breath and inhale his musky, piney scent didn't sway her. Nor did the overwhelming urge to throw her arms around his neck. She must remain absolutely still. This was a new kind of heaven. Better than hearing him sing and even watching him play football.

"Ty?" he said softly when it ended.

"Mmmm?" She didn't even move her lips.

"I have an idea."

She risked opening her eyes, desperate for a peek at his face. He couldn't think of her as a stalker, could he? She considered the possibility he kissed her to shut her up. The smile in his eyes made her think she could dissolve into a puddle at his feet. Except his hands still held her face, so at least that part of her had remained solid.

"Does it involve this date continuing?" she asked. She moved her arms to his waist. If opening her eyes hadn't woken her up, she figured she was safe.

He smiled. Her heart sputtered at the genuineness in it. "Yes," he said, planting another kiss on her lips, which seemed to distract him because he kept kissing her. She kept kissing back. "And food," he finished.

She pulled back and took a breath, hoping to regain some kind of control over the situation. "I know that's an important consideration for football players."

He slipped his hands from her face and took one of her hands in his, using it to pull her next to him. "It is," he confirmed. He led her around his car and opened the door for her.

* * *

She couldn't say why Anthony still wanted to share the same airspace as her or even talk to her, let alone hold her hand, gaze at her with an expression that mixed amusement with tenderness, or kiss her like he did back in the parking lot. When she'd seen Anthony's ex outside the restaurant, she thought she'd ruined everything. But he hadn't bolted, and inexplicably he still wanted her. It boggled her mind and made her sigh with contentment much too often.

Thirty minutes after they'd gotten the take-out, they pulled up to Anthony's aunt's house, and he pointed toward the backyard. "She has an awesome slide," he said, leading her up the sidewalk.

A tall woman with a blonde-haired, blue-eyed little girl on her hip opened the door. "Hey, Anthony." She blinked in surprise when she saw Ty. "Who's this?"

"Ty Daws, this is my aunt, Annie."

Ty stuck out her hand to shake Annie's. Annie's gaze darted between that hand and the one Anthony held. "Oh . . ." Her welcoming grin widened. "Nice to meet you, Ty."

"You've been talking to Nikki," Anthony accused dryly.

"I called last night to check on her." Annie bent over to put the child on the floor. The little girl bent her chubby knees and refused to stand, so Annie plopped her down. "I'm a little worried. I think she counted—"

"I know." Anthony nodded and looked sideways at Ty.

Annie scowled and sighed. "Fine. What's up?"

"Can we use your backyard?" Anthony held up the McDonalds bag.

Annie's grin returned. She gestured to the sliding glass door in the kitchen. "Go right ahead."

"Rocky?" The little girl toddled over to Anthony and held her arms up.

"Hi, Izzy."

"Rocky?" Ty repeated. Too cute. She thought her smile might break through her cheeks at the way he crouched and let Izzy throw her arms around his neck. He buried his nose in her wispy curls and kissed her head.

"My nephews and Izzy can't say any of my names," he explained. He kissed her again and lifted her into his arms. "Sorry, Iz. There's another girl I need to pay attention to tonight."

A soft *hmm* drew Ty's attention back to Annie. Her raised eyebrows suggested Anthony's reaction surprised her. She noticed Ty's gaze and grinned. "Come here, Izzy. Let's leave Anthony alone for tonight."

Anthony "flew" Izzy, airplane style, over to Annie's arms. Izzy giggled and shouted, "Gen! Gen!" and frowned adorably when Anthony left her in her mom's arms. He grabbed Ty's hand again and led her outside.

"You're pretty close to your aunt," Ty said. It seemed crazy that a date that'd started off so awful had turned out so amazing. Happiness kept bubbling up in Ty's chest—Anthony's hand in hers, his obvious love for Izzy, this beautiful day . . .

"She was the surprise in my dad's family. Youngest by ten years and closer to my and Nikki's age, so we all sort of grew up together." He dropped Ty's hand and pointed to the ladder on the wooden structure that held the slide. She hurried up it and waited impatiently for him to ascend.

"So Nikki is your sister?" she asked.

He nodded. He'd scaled the ladder in two steps. "Yep." He sat with his back to the slide. She sat facing him, letting her feet rest on the cool yellow surface and loving how they sat right next to each other, legs touching.

Ty reached in the sack and grabbed her double cheeseburger. "Is everything okay with her?"

Anthony's smile wavered. Indecision flitted through his eyes before he turned away, focusing his attention on getting the first of the six burgers he ordered from the bag. "She's been . . . sick before, so Annie worries about her." He looked back at Ty, his mouth already full. "Great date, right?" He held his smile in place, and she went with the change of subject.

She laughed. "Sure. I did promise you out of the way, so I guess I came through on that."

He nodded, his smile slowly returning to normal. She hadn't noticed the worry in his eyes until it disappeared. "Unless you count the audience." He pointed to the sliding glass door, where two boys with hair a few shades darker than Izzy's stared out at them.

"They're pretty adorable. I think I'll let them slide." Ty waved. "They probably can't help themselves with a cousin like Rocky Rogers."

Anthony chuckled. "True." He eyed her still untouched cheeseburger, already unwrapping his second. "We might be here awhile at this rate."

"I'm trying to savor these moments, make it last. After the train wreck I caused, I might not get a second date with you." She reached into the bag for fries. She was good with however long it lasted, right? She'd told herself that for a while. She'd get to say she went out with Anthony Rogers, that she'd ruined any hope for a relationship by bombing it big time. Not a lot of girls got that privilege. The mini-skirt girl at the party never had, Ty guessed. The date-bombing part. She ignored the idea that mini-skirt girl had probably gotten plenty of opportunities at the dating part.

"You think I kiss every girl like that?" He leaned closer.

"Honestly?" She choked on the word, thanks to his unsettling proximity. "Yes."

Smiling, almost to himself, he rested back onto the slide opening. "I've kissed a lot of girls," he admitted. "But not like that."

She swallowed. Her first bite of cheeseburger lodged in her throat. She'd like to answer, but it was impossible. As if she hadn't humiliated herself enough, Anthony would have to do the Heimlich, which wasn't near as romantic as mouth-to-mouth. Finally—thankfully—it slid down. She coughed, trying to do so softly, and had to reach for her soda. All the while watching Anthony silently laugh at her.

"So—" she cleared her throat, "do you think you want to fill me in about Keesha? You know, what I didn't glean from Facebook?"

Anthony laughed again, but this time Ty knew he forced it. She turned away to cringe at herself.

"How about we start with you?" he said. "Tell me about your big, broken heart."

"Sorry to disappoint; there isn't one." Ty nabbed another bite, chewing at least fifty times before she attempted to swallow again.

"That's not possible. Unless . . . well, you were someone else's big, broken heart." He reached for another hamburger and a handful of fries, scooting back toward her as he did so.

"Not that I know of."

"You're telling me there's not some guy out there who discovered your epic knowledge of football and didn't immediately drop down on one knee?"

Ty eyed him challengingly. "Want to be the first?"

He grinned. She loved how the idea of proposing didn't send him running into the house. "Tempting, Ty. Very tempting." He chewed thoughtfully. "So no love gone wrong?"

"Not unless you want to count tonight."

This time he coughed and had to grab for *his* soda. She laughed to herself. "How did you meet Keesha?" she asked, going forward.

"You know, I'm focusing on the present now, instead of dwelling on my past." He smiled at her shakily, and she felt a teeny bit bad for pushing it.

She burst into laughter. "That sounds like something from a bad dating advice book. I guess you've had a lot of practice on what to say when the new girls ask about all those exes."

He dropped his head, looking sheepish. "I did read it online. They said it was the best way to steer the conversation away. That or take a trip to the bathroom."

"Chicken." Where had all her daring came from? Probably that kiss.

He grinned. "Maybe."

She angled forward then paused inches from his face. He lowered his burger, meeting her eyes with the same playful challenge. "That's not the Rocket Rogers I know," she said.

He seemed to wait patiently, though she noticed his gaze darting between her eyes and her lips. "You'll have to keep my secret."

"Mmmm. I'll think about it." She wanted to close the gap now, but she also liked the way he stared at her, seeing the want in his eyes too, suspecting he might be falling for her, even a little. It made the future heartbreak more bearable.

Instead she went for playful and safe. She shoved her hand against his chest and sent his surprised figure—and fries—flying down the slide.

Once he tumbled out and regained his balance, he pointed at her. "You're going to pay for wasting my fries, missy."

She already clutched a nearby bar, trying not to collapse with laughter. His face, his tone, the word *missy* made her laugh so hard her side hurt. He sprinted around to the ladder, mounting it even faster than before. She couldn't get away. On this tiny playground set, his long arms reached into every corner. Despite her best maneuvering, he wrapped his arm around her within thirty seconds, dragging her toward him. When he'd pinned her against his chest, flailing and putting up a fight, he grabbed her fries and dumped them all in his mouth. Once he chewed them satisfactorily, he lowered his face to hers and kissed her. A wet, messy kiss that left them both laughing. And her spinning.

"Tell me the truth," she said once she'd drawn in enough breaths to recover, "how many girls have you kissed like *that*?"

* * *

Rosie was out on a date when Ty got back, so she didn't have to recount her awful failure or the blissful end to the date. She texted Walsh about it instead. That way she didn't have to share the mushy parts she wanted to keep to herself, but she could still brag about it—and have someone to commiserate with about the epic fail the date began with.

When she knelt beside her bed to say her prayers, she felt guilty. She couldn't keep Anthony off her mind. *Please, let me keep him. Let this be right. Let him be mine . . . forever. Please.*

Chapter Ten

Rosie meandered into the kitchen late the next morning looking worn out. Ty figured her date the night before must have been successful if she'd stayed out so late, but Rosie's expression didn't seem like one of triumph.

Probably not like the look on Ty's face. She stifled yet another grin behind her hand. "Late night?" she asked as she dumped the milk from her cereal into the sink.

"Meh." Rosie shrugged and pulled the fridge door open. "What about you?"

"Not bad."

Rosie stood and glowered at Ty over the top of the fridge door. Then her expression turned critical. "What?"

"He came over and asked me out last night."

Rosie shut the door. "Rocket did? For real?"

"For real, and it was a total disaster." Ty laughed when Rosie's expression fell.

"I do not get you, Ty Daws. Why in the world would that make you happy? What's going on?"

"Well, he kissed me, like real kisses—"

"Kisses plural?"

She nodded.

Rosie dropped into a chair at the table. She grinned and whispered, "Finally. Tell me everything."

Ty enjoyed a moment of silent gloating before she opened the closet by the front door. "No time. Sorry." She grabbed a jacket.

"Where are you going?"

"Anthony and I are going to watch his cousin's flag football game with David and Sean."

Rosie frowned—not surprising—but it looked more contemplative than anything. "More football, more buddy stuff," she said to herself. "But last night was progress. Good job."

Ty half expected her to break out a gold star and slap it on Ty's forehead. "Thanks." She rolled her eyes and headed out the door.

"Don't let it be too buddy-buddy! Take his arm or something. Maybe try and hold his hand, but don't push it. He never liked that," Rosie shouted from the doorway as Ty hurried down the stairs and to her car. She looked up and saw her roommate leaning over the railing. "Get him to ask you out again. Remember the stuff we talked about."

Ty waved at her and decided to ignore her advice. The last date she planned had tanked—at first. It had ended up fine without any help from Rosie.

* * *

After spending almost the entire weekend with Ty, Anthony still rushed to coaching football to see her on Monday. *Trouble, dude. Serious trouble. This is how it started with—*

Ty is not Keesha.

He said her name so rarely in his mind these days—and never out loud—it surprised him it didn't hurt more, like it used to. Did seeing Keesha release him? How had that train-wreck date (that got a lot better) made him forget his anger when all those other girls failed?

That made Ty big trouble.

He didn't care. Which made him smile. Then made him laugh.

"You realized our playbooks are due today, didn't you?"

How had Ty slipped into class unnoticed? "Huh?" he asked. Were there other people in the classroom? He couldn't tell except for the hiss of whispers.

"Our project? It's due today. And we didn't work on it at all this weekend." Ty giggled.

The words hardly registered. They had done much better things with their weekend than homework. He liked the tinge of pink in her cheeks and the way her whole face glowed. Now he was thankful for the whispers because they reminded him not to act like a love-sick fool. No, he'd have to wait for class to get over. Otherwise everyone would talk.

What happened to him? It was like he was down a couple touchdowns he'd given up, thrown in the towel, and given Ty the win.

Nothing wrong with having fun, he told himself, and he had a lot of fun with her. He deserved that. He hadn't enjoyed dating this much since Keesha, and for a guy that dated a lot, that said something. It wouldn't hurt to let things be for a while. Enjoy the ride.

"Who would want to ruin a weekend with homework?" he said.

She bent toward him. There. That magical, flowery-soapy scent that poisoned him in the best way possible. He took a good, long breath of it. Her smile widened.

She laid her hand on his knee. "I'm not a superstar football player. Brian isn't going to let this slide for me."

"I'll see what I can do. Besides, I think we have until four p.m. anyway." He curled his fingers around hers, the way he had since their disastrous-slash-awesome date.

"Besides a break for lunch, I have class until five." She sounded out of breath. The fact that after three straight days in his presence, he still affected her like that made his head swell more. Who said he needed to make a hundred girls faint? He liked making one loopy a hundred times over.

For now, he reminded himself. He wouldn't get carried away. "We'll have to do it over lunch then."

"We only have three plays so far."

He leaned closer. "Maybe you'll have to skip a class."

"I don't skip class for just anyone, you know."

"How about for Rocket?"

She shook her head. The flower-soapy smell deluged him. "Nope. But I will for Anthony."

"Deal." He took a pair of tickets out of his back pocket. "I have a surprise for you."

She must have recognized the telltale blue and white. She ripped them out of his hand, and her eyes went to the seat location. "Shut up," she cried, then with a glance around, lowered her voice to barely a whisper. "Shut up. You're kidding. These are for me?"

A warm feeling crept across his chest. "Of course they're for you. Sorry, your dad and brothers will probably kill each other over who gets to come. I wanted to get more . . ."

She squeezed his hand. "Maybe I'll take my mom instead. Oh, my gosh! I can't believe how awesome these are. If you dump me Saturday after the game, my life will still be complete."

Anthony burst into laughter. How could he take a girl seriously when she rated football tickets over her relationship with him? Except, that type of girl he *could* take seriously.

It took a second for her words to sink in. Dump her. Did that mean . . . ?

Don't think about it. It was better not to think about what it meant.

After placing the tickets inside her history book—which he knew was a compliment in and of itself—she took both his hands in hers. "Anthony Rogers, you have made me the happiest girl in the world."

Still chuckling at this serious pronouncement, he said, "Football tickets? That's all it takes?"

Mock innocence seeped into her expression. "What more could a girl ask for?"

How did she do that? How could she say something so meaningful without saying anything meaningful at all? The shock in his face must have been more evident than he thought. Her smile wavered.

"You're easy to please, Ty."

She shrugged and let go of his hands. He saw the blush, faint, but still there. Yep. She'd caught his hesitation. "We'll see. I don't know what you're going to follow this up with. Bowl game tickets?"

He put his hand in hers again, amazed at his need to please her. *Careful, Rocket*, an inner voice warned, but he didn't let go. "If you're good," he promised instead, glad to see a genuine smile replace the careful one.

* * *

It took all of Ty's willpower not to open the text message she got during her history of England lecture. Any other class, any other teacher and she would at least peek at it under her desk. But Mr. Fogle had hawk eyes. She thought he might be able to see through the desks.

So the second he excused them—three excruciating minutes after they should have gotten out—she whipped out her phone before even putting her books away. It *was* from Anthony.

We deserve a reward for getting that project done without even skipping class.

Not like he hadn't tried. And he had tempted her. More than he knew. *Agreed. Will it involve ice cream? More football tickets?* she texted back. She slipped her books into her bag and headed out into the busy hallway.

It involves me and you and a date. Possibly French fries.

Only if you promise to keep your hands off my fries.

That's not a promise I can make.

She laughed to herself, dodging a pair of feet she saw walking past in her peripheral vision, her eyes still on the phone. *No surprise there. I'm still in. Black tie affair?*

Casual. You can wear a black tie if you want though.

Since the crowd on campus at five p.m. was light, Ty could walk fast without having to dodge too many students, except for when she had to pause outside the Wilk to wait for a bunch of students coming out before she could go inside.

She glimpsed a familiar face in the glass and whipped her head around. She hadn't seen Dylan since their date. When he caught her looking at him, he melted into the crowd.

Her heart rate kicked up. Why did he disappear so fast? Anthony did tell Dylan to stay away, but normal people didn't vanish because they happened to bump into someone they shouldn't.

Ty shook her head, trying to shake the unsettled feeling. She didn't want to think about Dylan and his weirdness. She shouldn't have to. She had a date with Anthony, and she was willing to bet it'd be great.

When she got home, she went straight to her room to find the perfect casual outfit—without Rosie's help. For any other date, she'd love Rosie's advice. Usually Rosie did a great job of taking Ty's wardrobe and finding an outfit that played up her strengths without losing her personality. But ever since Anthony, Rosie had insisted Ty needed more . . . well, more "Rosie" in her clothes. Perhaps her roommate's advice got Anthony to notice her, but Ty wanted to be the one to "keep" him.

"What's up?" Rosie asked when they met in the hallway.

"Homework," Ty said without looking her in the eye. Ty darted into her bedroom and shut the door. Then locked it for good measure.

After an hour—and a large pile of discarded clothing—Ty almost wished she could let Rosie in to help. Almost.

A knock on her bedroom door startled her. "Yeah?" she called, yanking on her favorite jeans, which she'd already tried on twice.

"You still doing homework?" Rosie asked. Her voice sounded suspicious.

"Yup." Distracted, Ty tapped her finger against her cheek as she studied the three shirts she'd narrowed her choices to.

The door handle rattled, which disconcerted Ty. She hurried over, and hiding behind it, opened it a crack. "What do you need?" she asked, trying to keep irritation out of her voice.

"Why is your door locked?"

"You caught me in the middle of changing."

"For what?"

Ty shrugged, unwilling to give up the information she was going out with Anthony. She didn't want help with the outfit, and she didn't need a pre-date pep talk either.

Rosie frowned. "Did you plan anything with Anthony today?"

"Rosie, I can't talk right now. Sorry." Ty shoved the door shut and went back to pondering the shirts, ignoring the sound of frustrated stomps away from her door.

Finally she settled on her nicest Cougar T-shirt and a pair of bowed flats. She added a black scarf for kicks. She was still standing in front of the mirror when a knock sounded on the door at 7:23. She barreled out of the room, attempting to beat Rosie to the front door. Rosie would disapprove of Ty appearing so eager, but she would rather risk that than leaving Anthony alone with her attractive roommate for any period of time. Rosie might find a way to finagle his attention away. She'd proven herself good at getting Anthony's attention one way or another.

Rosie was reaching for the door handle when Ty shoved her aside and swung it open.

"Whoa!" Rosie cried before she saw Anthony resting against the doorframe. "Too eager," she whispered harshly from behind the door. She shook her head with disapproval and marched away.

Guilt for lying to Rosie earlier made Ty frown at the retreating figure.

"Hey there." Anthony's voice chased the guilt away.

She turned back toward him and gulped down a giddy giggle. "Hey, Anthony."

He reached up to finger the black scarf. "Nice touch." He grinned, using it to pull her nearer. "You look awesome. Ready?"

Ty closed the door. "I've been ready for hours."

Anthony tipped his chin toward her. It wouldn't surprise her if he saw right through her. "Oh, really?"

She feigned innocence. "Do girls normally spend a lot of time getting ready for dates with you?"

He slipped his hand into hers. Warmth jetted up her arm and across her chest. She had imagined a relationship with Anthony millions of times since she first saw him play football five years before. She expected to love every second. She expected it to fulfill all her dreams. She had never imagined how exactly, except for vague bonding over their shared love of football. But the crazy, spinning, fabulous, melting feeling still shocked her. Every time he held her hand. Every time he smiled just for her. Every time he *looked* at her.

Like now. He tilted his head back to survey her outfit. "Honestly, it's hard to say, Ty. You look so good it seems like it should have taken a long time. But you're always looking good, so who's to say it's not natural?"

She laughed. "You're good at this compliment thing. You've probably had a lot of practice."

He didn't answer, instead smiling and opening his car door for her.

When she slipped into the seat, she almost sat on a cowboy hat. "What's this?" she asked after he plopped down in the driver's seat.

He took the hat and dropped it onto his head. "It's my disguise. I'd hate to have fans swarming me while I'm trying to take you out on a reward date."

She pretended to appear skeptical, though, truth be told, people stopped them in the halls all the time to tell him good game or to ask him to sign the latest full-page picture of him on the front of the sports section in *The Daily Herald*. "Does that happen often?"

He started the car then reached up to swipe the hat down so it rested at a crooked angle over one eye. "Everywhere I go, babe."

Laughing seemed the best response. Otherwise she might puddle into the seat. The hat was silly, but oh, it worked. He wore a soft pair of jeans (she could tell because she rested her hand on his knee at the first opportunity) and a T-shirt, like her, only navy blue. But the black, worn-looking hat fit him. It showed off his playful side—the side that didn't need hundreds of adoring fans.

She cleared her throat. "Don't you think the number seven on the back of your shirt is going to give you away?"

He shook his head. "Hiding in plain sight."

"I see."

They pulled up to a somewhat run-down brick building, and the scarf felt too dressy. "What is this place?"

Anthony waited to answer until he'd opened her door for her. He pointed to a faded, wooden sign hanging crookedly over the door. "Juanita's."

He grasped her hand and led her inside. The interior surprised her. It was a bowling alley-slash-Mexican-slash-American restaurant. Barely over a half dozen tables crowded the front area, separated from a six-lane bowling alley by a short, bright-orange wall. The hardwood floors, both the dark of the eating area and the lighter color of the bowling area, gleamed, and it didn't smell like cigarette smoke or stinky feet. A family of six shared pizza at a small table on one of the far lanes, making the restaurant seem almost quaint.

"How did you ever find this place?" she asked, following him past a rickety sign that read, *Please Seat Yourselves.*

He forced a laugh. "Strangely enough, Keesha brought me here. One of her friends told her about it. That it's quiet and not many people know about it." He paused, gazing around the room and maybe avoiding looking at Ty. "She didn't like it."

Ty swallowed. He'd dropped more than a few hints over the weekend about Keesha liking the spotlight, liking people to know it was Rocket Rogers on her arm—but he'd loved her anyway. Ty could see that. Her and Anthony's best moments had been by themselves: his aunt's backyard; his living room in the middle of a Saturday afternoon when all his roommates were gone; the corner of the cafeteria, where he sat with his back to the other students while they huddled together, finishing their playbook and laughing over the one outrageous play they included.

"You're going to think I'm saying this to get on your good side, but it seems like a great place," she said boldly.

Anthony turned back to her, smiling. "I believe you." He pulled a chair out. "The food here is fantastic."

"You come here a lot?" she teased.

He scooted into the chair next to her. "Yes, but not with girls. Davey loves it too. I treat him every once in a while. Sometimes we bring Leprechaun but not too often. And we make sure to warn the cook ahead of time when we do."

"Well"—she chuckled—"I'm honored." She flipped open her menu. "Mmmm. I think I'm going to get zucchini fries. Maybe that'll stop you from stealing them."

"Unlikely," Anthony said without taking his eyes off his own menu. "We've tried everything here. There isn't one thing I don't like."

She pulled her brows together. "Really? Even the Rocky Mountain Oysters?"

He snorted with laughter. "Okay. Maybe one. On principle only. They could be good."

When she ordered the double bacon cheeseburger with both the battered zucchini fries and regular fries—"He has a problem," she'd said jabbing a thumb in Anthony's direction—he raised his eyebrows.

Once the waitress left, he lifted Ty's arm. "Excuse me, miss. Where are you going to put all that food?"

Her cheeks heated up. She should have kept her meal small, at least at first. Most girls probably did that with him. "What?" She pretended to huff to cover her embarrassment. "You don't think short girls have appetites?"

One corner of his lips pulled up. "We'll see."

She couldn't help it. That smile charmed her, so she moved in and stole a kiss. Who cared if he thought she was too forward. She wouldn't play this safe.

Anthony slipped his fingers behind her neck before she pulled away and eased her back toward him, kissing her again. Heat scorched her cheeks, and her heart pounded when he released her. She had the strongest urge to say thank you.

He was right about the food. She stuffed every last bit of it into her mouth, except the handful of fries she couldn't stop him from stealing. He chewed them up and "forced" a kiss on her with his mouth full of them. "Tradition," he excused. However gross, she loved that kiss. It was theirs. She knew he'd never kissed another girl that way. She could be sure of that at least.

They headed over to the lanes after dinner. Ty was a terrible bowler. She wouldn't impress Anthony with her skills there. He surprised her, though, by pulling her into his arms after they set their bowling balls down—his a swirly blue and white, of course; she went with pink. He started dancing with her to a slow, country song playing over the terrible speaker system.

"I thought this was a bowling alley," she protested.

"With this song on, it's too much to resist."

She could only nod and follow him. He didn't just sway back and forth, though she would've been happy with that. His steps were practiced.

He twirled her every now and again, grinning at what must be a surprised expression on her face. He danced too. Was there anything *not* perfect about this kid?

And when she thought this date, this night, this life, couldn't get better, he began singing while she rested her forehead against his chest. He dipped his head so those angelic notes—soft, half-whispered, but heart-poundingly beautiful all the same—drifted right to her ears.

He chuckled after half a verse, drawing his head away a fraction. "Sorry. Can't help myself."

She shook her head, unable to look up at him. "No. Don't stop. Please."

He paused. "You said that at the service thing."

"I've never heard anyone sing like you, Anthony. Don't stop."

They didn't bowl. They danced while he sang all the songs he knew and twirled her rowdily to the fast ones or the ones he didn't know. Every once in a while, she noticed the other patrons watching them—the older ones with remember-those-days looks on their faces, younger ones with knowing smiles. But mostly she rested her head against him, clutched his hand, and gave up the idea she would be able to walk away without regrets when he got tired of her.

Don't stop, she wished. *Please, please, don't ever stop.*

Chapter Eleven

As blissful as she felt, Ty needed to escape everything for a while, just to test if it was real. Did she really spend two hours dancing at a bowling alley with Anthony Rogers?

She went to her parents' house after classes on Tuesday. Since it was only two o'clock, her mom was the only one home.

"Hey, kiddo." Mom looked up from a cookbook when Ty walked into the kitchen. "What's up?"

Ty settled onto a stool and stared. And smiled.

Mom closed the cookbook, straightening up. "Are things going well with Anthony?"

Ty nodded. She swallowed. "Really well. I think . . . I think maybe I'm really, really falling for him."

"And Anthony?"

Ty appreciated that Mom covered the ecstatic smile with caution first. "I don't know." Ty leaned her head against the cool countertop then lifted it and rested her chin on top of her hands. "This is so scary."

Mom reached forward to grasp her hand. "Terrifying. I know. For me too."

Ty laughed. "He took me to this little bowling place last night with amazing food. But we didn't bowl. We danced, and he sang to me."

Mom bit her lip. "Sounds like he's falling for you."

"He could be. He's just . . . well, you know, he's Rocket. And maybe what's going on with us is different for him—at least from what I know—but maybe it's not different enough." She put her head back down against the counter and took a deep breath. She knew she needed to live more in the moment, enjoy what she had with Rocket, and forget about how it all could end. But a little voice kept nagging at her. She wanted Mom to tell her Rocket would stay—and she wanted for it to be true. At the very least, she needed to somehow shut that voice up.

"I'm sorry, hun. Maybe it's not."

Ty jerked her head up, scowling. Not what she wanted to hear.

"But maybe it is," Mom added with a grin. "You told me when you got into that class you didn't expect much, just the chance."

"That's not enough anymore."

Mom ruffled Ty's hair. "Aww, hun. Just go with it. Giving your heart to someone is a crazy thing. Crazy but exhilarating, and chances are you'll get it broken a few times. That's life. Give it everything you've got, if that's what you want. The rest will take care of itself."

Ty nodded. "Sounds familiar. Like what I said before."

"You're wise beyond your years."

"But what if . . . what if I'm falling in love with him?"

"I think that's definitely giving it everything you've got." Mom tilted her head and smiled unevenly. Ty could see now the relationship terrified her too, not knowing if Ty could handle a shattered heart. "Ty, he'd be crazy to give you up, and somewhere deep down, he knows that. I'd bet my life on it."

Ty sat up. "You think so?"

"From the first time I saw that picture of him kissing you—"

"On the cheek, Mom."

"Doesn't matter. I knew." Mom opened the cookbook, flipped through a few pages, and turned it to show Ty. "What do you think of zucchini pasta? Think Harly would notice?"

"Yes. Absolutely. He's Harly. His taste buds are superhuman."

Mom frowned. "True. Dang." She put the cookbook down and reached to take Ty's hands. "Sweetie, your Heavenly Father will take care of you, no matter what. You know that, right?"

Tears sprung to Ty's eyes. A lump formed in her throat. "I know."

"Have you prayed about it?"

Ty nodded and forced a smile. "Fervently."

Laughing, Mom pulled her into a hug. "Then Heavenly Father will definitely take care of this."

* * *

"You have that look on your face again," Anthony said.

Ty's head whipped back from staring over her shoulder as she walked into class and met Anthony's gaze. She smiled then frowned. "That look?"

"Like that day you said you thought someone was following you." Anthony's protective instincts kicked in, and when it concerned her, they came strong.

"Yeah . . ." She settled in her seat and turned toward the door, staring out. It must have been something big to keep her attention from him so long. "I have that same feeling. It's creepy." She sighed and turned back to him. A smile flitted across her face again. She peered over her shoulder one more time. "And I think maybe I saw Dylan." She must have sensed the anger that burst through him—or maybe the way he clenched his fists gave him away. She rushed on. "But of course, he goes to school here, so seeing him isn't a big deal." She put her hand on Anthony's arm.

He swallowed. Yeah. She was right. He didn't need to get all worked up about a guy who gave his girl the creeps. Except, she *was* his girl. He'd do anything for her.

He was a goner. And he didn't care anymore. Protecting Ty reminded him of how many fights he'd gotten into in middle and high school for Nikki. Some girls were worth it. He'd had a hard time admitting Ty was one of them, but she was.

He took another deep breath. Dylan creeped Anthony out too. He hated the way Dylan had looked at Ty. And not just out of jealousy. "Let me know if he does talk to you or anything. I'll find a way to be more forceful next time."

Her eyes danced. "That is so irresistible."

Just like that, his own smile returned. "You like it when I channel cave men?"

"When it's for me? Yeah."

He grunted. "Me. You. Lunch."

After a giggle escaped, she smiled sympathetically. "Math centers today."

"It doesn't sound like you're inviting me this time."

"As much as I would love to have you with me for pretty much every second of the day, I think Mr. Franklin would like the kids in his class to work at some point."

Every second of the day. He'd like that too. "I'm sure we can find a way to work math into a football game."

She laughed. "I bet you could."

"I'll give you a ride then."

"I can walk. Like I used to do all the time. It's only a few blocks."

He reached across the aisle and took her hand. "*Please* let me give you a ride?" How pathetic did he sound?

She leaned forward, her eyes softening instantly. "In that case, please do."

Class started. Anthony let go of her hand and pretended to pay attention to Brian. It was hard. Ty was way better looking, and every time Brian looked in their direction, he smirked. It was annoying. Anthony avoided it by staring at Ty, but she kept catching him—then smiling. He couldn't describe the quality of it. It reminded him of the way she asked him not to stop singing. Happy, but sort of desperate.

What did Ty have to feel desperate about? Him?

Every time he had to look quickly away, he noticed the other girls in the class, not because they were anything compared to Ty, but because they weren't looking at him anymore. They weren't paying attention to Brian, but they weren't trying to get Anthony's attention. Instead of worrying him, it made him laugh.

After class he and Ty held hands while walking to his car. He found himself scanning the faces of the people around them, wondering if Dylan was around. Why would he follow her? Surely he could torment other girls. Ty seemed to think his attraction came from her friendship with the football players. He didn't see Dylan. Instead he saw a lot of people staring at him and Ty. He frowned. *Seriously, people.* Half the campus walked around holding hands with the other half. Wasn't that what people came to BYU for? To get married? Degrees on the side?

"You're Rocket Rogers, Anthony." Ty's voice surprised him.

"Huh?" He looked down at her. She stared at him with a worried expression creasing her eyebrows together. "Did you read my mind?" Talk about wearing his emotions on his sleeve.

She laughed. The crease eased but didn't disappear. "Not quite. You're staring down everyone that looks twice at us. You're Rocket. Of course they're interested in a girl you're holding hands with. It just isn't done."

He looked at their hands. "Clearly it's done, smart aleck."

"Not often." The crease disappeared, melting into a soft look with that now maybe-explained hint of desperation. "And the girls are wild with jealousy." She moved closer to him, resting her head against his upper arm.

"The guys too," he said.

She grinned. "Thank you."

"Stating the facts, ma'am."

They reached his car. He opened her door before heading around the other side. He liked hiding away inside with just her.

"If you didn't want to hold my hand around other people, it wouldn't bother me—really." The comment seemed to burst out of her, and she wouldn't meet his eyes. "I don't need you to advertise to the world you like me."

Like me. Sort of an understatement, but he let it pass. He picked up her hand and squeezed it tightly inside his own. "Sometimes you say the weirdest things. Why wouldn't I want to hold hands with you?"

Scarlet flooded her face as she stared at him. "No. I don't mean that . . . Well, your love life is the topic of a lot of conversation, and we don't have to make it worse. I like things to be between you and me. I don't like sharing."

He pressed his face against hers. "You're funny," he said before kissing her.

"Centers," she whispered after a few kisses.

"Oh. Right. I'm supposed to drive you somewhere." He had to pull completely away. She sucked all resistance out of him. Scary. He'd declare his feelings on the big screen at the next football game if she asked him to.

"Yeah. To Harly's school." She sounded as reluctant as he felt about it.

Clearing his throat, he put the key in the ignition and started the car. "So, you're embarrassed about me, are you?" he teased.

"Most of the time, yes," she said without missing a beat. "But I have brothers, so I'm used to public humiliation."

A laugh escaped. He stared at her. "Are you for real, Ty Daws?"

"Stop sign." She pointed.

He braked hard, narrowly avoiding the car in front of them. She smiled.

"Did you decide who you're taking to the football game?" he asked.

"My dad. They had a hard-fought rock-paper-scissors tournament, and he won. I'm sure he cheated, but that's not to say my brothers didn't."

"Good for him." Anthony chuckled. He had a feeling he'd like her dad. Well, he figured that from the moment he heard the names of her brothers.

"The rest of the family is still coming, of course, just way worse seats."

"Man, now I feel all guilty." He intertwined his fingers with her again. He couldn't not touch her for five minutes together.

"Oh, don't worry. They'll survive." She winked.

"I'm going to assume you've always loved football." He watched her for as long as he could before turning back to the road. Maybe he should let her drive more often.

"Can't help it, can I?" She ran her thumb absently over the top of his hand. "I've been watching it and playing it practically since I was born."

"Were you one of those girls that bucked the system to play in high school?" Man, that would be cool, but he would have heard about her.

"Nope. I did the boring thing and played volleyball instead. But I've been in enough backyard games to acquire some serious skills, as you well know."

"If it hadn't been for your center, we would have creamed you."

"Pretend all you want. I understand if you don't want to tell your coach though. I can see it taking a big bite out of your ego if he replaced you with me." She turned in her seat to face him. "And can I assume you've always loved football as well?"

"You can, but like you didn't know that." He wiggled his eyebrows at her.

A slight, pink blush dotted her cheeks. "Well, it's not like that's listed in your biography anywhere, at least not on the BYU website. I didn't catch 'has played since birth' anywhere." She cleared her throat. "What I would like to know is if there's anything you can't do. You sing. You dance. I assume you bowl, since apparently you frequent Juanita's."

On a whim he took the serious route in this conversation. "I'm not great at relationships."

To his surprise she burst out laughing. "Really? From what I've seen, you do them quite well. Too well, for my taste." She blinked, and the smile disappeared. "Oh. I'm sorry. You were serious."

He smiled. "Too well? You call a string of first and second dates 'too well'? And missing that my girlfriend was falling in love with my best friend?" He didn't mean for that part to slip out.

Ty swallowed. "She didn't . . ."

Anthony sighed. It was out there, as much as he'd like to reach out and take it back. Except he trusted Ty pretty much completely. "Yeah. I went to pick her up for a date and caught Matt leaving her apartment—with a good-bye kiss and a promise to him she'd talk to me that night. Only the explanation wasn't necessary anymore."

She squeezed his hand, hard. "Did you beat the crap out of him?"

How could he not love her? She knew him so well. He laughed. "Well. I punched him. Hard as I could. Right in the jaw. Stupid kid didn't even fight back. Just said he deserved it and walked off."

"How could she let it go so far without saying something to you?" Ty murmured, and he knew she didn't expect him to answer, thank heavens. She rested her head against his shoulder. "I'm sorry."

He dropped a kiss on top of her head. "Thanks." He pulled up in front of Harly's school.

She opened the door but bent toward him and took his face in her hands. "Just so you know, I still think you do relationships well, especially this one." Without further explanation, she disappeared from her seat. He watched her walk up the sidewalk, and she rewarded him with a wave before going inside.

He grinned. Yeah. He thought he'd done pretty well too.

* * *

Anthony shut the door of his car and headed for the locker room. He caught sight of Brian making his way across the parking lot. His friend stopped and waited for Anthony to catch up.

"Got your head in the game?" he asked, falling into step with Anthony.

Anthony shook his head at the mischievous smile Brian wore. "What makes you think it wouldn't be? Name one time ever my head hasn't been in the game."

Brian chuckled. "All right. But I can see you have reason to let it wander."

"What's that supposed to mean?"

"Dude, you're happy. Maybe a bit giddy. Everyone can tell." Brian clapped a hand on Anthony's shoulder.

"You're making me sound like a girl." Anthony shrugged off Brian's hand but smiled anyway. "I'm not giddy, but I'll admit Ty is something."

"Something different?" Brian said. Anthony remembered the conversation they had before class and the way Brian talked about letting a girl—specifically Ty—into his life.

"Different, yes." Anthony held up a hand to stop whatever he expected would burst out of Brian's mouth at his admission. "But not *that* different. We're having fun. Nothing serious."

"Yet."

"Hey, weren't you the one warning me to get ready for the game? Now you're forcing thoughts of Ty on me, trying to distract me."

"Forcing?" Brian punched Anthony in the shoulder. His expression turned serious. "One more piece of advice. Don't let Keesha ruin this too."

Anthony paused, feigning confusion at his friend's comment. "How could Keesha ruin it? I haven't talked to her in months. Plus she's married now."

"You know that's not what I meant," Brian answered. "But for now, back to football."

Anthony nodded, forcing his mind away from Brian's insinuation. Keesha had ruined a lot of relationships for him. Or stopped him from pursuing anything serious. He shook his head. He was out of the woods now, beyond that two-date graveyard he'd left so many other possibilities in.

"Football," he muttered to himself and replaced the speculations with a visual of some of the plays they'd run tonight. Brian caught the change. He held open the door of the locker room and grinned.

* * *

Ty rubbed her hands together and eyed the football team, still standing on the field. "We'll just wave. He'll probably have to hurry in to the locker room."

Dad smirked. "Probably."

She glanced at the people to the right and left, all waiting at the bottom of the stands to give one last congratulations on the team's win.

The huddle broke, and the team headed off the field. Ty spotted Anthony's head near the middle, intent in conversation with David. Yeah. They wouldn't be able to do anything but wave. She knew it shouldn't disappoint her. Anthony had gotten them amazing seats, fabulous seats. And he'd invited her to come to church with him the next day. She just . . . she just would love for him to come and shake her dad's hand. Dad would die of excitement.

Her gaze followed Anthony as the team drew nearer. He caught her eye, and she caught her breath when he started to weave his way to the edge.

"Hey." He reached up to put his hand over hers on the railing.

She almost couldn't speak. First he wanted people to see them holding hands and now talking to her after a football game. They sounded like simple things, but they weren't. Not to her.

Luckily a kid near her shouted, "Hey, Rocket! Good game."

Anthony nodded his thanks and turned back to Ty, though several other fans were vying for his attention.

"Yeah, what he said." Ty pointed to the little boy.

He winked. "Thanks."

"This is my dad."

Anthony shook his hand. "Vern Daws. I'm jealous. You got to play with Detmer."

Oh. My. Gosh. He knew who her dad was. Or at least did his research. She looked at Dad. His face reddened with pleasure.

"Yeah. Yeah, thanks. One season. And not a lot." He laughed nervously.

"Still. You'll tell me about it sometime?"

Dad nodded. "Sure. Of course. Thanks for the tickets. Made my season."

"You're welcome."

Dad cleared his throat and glanced apologetically at Ty. "You busy for dinner tomorrow night? We'd love to have you over."

Ty wanted to disappear into the flood of people leaving the stadium. Meet her family? After only a couple weeks?

Anthony grinned though. "I'd love to." She sighed with relief. He didn't seem freaked out. He turned his gaze back to her. "I'll see you tomorrow?"

"Of course. Good game. Did I mention that?"

"Feel free to continue." He squeezed her hand one more time and slipped back into the throng of football players, waving at the people who made renewed efforts to get his attention now he'd turned from Ty.

The minute he disappeared inside the tunnel, she slapped Dad on the shoulder. "Inviting him to dinner without my approval?"

Dad laughed as he turned to head toward the exit. "You don't want Rocket to come to dinner?"

"First, let's practice calling him by his name: Anthony. Unless he asks you to call him Rocket, at which point you may feel free to use that nickname. Second, it may be too soon. I'm trying not to scare him off."

"According to your mother, we're giving it all we've got."

Ty sighed but laughed when he put his arm around her neck and pulled her into a hug. "Seriously, though," he added, "great seats. Try not to scare him off."

Chapter Twelve

THE NEXT DAY TY HUMMED to herself as she strolled into the Joseph Smith Building, where Anthony's ward met for church. Rosie had hated the outfit Ty insisted on wearing—simple, dark jean skirt; plain, but still pretty, pink top; and flats, ordinary flats with a tiny, pink bow on the toes.

"Just because you seem to be dating, doesn't mean you should let your standards fall," she'd complained.

"You know I owe you many thanks for getting Anthony's attention for me, but I don't have to be a Barbie doll to keep it. I can just be me. He seems to like it," she'd responded.

"So strange . . . ," Rosie had murmured. Ty ignored her.

Now she let her gaze fall over the students still milling around the door of the classroom where Anthony said they held sacrament meeting. She wanted to see Anthony. As soon as possible. Even the few hours since she'd seen him the night before were too much for her.

Ty met Dylan's eyes instead. Uncomfortable prickles worked from her fingers and spread all across her arms. Dylan smiled and pushed away from the wall he'd been resting against. He raised his hand in greeting.

I can think of something nice to say, Ty thought, but she gazed around with an edge of panic. Even when she was in a room crowded with people, being near Dylan made her feel slimy. Something about his dark expression in the restaurant. The way he knew her favorite meal. His overall possessiveness while they were together. She shivered remembering it.

Then the familiar smell of Anthony's aftershave and a warm arm snaking around her waist chased all those shivers away—well, created a whole new, enjoyable set of shivers.

In front of her, Dylan's expression froze and then fell. He narrowed his eyes before backing away.

"Hey." Ty turned to greet Anthony breathlessly. "To my rescue once again."

Anthony looked around and frowned. "Perhaps I need to be clearer about what 'stay away' means." He dragged his hand along her waist as he moved in Dylan's direction, beckoning David with his other hand.

Ty caught his fingers in hers and pulled him back. "No. Don't. I think he gets it."

Anthony studied her. "Clearly he doesn't. If he thinks he can bother you because I'm not around—"

"He's just a guy, Anthony." She offered a teasing smile, hoping to ease the tense expression on his face, no matter how endearing his protectiveness was. She didn't want Anthony getting into trouble for fighting. Besides, Dylan wouldn't bother her with Anthony around. "Don't you think I can handle it?" she asked playfully.

His expression didn't lighten. "Just a guy?"

He read her so well *he* was almost scary. "A very awkward guy."

"I don't like the way he looks at you. Or the look on your face when you think you've seen him around campus."

"You're sweet." She squeezed his hand and hoped he'd drop the subject.

"What's going down?" David stepped to her other side.

"Ty won't let me give Creepy over there another talking to." Anthony's disappointed scowl entertained her. She tried not to laugh.

David glared at her. "Come on. Fun hater."

"Don't encourage him. We're at church." She tugged on Anthony's hand again. "Let's go in and sit down."

"Fine." Clasping his hand around hers, Anthony led the way into the chapel, David following like a bodyguard. She didn't have to look to know Anthony sent intimidating glares in Dylan's direction. Worry wiggled through her. She was glad Anthony had proved more intimidating to Dylan than David, but the angry way he reacted concerned her. However flattering that Anthony wanted to protect her, fighting wouldn't go over well at the honor code office.

Anthony lifted their enjoined hands to acknowledge someone inside the chapel, and it distracted her from her thoughts about Dylan. She smiled. Holding hands while walking around campus, surrounded by people they may or may not know was one thing. Here in his ward? This was a declaration of territory. And whether he did it because of Dylan or not, her heart beat quicker.

Could he be considering her seriously? Not just some fling with some girl? Maybe she'd graduated from the girl who presented him with a challenge to a girl who was a contender for his heart. She said a silent prayer. *This is good. I'm thankful for these little things.*

"What's that look for?" Anthony asked when they scooted into a row of chairs with a few of the other football players. "Still embarrassed to hold hands with me in public?"

"I'm afraid some of the other guys might get the wrong idea." She pulled the hymnbook out and flipped to the page of the opening hymn, eager to see what she'd get to hear Anthony sing today. "Master, the Tempest is Raging." Perfect.

"And what sort of wrong idea would they get?" He slipped the hymnbook into his free hand, still clutching hers. He glanced over the title before looking back for Ty's answer.

She gave him a playful grin. "That you like me." She waited for a confirmation of her earlier thoughts, something besides the hand holding to let her know he was in this relationship for real. *Game Plan Key: Know how the offense's formation can tell the defense what their next play will be.*

He scooted as close as he could and moved his arm around her back, holding her next to him. With his other hand, he reached for hers, clasping it tightly. "What do you think?" he whispered with his forehead resting against the side of her head. "Am I making it clear enough how I feel?"

It took her too long to find the will to breathe and force out the words. "Yeah. Maybe."

He tilted his head away a fraction and laughed silently as the organist played the opening bars. Two could play at this game. Giving him a smirk of her own, she rested her head against his shoulder. She could get used to this.

* * *

When Ty walked into her apartment after church, Rosie dropped the *Ensign* she'd been reading and looked up expectantly. "How'd it go today?"

The regular debriefs after her encounters with Anthony had started to get on Ty's nerves. When would it stop? Couldn't Rosie declare victory and move on?

"Good."

Rosie fell back against the chair. "Oh, come on, Ty. Details."

Ty paused next to the doorway separating their rooms from the main living area, hoping for a quick escape. "I think you can call this endeavor a success, Rosie. He held my hand in front of people at church. You know what that means."

Rosie sat back up and clapped. "It means he plans on keeping you around."

"Yep." Ty nodded, glad her roommate got the point, and headed into her room to change her clothes.

"But anything could happen to change that." Rosie sounded almost desperate as she followed Ty. "Especially since he's going to your parents' house for dinner."

Ty pinched her lips together. "It'll be fine." That was a lie, but she didn't want more coaching from Rosie. "I think I can handle things from here on out."

Rosie grunted. "Yeah, right." But at least she walked away.

Satisfied with that for now, Ty pulled out her phone and plopped on her bed before changing to text Walsh. *I think I'm in love.*

After not hearing from you for days, I expect something better than that. I've known about your love for Rocket for years.

Kicking her shoes toward the closet and resting against her pillow, she typed, *That was infatuation. This might be real.*

What about him?

It looks good. This whole thing is fun. He's fun.

I hope he's committed because . . . everybody's coming over for dinner. Even Uncle Lee.

Ty sat up. *WHAT?*

Maybe I told Ben that Rocket was coming over, and he told his mom, so maybe now everyone's coming.

She collapsed back onto the bed and groaned. She'd never admit it to Rosie, but her roommate might be right. *I'm so going to get you for this.*

* * *

When Ty arrived on Anthony's doorstep so they could head to her parents' house, she greeted him with clammy hands and wide eyes. "What's wrong?" he asked, sticking his head out the door and expecting to see Dylan dogging her steps.

"It's not too late to change your mind. My parents would understand." She stepped inside.

Anthony grinned. "About dinner?"

"It's not just going to be my parents and brothers, and I would understand if you wanted to ditch. I pretty much want to ditch."

"Do they expect me to propose tonight?" he asked teasingly.

Her face drained of color. "No. No way."

Donning a mock frown, he pulled her closer, tucking his chin so he could see the crazed look in her eyes. He should feel bad for being amused by it. "I think my feelings might be hurt."

A smile peeked through her lips. "Anthony, don't worry. I've got my wedding dress cut out of a bridal magazine already. It's glued inside my journal, and underneath I've written *Mrs. Rocket Rogers*."

Stuff like that should scare him. Instead, Anthony used his other hand to pull her chin up to kiss her while he laughed. "Good to know," he said against her lips.

She pulled away sooner than he wanted. "Anthony, seriously though. Walsh told my cousin you were coming over for Sunday dinner, so then, of course, my aunt called my mom and then, well, called all her sisters, and they're all coming. Mom didn't know how to tell them they couldn't."

Anthony knew this should intimidate him, but instead he laughed. Because they were coming to meet Rocket Rogers not Ty's boyfriend.

He was calling himself that already? Boyfriend?

"Are these your mom's sisters or your dad's?"

Ty stared up at him, looking perplexed. "Seriously? My dad's. But . . . it's a lot of people."

"They would think I was a pretty big jerk if I didn't show."

"We'll come up with a good excuse. I'll take all the blame—tell them I told you not to come."

He gripped her by the shoulders and held her at arm's length. He gathered as much seriousness as he could muster. "Is there something you need to tell me about your family? Something that might warrant you being so adamant I don't meet them? Let me guess, your other two brothers aren't really named Walsh and Steve, are they? You made that up to impress me."

The tension slid out of her arms. She stepped closer and took a deep breath. "My Uncle Lee is a Utah fan."

"That's it. This is over."

Laughing, she put her arms around his neck. "You are the best ever. Don't let anyone tell you different."

"I'm aware, and I'm pretty sure no one has ever tried to tell me that except maybe Beast and my sister."

Nikki called as they drove over, reminding Anthony he was supposed to go over there. Being around Ty so much lately had made a lot of things slip his mind—like checking up on her more. He'd promised his mom when she left on her mission he'd keep an eye on Nikki.

"Hey there. You still coming over tonight?"

He looked at Ty, who smiled but eyed him curiously. He hadn't said any more about his sister since their date at his aunt's house. He returned her smile but then looked back at the road.

"Actually, no. Ty invited me to dinner at her parents' house."

"And you're going?" Nikki said at the same time Ty protested, "I did not. My dad did."

Chuckling, Anthony corrected himself. "I mean, her dad invited me over. And yes, I am."

"Well, well, well." He could hear the knowing smile in her voice—and then the whispered, "Well, well, well, well." He pushed away the worry. She couldn't always help it. "Getting kind of serious, isn't it?" she asked.

"Easy there."

"Sorry. So when are you bringing her to meet me?"

He turned toward Ty again. She'd been staring at him. She reddened and turned her gaze out the window.

"Um . . . ," he hedged.

"It's been a while since you brought someone over. I'd accuse you of being embarrassed, but you'd take me seriously, so I'll just say, I can handle it, Anthony. Whatever. And she sounds special."

That's what she'd said about Keesha. And Keesha was special, but she didn't handle meeting Nikki well. She'd hardly said a word the whole meal and came up with an excuse to rush home after dinner—making her discomfort obvious to everyone.

"Anthony?" Nikki asked after several seconds of silence. "That night with Keesha bothered you more than me; I told you that. She would've gotten used to it. Ty would too. Bring her over sometime."

He couldn't. Not yet. Maybe not soon. This thing with Ty was fun, and he didn't want to disappoint himself already. "Yeah. Sometime."

Nikki sighed. "Okay. Have fun. Come over tomorrow night. I'm making fried chicken and potatoes and everything."

Her comfort meal. "Sure. You're good, right?" He listened carefully for her answer, ready to drop Ty off and head over there if he heard anything amiss in her voice.

"I'm great. I promise. See you tomorrow." She sounded fine. Happy.

"Okay. See you tomorrow."

* * *

Ty knew it was weird that, as they walked up to the front door of her house, Anthony's steady hand kept her moving. He'd seemed hesitant earlier in the car, but he promised it was because he forgot he was supposed to eat with his sister. She'd begged him to go there instead, but Anthony insisted he still wanted to come, that he couldn't wait to meet her other two brothers and her mom.

But in less than a minute, he would meet *everyone*—all her dad's sisters and Uncle Lee, the Ute fan. How could Anthony act so nonchalant? *Please let them be normal around him.* She could trust her parents and her brothers—well, she could *mostly* trust her brothers—but the rest of them? It frightened her.

Anthony chuckled, and she tried to let it ease her again, like his teasing did back at his house. "Just so you know," he said under his breath, "they can't say anything that's going to scare me away."

That worked. Calmness eased through her chest and tamed the butterflies in her stomach. "Don't be too sure," she said anyway, clutching his hand. It would be just her luck if it was her family that sent him running and not something she did.

He brought her hand to his lips and kissed it.

Harly threw open the front door. Anthony finished the kiss quickly before turning. "Hey, Rocket!" Harly shouted.

"Harly," Ty whispered urgently. "Remember what we talked about?"

He stared at her with a blank look. "No."

Anthony sniggered as Ty drooped her shoulders in defeat. "Getting him to call you by your real name is a work in progress, I guess," she apologized in a low tone.

"Don't worry about it." He turned back to Harly. "Hey there, pal." He grinned and dropped her hand to pick Harly up and throw him over his shoulder. Anthony strutted over the threshold with a squirming Harly on his back.

Stevie barreled down the stairs. "Rocket's here!" he cried. "Hi, Rocket. Ready for some football?"

Sighing, Ty held her hand out toward the boy who had joined them. "Anthony, this is Stevie. Stevie, this is *Anthony*."

"Ooops. Hi, *Anthony*."

"Great to meet you, Stevie." Anthony wasted no time throwing Stevie over his other shoulder, making it seem easy to haul around an extra 150 pounds.

"Can we play football, Rocket?" Harly asked, trying to turn and face his idol from the awkward position over Anthony's shoulder.

"I don't think your mother would approve, Harly."

"Today is a special occasion." Harly sounded out of breath already. "She said so. Mom says as long as I don't ask you embarrassing questions like if you're going to marry my sister, then I can do whatever I want."

To Ty's utter happiness, Anthony grinned at her over his shoulder. She shrugged and led the way to the kitchen.

Mom, Aunt Maddie, Aunt Kim, and Aunt Julie all stood around the kitchen island. They looked up when Anthony strode in.

"Sister Daws?" Anthony hesitated for the first time since entering the house.

Mom scooted around the island. "Yep. That's me. We're so glad you could come, Anthony." She put out a hand and then retracted it with a laugh, since Anthony still held both Harly and Stevie, who had at this point succumbed to their fates.

"I found these two Sabbath-breakers in the front room. They tried to convince me to play football with them."

Mom didn't miss a beat, which Ty loved about her mother. "I'm glad to see you have them in hand. Literally."

Anthony plopped them down. Both boys looked up at him with adoration. So, including Ty, that made three people in the room wearing pretty similar expressions. Anthony reached out to shake Mom's hand.

Mom pointed back to the three women standing behind her still in awe that Anthony Rogers stood in the same kitchen as them. "These are Vern's sisters—Maddie, Kim, and Julie."

Anthony waved. "And which one of you married a Ute?" he teased.

Ty snorted a laugh into her hand. Aunt Maddie, the youngest, turned a brilliant shade of red. "That would be me," she stammered. Then she shrugged and cleared her throat. "I couldn't help myself."

Anthony laughed, but Aunt Maddie's blush didn't ease. "I guess they have to have wives, right?"

"I suppose so." Aunt Maddie offered a high-pitched, nervous titter.

Ty's dad walked into the kitchen from the family room on the other side. Uncle Lee hovered near the doorway—Ty figured he must have heard the preceding remarks—but Uncle Joe and Uncle Rich came in, filling the room almost to capacity.

"Good to see you, Anthony." Dad shook Anthony's hand with vigor. "This is Joe and Rich and Lee. There'll be a test after dinner to see how many names you remember."

"Of course. Kids too?" Anthony asked.

"Definitely."

As if on cue, footsteps thundered down the stairs. "Walsh said Rocket's here!" a cousin shouted.

"And we're gonna play football with him!" Harly yelled back.

Mom cleared her throat and shook her head. "Anthony and Ty have to help me set the table, Harly. No such luck."

Harly scowled. "But he's a *guest,* Mom!"

Anthony bent over and whispered something in Harly's ear. Harly's face lit up, and Anthony pointed at him. "But remember, you can't tell anyone."

"Yes, sir, Rocket." Harly bounded out of the room shouting, "Yes! Yes!"

Ty stepped to Anthony's side. "What'd you have to promise?"

"To come play football later this week," he answered in a low tone.

Grabbing some plates from the counter, Ty said, "You stay here and regale your fans with your exploits. I got this."

"Are you sure?"

"Oh, yeah." Ty eyed the family still crowded in the kitchen. "They'd probably follow us into the dining room anyway."

"I'll help." Walsh emerged from the crowd and grabbed the other stack of plates.

"That's quite a sacrifice," Ty said when they were alone in the dining room.

Walsh shrugged. "He's coming later this week, right? Plus, I get the feeling he's sticking around awhile."

Ty blushed. "Yeah. Hopefully." She rested against the doorway, listening for the conversation across the hallway in the kitchen. She couldn't hear Uncle Lee's voice—yet. Once he got up the nerve, Ty knew he'd say something. He hadn't had anything good to say about Anthony during the games Uncle Lee and Aunt Maddie watched with them the year before.

"Can Anthony hear?" Walsh asked.

Ty tilted her head. "Huh?"

"If he can hear, then he's heard worse than anything Uncle Lee can say. Uncle Lee isn't the only Ute fan in Utah. Or the only person to ever criticize Rocket."

"True," Ty conceded.

Dinner went well. Besides some good-natured ribbing, Uncle Lee behaved himself.

"Now the good part." Dad propped his elbows onto the table once everyone had a bowl of ice cream and a slice of Aunt Julie's apple pie in front of them. "The questions."

"Dad—" Ty blurted.

Dad held up his hand, a teasing grin on his face. "If Anthony's brave enough to come here and face all of us, I think he can handle a good grilling, can't he?"

Anthony settled in his chair, draping his arm across the back of Ty's. "Certainly. You first?" He must've known Dad would have the most embarrassing question. Well, besides Harly.

Dad rubbed his hands together, and only the pressure of Anthony's leg against hers kept Ty from fleeing the room in terror. "Your best football moment ever," he said.

Ty reached over to swat Dad, and Anthony laughed. "I used to say it was the day Coach called to ask me to play for BYU, but that was nothing compared to beating Notre Dame in South Bend. How about you?" Anthony shot back.

"No question. Watching Walsh run in the touchdown that clenched the state championship for them last year."

Anthony nodded slowly. He turned to Walsh. "I've heard you're quite the player. Not as good as your sister, but she's a tough one to beat."

Walsh slapped his leg in mock amusement. "She wishes."

"My turn." Mom stroked her chin, her eyes twinkling. *I can trust her*, Ty reminded herself, but with such a good mood around the table, it would be like Mom to throw something crazy out there. She might think it was a good time to surprise a serious answer out of Anthony about his intentions with Ty.

"What's your favorite play?" Mom asked. Ty sighed with relief.

Next to her, Anthony chuckled and nudged her with his elbow. "I can handle this," he whispered. Aloud, he answered, "Quarterback draws, of course."

Harly jumped up onto his chair and raised his hand. "Pick me, Rocket. Pick me!"

Anthony pointed to him. "Harly?"

"Why does everyone want you to marry my sister?" Harly dropped onto his seat and rested his elbows onto the table with a serious look in his eyes.

Ty opened her mouth to retaliate somehow, but a burst of laughter from Anthony and then the sound of him quickly clearing his throat stopped her. He fought a full-fledged grin.

"Well, Harly," he began and took a deep breath. She admired both his reaction and his attempt to seem serious for Harly's sake. "I think it's because I'm so handsome and, perhaps, for my amazing football skills." He turned his attention back to Ty, one corner of his lips lifting. Butterflies whipped through her stomach. *Wrong answer,* she thought. *I want him because he's so kind and loyal and funny and . . . everything.* Anthony's smile widened the longer she stared at him, probably in that same silly doe-eyed look she sometimes couldn't help.

"My turn," Uncle Lee said from the end of the table.

Ty stiffened, her butterfly moment gone just like that. "I think that's enough for one day. Save some for next time." Except for Uncle Lee. He wasn't invited back unless Anthony was safely sealed to her for eternity.

"Oh, come on, Ty. That's not fair." Uncle Lee scowled mockingly.

Anthony nudged her with his shoulder. "Think I can't handle a Ute?" Everyone laughed.

"You shouldn't have to," Ty said amid the laughter.

He looked up at Uncle Lee. "Take your best shot."

"Tell the truth," Uncle Lee started, and she knew something bad was coming. "Were you really down before you lost the ball?"

Silence gripped the table for several seconds. No one needed to explain what Uncle Lee meant. They all knew the infamous play in the Utah-BYU game the year before. With Utah linemen rushing him, Anthony had scrambled out of the pocket. A lineman caught up, taking Anthony to the ground. Amidst the chaos, a Utah player came up with the ball and ran for thirty yards before the officials reviewed the play and gave the ball back to BYU. The Cougars scored on the next play and went on to win the game by one touchdown.

A loud *thump* underneath the table near Uncle Lee interrupted the silence. "Lee!" Aunt Maddie hissed. She turned to Anthony, her face deep red. "I'm sorry. You don't have to answer that."

The smile that had frozen awkwardly on Anthony's face slipped into a smirk. He stared Uncle Lee right in the eye. "No problem. It's an easy one too. Of course I was." He didn't waver.

Uncle Lee finally laughed. "You gonna marry her?" he prodded.

Anthony smile dropped off, and Ty panicked. She should've insisted Anthony go to Nikki's, even if she had to drive him there herself. "Uncle Lee!" she protested.

"Lee." Aunt Maddie smacked him on the arm. "Back off."

Uncle Lee chuckled. "Of all the BYU players, I could probably like this kid. I think he should go for it."

"Who wouldn't want to marry Ty?" Anthony shrugged the question off, and his smile returned. Hollowness filled the joke, far different than the lighthearted answer to Harly's same inquiry.

Mom stood up and pointed a finger at Uncle Lee. "Dish duty, pal."

He held his hands up in surrender. "Okay, okay." Pushing his chair back, he looked over at Anthony. "Up for some dishes?"

Anthony kissed Ty's cheek and stood. "I won't say no to a challenge."

"Be nice." Aunt Maddie and Ty admonished at the same time.

Anthony leaned over. "I told you. I can handle this. There's nothing he can say I haven't heard before."

"You shouldn't have to," she repeated, but the smell of his cologne had already started to wash away her unease. "Not with my family."

"I want to be here, Ty." He wiggled his eyebrows. "And I want to help your uncle. See what he can dish up." His eyes twinkled with mischief. "I want to be here. With you."

She relented. She couldn't help it. The way he gazed at her had her all lightheaded and dizzy. But he was serious. She knew he wasn't teasing her. "I'm more worried about Uncle Lee now."

"I bet." He dragged his hand over her shoulder and followed Uncle Lee to the kitchen.

It was beyond surreal. Her. Anthony Rogers. Dating. Him meeting her parents. Like some crazy dream. She had a hard time telling herself she wouldn't wake up.

Chapter Thirteen

As the next week progressed, fewer and fewer people stared when Anthony and Ty left coaching football hand in hand. It even started to feel natural to Anthony, who hadn't held a girl's hand in public—except Keesha's—since his freshman year at BYU. It reminded him that the inevitable next step was to introduce her to Nikki. But not yet. He couldn't. He needed to know Ty better first.

"You know," he said as they headed to the Wilk for lunch on Friday. "I feel like I'm at a disadvantage with you."

Ty burst into laughter and looked up at him, cocking her head to one side. "You. At a disadvantage. With a girl."

"Not *a* girl. You."

"And how is that?" She shook her head at him.

"You know a lot about me"—she turned her gaze to the ground. Smiling, he tugged her closer—"so shouldn't I get to stalk you somehow?" he finished.

She waved her hand at him, pretending to be nonchalant. "Stalking is such a strong word . . ."

"First food, then interrogation." Anthony paused inside the door. "What looks good?"

"I brought our lunch today." She led the way toward the crowded tables, standing on her tiptoes, like that would help her see an empty spot. Then she froze, staring across the room.

Anthony followed her gaze. "What is it?" he asked.

She shook her head and continued searching for a table. "Nothing." Her lips pulled down in a frown, and she tried to mask the nervous expression filtering into her eyes.

He took her arm. He knew that look. "Ty?" Looking over her head, he zeroed in on the area she'd reacted to and found Dylan a few tables away from where Anthony usually met Ty for lunch. Irritation made the hairs on the back of his neck stand up. Anthony made a serious effort to think like she wanted him to—a coincidence, a guy with a crush.

She sighed. "It's not a big deal. It's just the second time this week Dylan has been in the cafeteria the same time as me."

"Did you used to see him here? You know, before your date?"

Her hesitation was answer enough, but Anthony waited for her to respond anyway.

"No . . . ," she said.

He moved in that direction. What would it take to get it through Dylan's head he needed to stay away from Ty? Ty's arm circled around his waist, which certainly wouldn't hold him in place if it weren't for the way it made his heart race.

"But I wasn't looking for him before," she finished in a rush. He turned back to her. "Rosie and I made pizza for dinner last night. There were lots of leftovers," she said, tilting her head toward him and smiling.

Anthony dropped his shoulders. "Why won't you let me talk to him?"

"Talk?" She raised her eyebrows.

"I need to be clearer about defining what it means to leave you alone."

"It could be a coincidence." She slid her hand into his and tugged.

"But you don't think it is," he guessed, considering the way she reacted when she saw Dylan.

"Even if it's not, why make a big deal out of it?"

"Is there something going on between the two of you that I should know about?" Reluctantly Anthony allowed her to lead him away.

"Ha. Although, if things go south with us, at least I have a backup." She smirked, ignoring Anthony's scowl and pointing into the mass of students. "Look. There's DJ."

Anthony knew she'd dismissed the subject, so he let it go too. "How am I supposed to interrogate you about your deepest, darkest secrets with him around?"

"Okay. I'll tell the hostess we prefer the corner booth." She pointed again, this time to an unused table on the fringe. "But you already know my deepest, darkest secret."

"And what would that be?" Anthony had to let go of her hand to pick through the maze of students, backpacks, chairs, and tables. He did his usual nod and wave for students who called out his name, keeping his attention focused on the girl in front of him.

She paused and turned to him, lowering her voice. "I want to marry Rocket Rogers," she said with a straight face.

Two different sets of chills raced through Anthony. "There's got to be something better than that," he choked out.

A grin shot across her lips. "Nope." She pushed her way through to the table and dropped her backpack on top, pulling out a bright-orange, soft-sided lunchbox.

While Ty extracted paper plates, napkins, juice boxes—he smirked behind her back—and plastic containers full of leftovers, Anthony plopped into a seat and dug his laptop out.

"Facebook ought to tell me what I want to know."

"There're no past relationships on there, so don't waste your time." She scooted a paper plate across to him. "Hope you don't mind cold pizza."

"Isn't that the best way to eat it?" He crammed half the slice into his mouth before logging in and clicking Ty's name. "Thanks, babe," he said, his mouth still full. He clamped it shut and tried not to show his embarrassment. He never ate like this around girls, but more often than not, he didn't feel the need to impress her. He didn't need to keep up appearances with her or worry about his precious reputation with the ladies. She didn't notice his lack of manners anyway. She slid her own plate to the spot next to him and settled in, her shoulder touching his arm.

"No problem." She took a bite and chewed it. "So," she asked, "when do I get to meet *your* family? It's only fair I be put through what you were."

Funny you should mention that, he thought. He leaned on his elbow and decided to keep it lighthearted. Feigning seriousness, he said, "I'm not related to any Utah fans."

She laughed. "Touché."

Ty wanting to meet his parents should scare him. In his brain, alarms went off, blaring at him about how serious this was getting, about how *quickly* this was getting serious, about how Nikki could see it too. But in truth, he'd like nothing more than to introduce Ty to his mom. She'd adore Ty. So what held him back from taking her to Nikki's house? Didn't he trust Ty?

"I wish I could," he said. When he looked up, he noticed a worried expression settling in her eyes. He squeezed her hand to reassure her. "My parents are on a mission in Chile."

Shock replaced the worry. "Your parents are on a mission? Now? While you're playing for BYU?"

"I guess they've seen enough," he joked. She hit him on the arm. "I know they're still watching me, Ty, and that's enough. They don't need to be here to watch me throw the same passes and run the same routes they've seen for the last twenty years. And they'll be home in December, in time for a bowl game even."

"You couldn't run a naked boot when you were four years old."

"You'd be surprised."

She laid her head on his shoulder, holding her pizza up but waiting to take another bite. "Well, I'll never get sick of watching you play."

"That's the best thing I've heard all day." He finished off his first—excellent—slice and reached for another. She'd crammed at least eight more slices in the rectangular container. Involuntarily the sides of his lips curled into an appreciative smile. Yes, she sure did bring lunch. Plenty of it. He wondered if there was anything about her not to like.

I would be a dummy to ever let this girl out of my sight. He took a bite of his second slice, going back to searching her Facebook posts from before he met her.

"Um . . ." she interrupted.

"Yeah?" He clicked around her page.

"What about Nikki?"

He looked up. "Oh. Well."

She lowered her pizza and stared at it in her hands. "I didn't think that'd be as big of a deal as meeting parents." She bit her lip. "Is it?"

With Nikki? Yeah, it was. The words to explain everything waited on the tip of his tongue. He wanted to tell her, but it wouldn't come out. "No, not really," he lied. "She's just . . . busy a lot. I'll talk to her."

Ty nodded, still not looking at him. "Okay. Great." She forced a pathetic smile and took another bite.

Anthony wanted to pull her close and bury his head in her hair, comfort her somehow—but if he did, she'd know he lied, know there was a reason to comfort her. So he went back to studying her Facebook profile and injected false lightness into his next words. "Yes, this is very interesting."

"More like embarrassing," she mumbled, seeming more interested in her pizza than anything else. He was such a jerk.

Still, the articles and videos of him popping up across the screen made him stifle a chuckle. "Well, it's no wonder you know so much about football. You're well-read—and watched."

"Stop it," she pled halfheartedly. "I've already confessed to stalking you and being obsessed."

"I don't see any relationship statuses." He turned to her, disappointed.

She shrugged. "I told you. There were never any worth announcing to the world."

"And now?" He laid his arm over the back of her chair.

Pink rose to her cheeks, and she didn't look as hurt anymore. "Seeing as how you're such a public figure, it wouldn't be fair of me to post anything until you have."

"Oh." Anthony laughed at her girl logic. He flicked a button to put his laptop on standby then shut it. "Okay. I give up. You're going to have to tell me everything."

She rolled her eyes toward the ceiling and pushed her lips together in thought. "My absolute most favorite food in the world is hamburgers."

Anthony moved his chair so he sat as close to her as he could. "Right. Okay. That's a start. How about . . . how did you decide to major in history?"

She stared at him, head resting in her hand, while she came up with an answer. "I had a teacher in high school who got me interested in it. He had all these activities to help us get inside people's heads in the past—to understand things from more than just one perspective. To see them as stories, like I told you before."

"So why teach high school? Don't girls in education normally want to teach cute little kids in elementary school?" he asked.

"I want to be able to discuss and interpret history. I don't want to just relate facts." She took another couple bites of her pizza, still her first slice, and pushed the Tupperware box toward him.

He grabbed another slice and grinned before biting into it. "Interpret? It's history. Either it happened or it didn't, right? Like that first bowl game you told me about." He enjoyed the way her eyebrows shot up, surprised that he remembered. "The score was 49 to 0, and Stanford gave up. What is there to interpret?"

"You sound like Mrs. Frazier." She shook her head. "Don't you wonder if there's more to the story?" She leaned forward again, her eyes dancing with excitement. "That 49 to 0 score isn't that bad. Last year, TCU beat Ole Miss 42 to 3 in a bowl game. Hardly better, right? But Ole Miss didn't call it quits at the end of the game. What kind of attitudes and stuff led to Stanford conceding with eight minutes left? You see what I mean?"

She definitely had a point. When Anthony had first met her, he chalked up all her sports talk to trying to gain favor with him, but the excited way she got into even the history of it? How could he have ever thought she had anything in common with hangers-on like Sophie Pope or the High-Heel Girl from their coaching class? It was about more than football with her. It was family togetherness and players and teams she wanted to get to the heart of. It was endearing.

"You're right. It is weird—and maybe not so black and white. Who's Mrs. Frazier?"

"The history teacher I'm interning with. You'd think someone who studied the subject would be more interested in it. She's so resistant to my ideas about things to do to get the kids excited."

"Forgive my skepticism, but kids excited about history? Sounds like a stretch. You can't exactly teach about the history of bowl games there, can you?" She rolled her eyes and then looked disappointed in his reaction so he hurried on. "I know you hate confronting other people, but let her know how excited you are to help them learn. How can she turn that down?"

"I guess you're right . . . maybe." She studied her pizza again.

"So practice on me. Why is it essential for kids to understand why history is important?"

She shook her head at his forced enthusiasm. "Okay. Fine. Another example. How about my Uncle Lee's rude observation last Sunday? Between the three of us, we would give three different accounts, right? You were on the field, and he and I watched from the stands—not together, thankfully. Still, if we wrote it down for history, people would have to take into account a lot of things when they read it—our circumstances, our preexisting opinions, you know?"

Just to be argumentative, Anthony asked, "You disagree with me as to how that play went down?"

Eyes wide with mocking innocence, Ty shook her head. "Absolutely not. You were there, and you told me what happened. I choose to interpret the event how you saw it."

"Good girl." He shook his head. "But seriously, you expect teenagers to respond to that kind of stuff about the American Revolution?"

"No. But a girl can dream, right? They'll all fall asleep, and I'll be forced to fail them. Mrs. Frazier's probably right."

"That sounds depressing. Perhaps you ought to consider a different career path."

"Like getting married or something?" she challenged, holding her pizza at chin height.

He looked away. "This pizza is pretty great. Hope it's not the last time you cook for me."

She didn't answer, and when he looked back, her lips twitched with amusement. It distracted him for several seconds, studying them.

"I could always coach football on the side," she answered. "And I'll cook anytime you want." He didn't get a chance to respond.

"Figures you two would be off hiding somewhere." David's voice alerted Anthony that he approached from a few tables away. Torn between gratitude his friend alerted them to his presence and irritation David interrupted his lunch with Ty, Anthony turned, not bothering to move his arm from behind her chair or scoot away. Sean lumbered behind David, scowling at the obstacles preventing a smooth crossing of the sea of tables—despite the almost panic-stricken students who scooted out of the way when he approached.

David plopped down a tray laden with a footlong sub sandwich, an enormous portion of fries, and several other minor courses. His eyes caught sight of the pizza, which Anthony pulled toward himself. "Mine," he warned and looked pointedly at Ty too.

David grinned. "Somebody didn't learn how to share in kindergarten."

Ty laughed, which annoyed Anthony, but he shouldn't let it get to him. David and Ty were friends. Just friends. "It looks like you have plenty of food to go around, Beast," she said. She reached into her backpack and grabbed a book before pointing at all three of them. "No talking about football, okay. I have to read these last ten pages before class."

Sean swallowed half of one of the sandwiches crowding his tray. "Didn't anyone teach you not to wait until the last minute to do homework?"

Ty smiled as she flipped through the book. "I had better things to do."

Anthony winked at Sean, who groaned and devoured another large section of his sandwich. "I told you we shouldn't have come over here," he said to David.

"How else are we supposed to see Dreamy these days—or Ty for that matter? He's been very possessive lately," David said.

"Can you blame me?" Anthony asked.

Ty ran her hand under a sentence and reached for another slice of pizza from the Tupperware still in Anthony's hand.

"No," David said.

Anthony punched him before starting in again on the pizza.

* * *

"Ty? Is that you?" Rosie called from her bedroom when Ty walked through the door. *Too bad Anthony's at practice. I would have stopped at his house.*

"Yeah." She headed to the kitchen for a snack.

Rosie hurried out of her room. "I saw you and Anthony eating lunch together today."

Ty smiled and tried not to express her annoyance. She thought she'd taken care of this before Anthony went to meet her parents. Rosie still wanted to analyze (and overanalyze) her time with Anthony?

"Yep." She dug the empty Tupperware box out of her backpack and dropped it into the sink before mentally flipping through her list of great recipes. She wanted to come up with something yummy to take for "left-overs" tomorrow. Lasagna? She opened the fridge, doubting she had all the ingredients.

"So what did you talk about?" Rosie rested against the table next to the kitchen window.

"My deepest, darkest secrets; history; and Anthony's inability to share." Ty ticked off the topics on her fingers.

Rosie pursed her lips and rocked forward. "What deep, dark secret did you tell him?"

"That I want to marry Rocket Rogers."

Rosie gasped. Ty had to shut her eyes to keep from rolling them at her roommate's overdramatic response.

"What, Rosie?" she asked when Rosie didn't respond.

"Just because he seems smitten with you now doesn't mean saying stuff like that won't blow this thing. What did he do?"

Ty hated to admit it startled him. "He stuttered a little bit but recovered quickly." She turned back to the fridge, pretending to search for meal ideas. "Honestly, it didn't seem to bother him." She decided not to mention she asked to meet his parents. Or the way he reacted to her asking to meet Nikki and his excuse to get out of it. Rosie might have had a heart attack.

Ty's reassurance didn't faze Rosie. She tapped a finger against her lips. "Yeah, until he stops calling," she said bitterly.

Biting back laughter, Ty pushed aside some milk. "Is that what you think happened between you two? You said something that scared him?"

"Who knows?" Rosie threw up her hands. "Maybe."

"It was fine." Ty shut the fridge, frustrated with both her lack of culinary ideas and Rosie's pessimism. Should she tell Rosie Anthony probably didn't call because he didn't call a lot of girls back? Because a girl broke his heart a year ago and he didn't want to trust another one again, not even Ty.

"Have you talked to him since?"

"Yeah. The rest of lunch, remember the other topics? History? How he can't share?" Ty picked up her backpack and walked out of the kitchen. Maybe she could escape into some homework.

"And since lunch?"

"He texted me before he went to practice."

"That's good." And somehow, Rosie sounded serious.

On second thought, Ty couldn't stay there. She slipped her backpack on and headed for the door.

"Where are you going?"

"I need to get some reading done. I think I'll go to my parents' house."

Rosie scowled. "We should talk about the other things you guys said during lunch. Who knows what else I need to warn you against."

Ty shook her head. "Thanks, but no thanks, Rosie. Everything is fine between Anthony and me."

"Not for long," Rosie muttered, turning her back on Ty and heading to her bedroom.

* * *

An hour later, Ty wasn't reading like she should have been considering she had a thirty-page article she had to be familiar with for a discussion in her history of England class. Instead she laid back on the trampoline in her parents' backyard, staring up at the pale blue sky.

She knew Rosie wasn't right—her roommate didn't have the slightest clue how well Ty and Anthony's relationship worked—but that didn't mean her words didn't bother Ty or wiggle into Ty's brain and squirm around.

Yeah. So Anthony stumbled a little over her bold statement, but he didn't seem to care later. It hadn't stopped him from being publically affectionate with her for the rest of lunch or when he walked her to class afterward.

He did act strange about Nikki. That wasn't new though. He'd been vague about his sister since their first date. Maybe they didn't get along. He'd wanted to introduce her to his parents, and that was something.

So sure, Rosie knew about guys and relationships, but Ty knew Anthony. Inside and out. Embarrassingly well. Only one other girl had ever reached the level of commitment Ty stood at with him, and he'd almost married her. Ty didn't think Anthony would propose anytime soon, but they had a great relationship and an even better friendship. She didn't need Rosie anymore. Was that why her roommate insisted on acting so pessimistic about the whole thing?

A body landed next to her on the trampoline, interrupting Ty's thoughts and sending her rebounding into the air, screaming and flailing. When she came down next to Walsh, she clutched her chest and looked around for her history folder. It lay on the ground next to the trampoline, papers scattered everywhere.

"You almost gave me a heart attack!" Her heart thumped wildly underneath her fingers.

"No wonder. You were totally zoned. Wait. Let me guess—Anthony?"

She shoved him in the shoulder, laughing anyway. "Yes, if you must know."

"Well, I'd expect some kind of stupid, silly grin on your face considering the way you two acted at dinner the other night. Not that frown."

"My roommate thinks I'm going to blow it with him," Ty said.

"What does she know? Why would Anthony give up a girl who knows football better than most people on the planet?" Walsh sounded baffled.

He made it easy not to take herself too seriously. "And when that novelty wears off?" she asked.

He propped himself up on his elbow and stared at her, confused. "Why would it?" He was so teenage boy. Of course nothing mattered except football. "And if it did, there's always, you know, kissing."

She shook her head and shoved him again, grinning. "Yeah. I suppose there's that." Tension had already started to drain out of her, and Rosie's worries seemed unfounded. She should've gone and found Walsh a long time ago. Her brother's simple worldview had often solved her problems.

"No, but seriously, Ty"—Walsh sat up—"if I ever find a girl like you, I think I'm going to ask her to marry me on the spot. You're so easy to be around, not like most girls."

She turned back to the darkening sky. "Of course you think that. You're my brother, and you still have a mission to think about." She took a deep breath. "But I have to be myself with him no matter what. If I blow it, then he's not the right one." It felt good to say that out loud.

Walsh stood up. "Well, that would be a bummer." Before she could react, he started jumping again, sending her flying all over the trampoline, unable to stop herself because she was doubled over with laughter. But she didn't care. Walsh had saved her, and for now, that was okay.

Despite her bouncing, she sent a simple prayer heavenward. *Help me remember to enjoy this. And I don't say it enough, but thank you for now. Thank you for Anthony . . . and Walsh.*

Chapter Fourteen

Rosie hadn't tried to shake Ty down for information for a few days, which made Ty suspicious. Especially when Rosie greeted her at the door late Saturday morning after Ty returned from some hardcore studying at the library.

"Where have you been?" Rosie asked.

"The library." Ty laid her bag on the couch and sank next to it, closing her eyes and thinking she might fall asleep right there. She'd stayed up late the night before watching BYU's game against Boise State, then Anthony called to talk about the game with her, and she didn't end up getting to sleep until well after midnight. She'd had to drag herself out of bed to make it to her eight a.m. study group.

"On Saturday?" Rosie's voice dripped with disbelief, like she thought Ty had taken to making up absurd stories to get out of telling her she was with Anthony.

"Study group. I have a test on Monday."

"Well, get up." Rosie yanked Ty off the couch.

Blinking the near sleep away, Ty stood next to the couch and stared at Rosie. "Why?"

"We're going to Utah Lake." Rosie took Ty's arm and hauled her toward the bedrooms. "Get a move on. We're leaving in, like, twenty minutes."

"Why?" Ty stumbled along behind, trying to remember ever planning such a thing.

"Because you need to get out more. Go change. Hurry."

"Rosie, I don't want to go out to the lake today. I was up early, and I have a lot of homework to get to today. Plus, I haven't seen Anthony since Thursday. He should be home sometime this afternoon, and I want to be here."

Rosie pushed her toward the bedroom. "Get dressed. You'll feel more like going once you're in your swimsuit."

"Rosie . . ."

She gave Ty one last shove into the room and stalked out. Sighing, Ty shut the door to get changed. Once Rosie had her mind set on something, it took more energy than Ty had this morning to slow her down. She remembered a comment Anthony made the other day at lunch about her not liking confrontation. That definitely applied to her situation with Rosie, but she'd worry about it later.

She reluctantly scavenged her swimsuit out of her drawer and put it on, though she wasn't sure the seventy-degree weather was warm enough to entice her into the water in October. She topped the suit with sweats and a T-shirt and then grabbed a hoodie, just in case. As she walked into the living room to inform Rosie she had complied, a knock sounded.

Ty couldn't help but hope Anthony would appear at the door, coming over to claim her before she had to go to the lake. Instead, two guys stood outside. She recognized Cameron, their home teacher, but she didn't know the shorter one, a chubby blond. What Rosie had made out to be a fun day at the lake with friends had turned into a date.

"You guys ready?" Cameron asked.

Ty grabbed Rosie's arm. "What's going on?" she whispered.

Rosie scooped up a large tote with towels poking out of the top. "We're going to the lake. I've already explained this." She grasped Ty's hand and pulled her out the door, like she knew Ty wouldn't leave the house on her own. "We're ready," she said brightly. "Did you guys pack lunch?"

The chubby blond nodded. "Of course."

"Rosie!" Ty tried to keep her voice down as they descended the stairs. "You didn't tell me this was a double date. I can't go on a date with another guy—I'm dating Anthony!"

"Lighten up. You haven't been together long enough to assume you're exclusive." Rosie strode ahead to join Cameron, and Ty knew she was stuck.

When they reached the car, Rosie got in front with Cameron, leaving Ty to slip into the backseat with the other guy. Instead of wading her way through an awkward conversation, attempting to avoid the fact she didn't know him, Ty decided to be blunt.

"Hi. I'm Ty." She stuck her hand across the seat toward him.

"Justin. From your family home evening group."

"Oh. Yeah. I haven't been to FHE in weeks." She forced a smile. She wanted to take a few swings at Rosie's head with the beach bag. Why did her roommate keep getting her into these situations? And why couldn't Ty be brave enough to stand up to her?

Justin shook Ty's hand. She couldn't read the half smile, half smirk he gave her. Maybe she was too tired. Maybe she was already in so deep with Anthony she didn't understand guys anymore.

The minute the car started moving, she wanted to tip her head back against the seat and go to sleep.

"Tired?" Justin asked.

"Yeah. I stayed up late watching the football game last night." Ty attempted to rub the sleep out of her eyes and focus on Justin. She could at least be polite.

"Of course."

Ty looked up and caught Justin's gaze flicking upward in irritation. "You don't like football?"

"Me? No, I like football fine." He turned to stare out the window.

"It was a pretty good game." Ty didn't know why she tried to continue the conversation when he didn't seem to care.

"Yeah. Great. Rocket did great." When Justin mentioned Anthony, he looked Ty right in the eye, waiting for a response.

She blushed. "Like always." Now she stared out the window. Feeling bad, she turned to try again. Justin had turned his attention to the back window. "Are there others coming?" she asked, craning her neck to study the traffic behind him.

"Not that I know of, but I keep expecting Rocket to pull up and snatch you from the car."

"Huh?"

"From what I hear, he doesn't like you going out with other guys. But I guess at least I won't get stuck paying for an extra meal." Justin chuckled.

Despite the heat sweeping across her face—a mix of embarrassment and anger—Ty managed a quick retort. "Yeah, well, Dylan wouldn't have been stuck with the extra meal either if he hadn't ordered it for me." She narrowed her eyes. "How do you know him anyway?"

"He's in my institute class. Bragged about taking out Rocket's girlfriend and how things were working out really well for you guys until Rocket showed up."

"Working out well? Ha." What had Dylan told everyone about their date? Apparently he left out all the creepy parts, like his bad joke telling and knowing her favorite dish at Olive Garden.

And it was weird Dylan went to an institute class when he probably already took a religion class at BYU. Maybe to widen his choices for dating? She could only hope. Shrugging it off, she resumed her perusal of traffic from her own window, wishing Anthony *would* pull up and whisk her from the car. Neither she nor Justin attempted conversation the rest of the way. Rosie and Cameron didn't seem to notice.

At the lake, they unpacked the lunch, and conversation flowed easier. Cameron and Rosie included the other two; although Rosie seemed distracted. Still, when they finished, Justin leaned back in the sand and pulled his hat down over his eyes.

Cameron helped Rosie up, and she shed her sweatpants, following him to the edge of the water to wade. The trip to the lake felt more and more like Cameron and Rosie wanted to go out and, for some odd reason, had dragged their friends along. Justin seemed about as glad to be there as Ty was.

Well, Ty could guess Rosie had ulterior motives for getting Ty away from their apartment. She rolled up the bottom of her sweats and headed off down the beach. She should have texted Anthony before Rosie hauled her away, but he probably wasn't even back from Boise yet.

She surveyed her group down the beach. Justin still lay across their blanket, the rise and fall of his chest the only sign of life in him. "I could be napping comfortably in my bed," she said to herself.

She knew Rosie wouldn't want her calling Anthony right now, but she slipped her phone out of her pocket and called him anyway. She needed cheering up.

He answered on the second ring. "Good morning, sunshine."

"For your information, I have been up since a quarter after seven." She grinned. Yup. Worked.

"Why in the world?"

"Study group. I have a test on Monday in my biology class."

"Isn't that one of those classes you're supposed to take your freshman year?"

"Science stinks. I put it off as long as I could." Ty looked back down the beach to make sure Rosie wasn't spying on her.

Luckily the waves and Cameron held all Rosie's attention.

"And does the benefit of a few years help?" Anthony asked.

"No. It's just as bad as it would have been freshman year. Only now I have four other hard classes to deal with too." She kicked at the rocks absently.

"Well, coaching football is easy."

"That's the worst one. I never seem to get my homework done for it until the last minute, and my study partner is the worst. He's very distracting."

"I'd tell you to do something about that, but . . ."

"Exactly." She laughed. "When will you be home?"

"Probably in a couple hours. Can I come over?"

"Of course, but call me first. Rosie made me come to the lake with her and some friends. I'm not sure how long we're going to be here." Ty looked over her shoulder again. Cameron and Rosie stood by the blanket. Even from this distance, she saw the scowl on Rosie's face. She altered her course back toward the blanket, trying to angle her body to hide the fact she was on the phone.

"You're at the lake with a bunch of girls? That sounds . . . exciting," he joked.

She paused. She didn't want him to know she was on a date, but she didn't want to lie to him either. "Um, Rosie brought a couple guys along. She pretty much forced me into it, literally dragged me from the apartment."

He didn't answer for several seconds. "So you're on a date?" His tone was falsely light, like when he'd tried to pass off his reluctance to introduce her to Nikki.

"Well, um, I guess, technically. But this guy she brought to entertain me is sleeping right now." She hoped he'd hear her desperation. She didn't want him to think this was more than it was.

"Ha, ha. Yeah, that sounds pretty bad," he said. She cringed at his awkward tone. "Well, I don't want you to be rude on your date, so I'll talk to you later."

"It's not a date . . ." she protested.

"Okay. Have fun. Bye."

It didn't sound like he'd heard her at all. "Okay. Bye." The call ended.

Ty would've liked to sit and scowl at her phone and freak out about why Anthony acted the way he did. It couldn't be that he thought she liked Justin romantically, right? She always went on about how great dating Anthony was, and though she hadn't said the words, she thought she made her feelings for him obvious. Why else would she make comments about wanting to marry Rocket Rogers? You didn't joke about that stuff unless somewhere deep down you meant it.

But Ty had to stuff her phone in her pocket and look like the conversation she had didn't trouble her. Rosie didn't ask who Ty was talking to, but she didn't have to. Ty could tell she knew.

"How's the water?" Ty asked.

"Not bad," Cameron replied. "Still warm from the summer. It's getting out that gets you." He grinned and picked up a towel for Rosie, rubbing it across her shoulders. Ty watched with interest at the way Rosie jerked away at first, then forced a smile and relaxed at Cameron's touch. Considering the way Rosie acted around him at their last home teaching appointment, Ty thought her roommate liked him. Plus he was pretty good looking and the type of guy Rosie normally dated.

"Don't you want to at least wade?" Rosie asked. She sounded tense, but it could be the chatter of her teeth. Ty hoped it was that.

"Maybe I'll wade. Later." She plopped onto the blanket and dug around for the chips. She looked over at Justin, who still appeared sound asleep.

"What a party pooper, right?" Cameron nodded at Justin while he spread his towel out on the sand.

"To tell you the truth, I'm a little jealous," Ty joked. "I had a pretty late night last night and had to go to a study group early this morning. I was kind of planning on a nap." She offered Cameron the bag of chips. He took a few before reaching over to help Rosie smooth out her towel.

"I brought some cards." Rosie rummaged around in her tote bag and produced them. "Should we wake Justin up?"

Inwardly Ty voted not to. He was less awkward sleeping.

The day didn't absolutely tank, but after the card games and two or three trips to the water to wade, Ty needed a nice long nap—or a few hours cuddled up next to Anthony. She was tired and only making a minimal effort to keep her phone checks from Rosie. Time crawled, and Anthony hadn't called, though it'd been well over the two hours he mentioned when they talked on the phone.

When they pulled into the parking lot at Rosie and Ty's apartment, the sun had begun to set. It had been the longest day of her life. She had wrapped her mind up so much in what might be going on in Anthony's head, she wasn't participating in Rosie and Cameron's conversation, and Justin hadn't attempted to talk to her since they quit playing cards earlier.

"Thanks! Had a great time!" Ty lied as she hurried up the steps to the apartment, phone already to her ear. This time it took Anthony several rings before he picked up.

"Hey."

"Hey, there. I'm back." Ty tried to sound chipper.

"Oh, great." Anthony didn't sound like he meant the *great* part. "Sorry I didn't call when we got in. I took a nap."

"It's okay. You probably deserved it. I could sure use one." She laughed. It sounded shrill and totally unbelievable. "You still want to come over?"

He hesitated. She tried not to hyperventilate while waiting for an answer.

"Of course," he said after what felt like several more hours. "I'll be over in a minute."

"Perfect."

Rosie hadn't come up to their apartment by the time Anthony showed up, and Ty could only hope her roommate had gone off with Cameron to get the one-on-one date they should have planned to begin with.

Ty threw open the door after two knocks, grinning with relief, but she resisted the urge to throw herself into his arms. The way he stood—hands in his pockets and leaning away from her—and the way he'd left their phone conversation kept her away.

"How was the trip?" she asked, plopping on the couch and patting the seat next to her. "You played great. I know I told you last night, but . . ." She waited for Anthony's customary teasing that he didn't mind her praise, but it didn't come.

"Thanks," he said. He rested against the bookcase instead of sitting.

"You're probably still tired." Well, she hoped that explained his behavior, but she knew it didn't. "Want to watch a movie . . . ?"

He stared at her. "Can I ask you a question?"

She gulped. "Of course."

"Do you want to date other people?"

"Date other people?" Was it a suggestion or an accusation?

"Yeah. So we're keeping this thing with us pretty casual?"

She studied his expression—cool, collected, no hint of the annoyance she thought was the reason he hadn't called her all afternoon.

"This wasn't really a date. He didn't ask; I didn't accept. I told you, Rosie literally dragged me out of the apartment," she said, testing the waters to see if this would placate him at all.

His eyes narrowed for an instant before he shrugged. "Oh?"

"I didn't want to go . . ." But she knew he didn't care.

His gaze strayed away from her to everywhere else in the room. "So," he said, his voice detached, "it's not a big deal. I want to make sure we're on the same page with this."

Ty stared at her hands. She'd told herself she would go all out for Anthony, leave nothing on the table. And if he didn't like what he saw, at least she knew she gave it everything. So she should shout out something like, *I don't want a casual relationship with you; I want it to get as serious as it can.* But now, of all times, Rosie's cautions pounded against her. How could she tell him she thought she loved him? How could she say it first when she didn't know how far into this relationship Anthony wanted to go? When he might be here because he thought dating her would be fun for a while.

She took a breath and looked up. "I guess that's up to you."

He scowled. "Up to me? What's that supposed to mean?"

"I . . ." What could she say? She couldn't be honest. She knew she should, but Rosie was right. Her comments at lunch the other day about how far she wanted this relationship to go had startled Anthony, and she had been joking. What would he do if she said something serious about their future?

He sighed, probably ready to clear it up so they didn't have to have any more serious talks about their relationship. "Well? So is this thing casual or what?"

She couldn't look him in the eye. "No—well, what do you think?" She wrung her hands together.

The apartment door opened, and Rosie walked in. In a flash, her annoyed expression turned to a smile as she surveyed Anthony. "Hi, Rocket."

Anthony frowned at her and shook his head. "I'll talk to you later, Ty." He crossed the room in a couple quick strides and disappeared out the door.

"What was that?" Rosie shut the door behind him.

Ty fought against a lump forming in her throat. *This is not a big deal,* she tried to tell herself. "I'm not sure."

Rosie's face drained of color. "What happened? What did you say?"

"What did *I* say? Me? You forced me to spend half the day on your date at the lake, and telling him about it led to a conversation about the status of our relationship—which, I guess is that we're both just in it for fun and games because, again thanks to you, I didn't have the guts to tell him I think I love him." She stood up and stalked to her room, swallowing over and over to keep that stupid boulder blocking her passageway from erupting into full-blown tears. They hadn't really fought. No point in crying.

Rosie followed her. "It's a good thing you didn't say something like that! He'd be gone for sure. We can fix this. It takes time to ease him into the idea of a serious relationship. We can do it."

We, we, we. Ty didn't miss that or the excited tone in Rosie's voice. "Rosie, this is between me and Anthony. *I'll* fix this. I told you, I can handle it from here."

"Clearly you can't. You almost told Rocket Rogers you loved him. How well do you think that would have gone over?"

Ty wanted to scream in frustration. "What good will not telling him do if this ends and he has no clue how I felt about him?"

"We'll cross that bridge when we get to it. For now, play this cool, like tonight wasn't a big deal."

Ty clenched her jaw and dropped onto her bed, pushing her face into her pillow. After a couple calming breaths she lifted it enough to say, "Good night, Rosie."

Rosie paused before sighing. "Fine. Good night." She closed the door with a louder-than-necessary snap.

* * *

Anthony swung the door shut behind him then caught it at the last second to keep from slamming it. *I guess that's up to you.* She didn't want to decide? He put himself out there, further than he had in over a year, and she *knew* that. She knew that and still went out with another guy, and he didn't want her to.

Hadn't he made his feelings clear? He'd met her parents. Rescued her from an obsessed guy. Taken her to *Juanita's*! Sure he wasn't the best at putting into actual words how he felt, but she knew his past. Why the heck couldn't she say whether or not she wanted to date other people?

She had the desperate look on her face he'd sometimes caught in her expression. What was she scared to tell him? Maybe she worried about scaring him off by saying anything too serious. That would make sense.

He could handle that.

But Ty was so thoughtful. So kind. The more he got to know her, the more he wouldn't put it past her to hang on for his feelings. She must know he had fallen in deep. She'd followed his every move for years. She knew they'd gone further in this relationship than he had since Keesha. Maybe she just didn't want to break his heart.

Please tell me that's not the reason she's sticking around. So much worse than Keesha clinging to their relationship because he was Rocket Rogers.

Anthony looked up. David stared at him from the hall. "What?" Anthony snapped.

"Well, last time you came home from a date this early—it wasn't good." David wasn't joking around though. He looked concerned. Great.

But David was his best friend. "I think Ty and I had a fight. Maybe. Not really, but it feels like it."

"What could you two find to fight about?"

"She went on a date."

"She went on a date?" The skepticism in David's voice was thick enough to spread over toast.

"She says Rosie made her go to the lake with a couple guys, but when I asked if she wanted our relationship to be casual, she skirted around it. Wouldn't give me a yes-or-no answer." Anthony sighed and noticed David's jacket. "Where're you going?"

David hesitated, but he didn't push Anthony to talk anymore. "To Sophie and Ally's. Want to come?"

Anthony should go back to Ty's. Figure out some way to talk to her alone. "Yeah." He followed David out the door.

They didn't talk on the way over. Was that good or not? David rarely treated Anthony's relationship woes—mostly minor in the past—with any seriousness. Anthony expected at least a couple jibes along the lines of if Ty wanted to date other guys, she could always call David. The quietness led to thinking more about her.

Thankfully, it wasn't just Sophie and Ally at their apartment. A lot of his team had stuffed themselves into the tiny living room and even smaller kitchen, along with the usual groupies. A crowd. He needed that.

"Where's your sidekick?"

Anthony, only two steps inside the door, looked up to see Sophie standing in front of him. His defensive, protective instincts kicked in. Sophie looked too hopeful, and it annoyed him. "You mean, my girlfriend?"

The smug look dropped off Sophie's face. "Whatever." She didn't step away, and her closeness made him uncomfortable. How could he judge Ty for her trip to the lake? At least she didn't go voluntarily. The longer he stood in this familiar living room, the more he wanted to go find his *girlfriend.*

"At home." He moved to skirt around Sophie. He'd stay for thirty minutes, tops.

"Oh, come on, Rocket."

Irritation prickled on the back of Anthony's neck. Why had he ever enjoyed Sophie Pope's company? Had she ever cared what he did off the football field if it didn't involve her?

"What does she have that I don't?" she asked.

Anthony took in her appearance in one sweep—and not a lingering one. Short skirt, like always, displaying long, tan, gorgeous legs. A snug, long-sleeve sweater he thought should be more modest than it was.

Besides the ability to respect herself? he thought and barely kept himself from saying it out loud. He'd never minded Sophie's appearance before, but next to Ty, she just looked like she tried too hard. "For one, she knows my real name," he said instead.

Her smug smile, which had started to reappear on the edge of her lips, dropped into a confused frown. She hesitated. "You're dating her because she calls you . . ."

He laughed. Outright. "Anthony," he supplied. Deep red swept up Sophie's face, though Anthony didn't know if it was embarrassment or anger. "And yeah, it's a start." He walked away. Sophie didn't stop him.

Anthony planted himself on the couch. Though he didn't treat the other girls with the same contempt Sophie got—they didn't start conversations by insulting Ty—he didn't encourage advances either. He spent the remainder of the time talking football with other guys.

David nodded understandingly when Anthony told him he was heading home. The crisp chill didn't bother him during the six-block walk. He actually smiled. What did Ty have that all the other girls in the room didn't? Everything.

There was football—not just that they had it in common or she liked it for him. Because she didn't. It was the way she loved it. He loved that.

There was the way she always thought about Anthony's feelings, but not in some hero-worship way. She did that for everyone. After years of waiting to date him, she turned down the first two opportunities for her brothers because she promised them something. He loved that.

There was her friendship. The way—most of the time—she could say anything to him, like wanting to marry Rocket Rogers, admitting to stalking him, or asking about Keesha. She adored him, and he loved that—*her*.

He stopped in the middle of the street when it hit him.

Why was he surprised? He'd been a goner since that first time he'd kissed her.

He loved her.

At first he wondered how he let that happen. Then with a chuckle, he saw it had happened right from the start, and he never stopped it. He never pushed her away. He didn't quit calling after a couple dates. He didn't take out another girl so Ty wouldn't get any ideas about them. He didn't do the things he usually did to protect himself. That was how it happened.

His smile stretched until it felt like it took up his whole face. He didn't mind. It didn't scare him. He could call the most perfect girl in the world his own, and he didn't want it any other way. Instead of falling into his old act of playing it cool, he should've told her that.

"Time to make it official," he mumbled to himself and took out his phone.

* * *

Ty was rubbing the water out of her hair with a towel when her phone lit up. She took a step across the room, toward her desk, and almost ignored it when she saw it was an alert for a Facebook notification. Not a text from Anthony.

But then his name caught her eye. She looked closer. *Anthony Rogers has changed his relationship status.*

Her heart stopped. Dropping the towel on the floor, she flicked her finger across the screen and jabbed at her Facebook app. It seemed to take forever for it to open and show her that she had six notifications. She ignored all but the top one: *Anthony Rogers has changed his relationship status.*

She tapped at it impatiently. Blank white page. "Come on!" she shouted, swiping her finger up and down on the screen, waiting for the page to appear.

"What's wrong?" Rosie called from her bedroom next door.

The blue box appeared on the screen.

Ty held her breath. Was it for real?

Anthony Rogers is in a relationship with TyAnne Daws.

Chapter Fifteen

Thinking about how Anthony announced to the world that she was his girlfriend kept Ty up most of the night, but that didn't stop her from grinning the entire time she was getting ready for church. He hadn't specifically invited her this week—something Rosie had brought up multiple times—but Ty didn't care. She placated her roommate by putting on a dress Rosie talked her into buying a few months before, a dress that surprised Ty when she ended up liking it. It had a full skirt and big, black hibiscus flowers. She even took the time to curl her hair.

She still finished getting ready with thirty minutes to spare, so she sat on the couch and read the same article in the *Ensign* four times and still got nothing out of it.

She left long before she had to, despite a glare from Rosie, and speed-walked across campus to the JSB until she realized if she didn't slow down, she'd show up to church all sweaty.

Anthony stood with David and Sean outside the door of the building. When she rounded the corner, he started walking toward her. She buried herself in his arms, sighing at the way they tightened around her waist. *Game Plan Key:* . . . She had nothing. She'd deleted it the night before.

"I don't want a casual relationship. I don't want to date anyone else. Ever again." She didn't mean for that last part to escape but couldn't take it back. She didn't want to.

He chuckled into her hair, making a few strands dance across her cheek. "Me either." He kissed the side of her forehead. "Is this us making up?" he asked.

"Was last night us fighting?" She tilted her head back to stare up at him. "We should save the real stuff for later. When people aren't passing us on their way to church."

"Not appropriate?"

She shrugged. "Probably not."

He pressed his lips against her forehead. "So we'll make up later?"

"Promise."

* * *

Walsh answered on the second ring and sighed instead of saying hello. "This is going to be mushy, right?"

The perma-grin on Ty's face grew wider. "You saw Facebook."

"Of course."

"I'm Anthony Rogers's girlfriend." She laughed.

Walsh laughed with her. "But seriously, aren't there *girls* you could go talk to?"

"Every time I talk to Rosie, all she wants to do is strategize. I just want to say it again. I'm Anthony's girlfriend."

"Do you mind if I put the phone down? Will I miss anything?"

"Wow, you're kind of taking the fun right out of it." But she still grinned. She didn't think she'd be able to stop for a while.

"In all seriousness, I'm happy for you. He'd be crazy not to date you."

"And make me his girlfriend?"

"And now I'm hanging up."

* * *

Ty laughed at the skip in her step on Monday morning. It was ridiculous that a simple thing like Anthony announcing his relationship status to the world lifted her mood this much, but it did. It meant everything to her. It meant he was serious. It meant she could admit being serious about him.

The feeling was only dampened by that pesky, nagging feeling someone was following her. She peered over her shoulder, her eyes scanning the students behind her. There. Again. Dylan. Remembering her conversation with Justin on Saturday, Ty whirled around to face Dylan.

He'd already half turned to walk back the other way when she called out, "Hey, Dylan." She waved at him with one hand while reaching into her bag for her wallet with the other. *Why does he change directions every time he sees me?*

He looked startled then excited, which sent a trickle of ice down her spine. "Hi, Detmer. So did Rocket finally give you permission to talk to other guys?" He stopped next to her. Too close.

She stepped back. "No," she said without realizing what she answered. "I wanted to give you this." She handed him a ten-dollar bill.

Dylan's eyebrows sliced downward as he stared at the money in his hand. "What's this for?"

"Well, when our date ended early, you told Anthony you didn't care if he paid you back, but from what I hear, you weren't too happy you had to pay for the meal *you* ordered for me." She emphasized her point by jabbing a finger in his direction when she said *you*.

Dylan held out the money and avoided looking at her. "I didn't . . . well, I mean . . . It wasn't . . ."

Ty didn't wait for him to form an answer. "Good-bye." She hurried away without another look back.

* * *

Ty tapped on the door of Anthony's house and glanced at her phone. She might be too early. With a half-smile to herself, she shrugged. She'd wait on his doorstep. Eager? Yeah. She didn't care anymore. Not at all.

But David swung open the door. "Is it—? Can it be? The official girlfriend of Rocket Rogers?"

Ty grinned and stepped past him into the house. She could tell him to take it easy, but she'd spent thirty minutes after classes staring at Anthony's Facebook profile page and the line where it announced to the world she belonged to him.

"Yes. Yes, it is," she said. She dropped onto their couch. "And do you happen to know where the official boyfriend of Ty Daws is?"

"He drew the short straw and had to pick up the pizza. He'll be here in a minute." David sat on the other end of the couch. "Shouldn't you be going to family home evening or something?"

She hit him on the shoulder. "It's possible I'll never go back. At least not to that group. Dylan convinced one of my FHE brothers I'm the worst date ever . . . not that it matters anymore." She grinned again.

David chuckled before answering. "What did Dylan say about you?"

"I like to leave dates before they're over and let guys pay for an untouched meal. He conveniently forgot to mention he ordered the untouched meal." Ty shivered at Dylan's creepiness. "But I took care of it today."

"Did you beat him up?"

"Thought about it."

"You could take him."

Ty laughed. "I gave him ten bucks."

"When did you see him?" David frowned.

"Up on campus today."

"What was he doing on campus?" He put his hands behind his head and rested his feet on the beat-up coffee table, kicking off three or four empty soda cans. His restful-looking pose contrasted with his tense expression.

"Going to class, I assume."

"Dylan goes to UVU."

A feeling akin to a bucket of ice getting dropped down the back of her shirt hit Ty. She thought of the dozen or so times she'd seen him around—the time he walked her up to campus, all the times she'd noticed him in the cafeteria. Why would he show up on the BYU campus if he went to UVU? Not just to see her, right? Not when Anthony specifically told him to stay away. She remembered the way he tried to flee when she saw him earlier that day, the way he disappeared when she saw him in the reflection of the doors at the Wilk.

"What?" David sat up. "What's that look for?"

She wiped her face of expression, hoping to seem innocent. "What look?" She shouldn't get worked up. He could be on campus to pick up stuff at the bookstore or meet with friends or a million other little things. Not just to see her. No, that would be too weird.

David scowled. "This look." He pointed to his face.

"Nothing. I've seen him around a few times, but I'm sure he has a good reason."

The scowl on David's face deepened. "Like looking for you."

She shook her head. "Don't. It's probably nothing. Leave it. And don't tell Anthony. He might get . . . protective." She couldn't even stop a momentary smile thinking about that during a serious conversation. "Listen, David, I don't want him getting into trouble because he can't keep his temper around Dylan. It's enough that he cares."

David hesitated. "If Dylan's coming up to campus just to see you—"

"Maybe he's not. Maybe he has friends or he's transferring. How can we know?" She held her hand out, pleading. "David, if you tell him and he does something to Dylan, he could get suspended for fighting."

David shook his head and looked away, taking his time before he responded. "Okay," he said, swallowing hard. "Maybe it's nothing."

"Pizza!"

Ty slapped a grin on when Anthony stepped through the door. He narrowed his eyes at David, then he grinned back at her.

"Not sure if I brought enough for you, gorgeous." He walked past the couch, balancing four boxes in one hand while he bent to peck her cheek.

"I'll need a whole pizza to myself." She jumped up to follow him to the kitchen, knowing she'd have to grab some before the rumble announcing Sean's approach got closer. She knew how quickly food disappeared in this house.

Anthony grabbed a few plates from the cupboard, handing one to Ty before flicking open a pizza box. "Was David behaving himself?" he asked, glaring toward the archway separating the kitchen and living room. He replaced the glare with a smile after only a second.

Ty watched David enter the kitchen. She caught another eye roll from him before he passed her. Ty winced, knowing that even the thought of losing her to a friend must bite at Anthony, considering what he went through with Keesha. Ty should've been more careful.

She wrapped her arms around his waist, taking a deep breath of his clean smell, a sharp, piney scent. "Total gentleman. He saw somewhere that I'm dating Rocket Rogers."

Anthony turned to kiss the top of her head. "Good."

"Seriously? It's dinner time. Can't we at least escape the mushiness to eat?" DJ said, following Sean into the kitchen. Ty darted in front of Anthony to grab pizza before it was too late. He laughed and scooped up four slices for his own plate.

"There are girls here all the time. Shouldn't you guys be used to, you know, kissing and stuff?" She put two slices of sausage pizza on her plate and backed away, out of the path of hungry football players.

David, Sean, and DJ all turned to gape at her, eyebrows raised. "No," they answered in unison. Anthony shifted uncomfortably.

"Hmmm." Ty grinned and leaned into her boyfriend's side. "We'll have to fix that." Reaching up, she pulled Anthony down to meet her. She gave him a long, sloppy kiss, trying to hold back laughter as long as possible amidst the protests of the other three. "Is there a kiddie table somewhere we can send them to?" she asked when she pulled away. "Preferably in another room."

Anthony bit back a smile. "I'll look into that." He took her hand and led her from the kitchen to the living room.

* * *

"Rocky!"

Anthony picked Porter up as he stepped inside his sister's house and swung his nephew onto his shoulders. "Hey, P. Where's your mom?"

"Setting the table for dinner."

Anthony headed toward the dining room to see if he could help. "And your dad?"

"Changing Eli."

As Anthony came around the corner from the entry way, he hesitated. Nikki walked around the table, brushing the bottom edges of the plates, her lips moving silently. He didn't need to read them to know she was counting. *Four . . . five . . .* She stopped and started around the table again, halting when she caught sight of Anthony watching her.

"Hey." She forced a grin. "Put Porter down. He's going to break his neck."

Anthony didn't argue as he lifted Porter gently off his shoulders.

"No fair." Porter scowled and stomped out of the room.

Anthony turned back. "Sorry. I know you hate that."

She shrugged and continued her perusal of the table, though she kept her arms folded and didn't move her lips this time. "No big deal."

"Can I help?" Anthony didn't wait for a yes before grabbing the bright teal napkins from her hands and taking care to place them exactly right.

"Where's Ty?"

Anthony looked up from arranging a napkin. Nikki stood at the head of the table, her hands clasped around the wooden rung of a chair. She frowned at him.

"She couldn't come." He avoided his sister's gaze by concentrating on the napkins again.

"Did you ask?"

He'd hoped she wouldn't press him. She hadn't for a long time. "She had a bunch of homework. I didn't want to bother her."

"I see."

He moved to the next setting, glancing at her before looking down to fold the napkin. "It's not a big deal, Nik. I'll ask her some other time."

"Okay."

He knew by her tone it wasn't. When he looked up, she'd left the dining room. He sighed.

After a few minutes, Anthony's brother-in-law, Joe, came into the room, Eli and Porter tailing behind them.

"Sit, boys," Joe said. "Uncle Rocky and I will get the food." He clipped Eli into his booster chair before heading into the kitchen.

Anthony followed. "Where's Nikki?" he asked, picking up a casserole dish.

"Upstairs." Joe grabbed a basket of bread and a bowl of potatoes. He paused. "You should've brought your girlfriend."

"I told Nikki Ty had homework."

"That couldn't be put off for an hour?" Joe asked. Eli let out a screech, and Joe headed for the dining room. Anthony followed again, setting down the casserole—his mom's famous and delicious baked macaroni and cheese.

Joe didn't talk again until both boys had their food, and they'd said the blessing. "Nikki thinks you're worried she'll scare Ty off," he said in a low voice as he dished his own macaroni and cheese.

"It's not that." Anthony shook his head. "I don't want to stress Nikki out. Make her worry about being too perfect for someone."

Joe put the spoon back in the macaroni and cheese. Anthony found himself staring at the golden-brown bread crumbs on top, looking as buttery and delicious as Anthony remembered his mom making it.

"Nikki made this three times today to get the topping right then made me take the other two to our neighbors so you wouldn't know and worry. She left Eli's toy basket out and a couple movies stacked next to the TV so the house would look normal and Ty wouldn't feel awkward with Nikki."

Anthony didn't take his gaze away from the macaroni and cheese. "I can't, Joe. What if . . . what if Ty's weird about it, like Keesha? What if Nikki does all that stuff again and Ty doesn't understand? What if she hurts Nikki?"

Joe didn't talk for a long time, and Anthony piled the biggest helping of the casserole he thought he could get down. He'd at least stuff himself silly in a meager effort to make Nikki feel better.

"Is she coming down?" Anthony asked.

Joe shook his head. "Not tonight."

Anthony scooted his chair back. He needed to go straighten this out. Joe put his hand on Anthony's arm.

"Let her rest. She's got a headache."

Nodding, Anthony complied. He pulled himself back toward the table and began working on the mountain of food he'd dished himself, even though he had no desire to eat anymore. After several minutes of silence and a few short conversations with the boys, Joe spoke to Anthony again.

"The thing is, what if you don't ever bring Ty over and *that* hurts Nikki?"

Chapter Sixteen

Ty's eyes flew open. She looked around her dark room, wondering what woke her. On the bookcase next to her bed, her phone rang. Frowning, she snatched it up. What was wrong? Why was someone calling her at four thirty a.m.? When she saw Anthony's picture on her screen, identifying him as the caller, her heart rate shot up.

"Hello?" she answered, hearing the panic in her own voice. "Anthony? What's wrong?"

He laughed. "Wrong? Why would something be wrong?"

"It's four in the morning." Ty's heart slowed—a little.

"Four thirty."

"People don't normally call this early just to chat."

"Well, I didn't either. I called to warn you I'm coming over to pick you up in about fifteen minutes."

Despite the absurdity and the early morning hour, Ty rested back against her pillow with a smile on her face. "Why in the world are you picking me up in fifteen minutes?"

"For a date. Wear good shoes. And it's a little chilly outside."

"What about class?" Ty now grinned as she slipped out of bed and headed across the room to turn on her light.

"Who cares about class?"

"Well, sometimes I do."

"Hopefully you'll get over that soon."

Ty rifled through her drawer for a pair of jeans. "I can see I'm not going to get out of this—"

"Were you trying?"

She ignored his chuckle. "So I'm going to hang up and attempt to make myself as presentable as possible with only fifteen minutes at four thirty in the morning."

"You'll be as stunning as usual."

Her heart rate spiked again. "Probably. Bye."

"Bye."

Decked out in a sweatshirt, jeans, a ponytail, and mascara (she had to wear *some* makeup), she met him outside so he didn't have to knock.

He looked down at her, smiling. "Stunning. Just like I thought."

"Suck up." She snuggled in next to him as they walked toward the car, and he moved his arm around her, squeezing her shoulders. "So what is so important I have to get up in the middle of the night?"

"Hiking the Y. And you'll see why when we get there."

She raised her eyebrows, holding her expression while he opened the door for her. "Hiking and sleep deprivation is your idea of romance? I might start believing you're not good at relationships. Is this your way of running off girls who get too serious?"

Anthony waited to answer until he'd settled in the driver's seat. "You've foiled my plans. I guess that means I'm stuck with you."

She rested her head on his shoulder. "Yup. Stuck."

"Mmmm. That's too bad. I had all these other girls lined up."

"I'm going to need names and addresses."

* * *

When they arrived at the base of the Y trail, Anthony took a backpack from the backseat. He set it on the trunk and sifted through the contents, pulling out a headlamp and fitting it over his hair. Ty couldn't help the giggle that escaped.

"Sexier than you could ever imagine?" He flicked it on and posed.

"I will never look at you the same way again."

He wrapped an arm around her shoulder, pulling her close to kiss her with the light shining in her eyes. Once he released her, he grabbed the backpack and hoisted it over his shoulders.

"Come on. We're wasting . . . moonlight." Anthony grabbed her hand and tugged her toward the trailhead.

As they walked up the steep path, Ty enjoyed the stillness of the morning with Anthony. It was lovely to walk with him at five in the morning, to gaze up at the mountain above her and see the grayness of the early morning sky, to peek at her boyfriend and giggle inside at the headlamp.

"What?" Anthony caught her more than once. "You can't take your eyes off me, can you?"

"Never have been able to." She nudged him with her shoulder. "Okay. Stop. I have to have a picture of this." She pulled out her phone, stood on her tiptoes, and snapped a picture of them both. "Perfect." When she looked at it, she saw what her mom meant about that besotted look. It might have been in her own expression too. She turned to gaze at him. "This was a great idea."

"Even at five a.m.?"

"Especially at five a.m." She waited for her reward. Anthony pushed back the headlamp—so thoughtful—and bent toward her.

"Excuse me."

Startled, Ty and Anthony jumped out of the way of an oncoming runner. "That was . . . unexpected," Anthony said. He reached for Ty's hand again.

They made their way slowly, so Ty didn't worry about breaking into a sweat or getting smelly or anything.

"How was dinner last night?" she asked. She'd distracted herself with homework to forget he hadn't invited her. She hadn't pushed him. As much as she wanted him to open up about his family, she figured it would happen when he was ready.

He turned to study her before he answered, rubbing his free hand along his pants. "Um. Good. It was delicious, but Nikki got sick."

Sick. That word again. "Is it anything serious?" Ty asked. Maybe if she gave him a good opening, he'd share with her.

It took him a long time to answer. He let at least two or three minutes pass in silence. "Not last night. No."

"So it's been serious before?" She shook her head at herself. "Sorry. I don't mean to pry, Anthony. I just . . . I just want to know you."

Using her hand, he pulled her into him and buried his face in her hair. "Yeah. I know." But he didn't answer her question. They walked again in silence, letting the conversation float away before either spoke again.

After a bit, Anthony started to swing their hands as they walked. "So you won't open up about your ex-boyfriends . . ." A clear change of subject, but his tone was warm, not uncomfortable, so she didn't let it bother her.

"Because there are none worth mentioning. None serious enough to bother with."

"None serious enough? So there *were* boyfriends," he prodded.

"Sure. Okay. There was . . ." Ty had to concentrate to remember back far enough. She didn't date a lot in high school. She hung out with guys a lot—football knowledge like hers had been hard to resist for most guys—but not a lot of dating. "Okay, Eric Nelson my sophomore year in high school. We went out for two weeks."

"Two weeks?" Anthony stopped on the trail and stared her down.

"He asked me to homecoming, and we went together. We went out for two weeks, then I dumped him."

Someone cleared his throat behind them. Anthony and Ty looked back to see another runner about ten feet away. Eyeing each other, they stepped off the path to let him pass.

Once they continued hiking, Anthony asked, "Why did you dump him?"

"He said you were the most overrated quarterback in high school football."

Anthony burst into laughter. "Now I know you're making *that* up."

She made a crossing motion over her chest. "Cross my heart; I'm telling you the truth. He was a second-string running back for the JV team. The varsity played your guys that week, and after we lost—by a mere twenty-one points—he said you were overrated."

Anthony tapped a finger against his chin. "I think I might remember that game. Closest one I played during my high school career."

"Yup."

"Your team probably would have won if you'd been playing."

"It's very likely."

"First kiss?" Anthony posed.

Heat engulfed Ty's face. Thank heavens Anthony hadn't put down the headlamp after their last kiss; it now beamed uselessly into the sky. "You mean, was Eric my first kiss?" she stalled.

He looked down at her and—curse him—adjusted the headlamp to get a good look at her face. "Yes. That's what I mean."

She squinted against the light and put a hand up to shield her eyes. "No. Eric Nelson was not my first kiss."

Anthony pushed the headlamp back up and took her hand, stopping in the trail to pull her close to him. "Ty, why is your face so red?"

She tried to bury it against his chest. "Exertion."

"Who was your first kiss?" Poorly disguised laughter shaded Anthony's question.

She pointed her face into his sweatshirt. "You."

His chest shook. "What did you say?" Using his index finger, he lifted her chin.

"You were my first kiss." Ty stared at him, trying to seem confident and failing.

The smile on Anthony's lips was small and his expression confused. "Really? That stupid kiss I gave you outside your apartment just to look cool was your first kiss?"

Ty tried to start walking again, waving her hand around to appear dismissive. "Like I said. Not a lot of guys worth it."

Anthony didn't let her get away. "I'm the biggest jerk in the world for that first kiss. Let's redo it." He cupped his hand around the back of her neck.

"Redo?" she whispered.

"Mmm-hmmm."

The first kiss had been pretty good. Ty wouldn't trade it for any other first kiss. She knew now what that kiss had done to Anthony. But this one was really good too. Soft, tingly, the glow of the headlamp surrounding her. Her favorite thing about kissing Anthony was the way she had to stand on her tiptoes and rest her fingertips against his chest for balance.

Another throat cleared, and someone brushed past Ty. "Sorry. Excuse me."

With a giggle, Ty had to look up the trail.

His arm around her shoulder, Anthony scowled at the person disappearing into the dimness ahead of them. "Is there some race I didn't hear about? Why is this place so crowded?"

"Anthony, it's the Y trail. It's popular with runners in the morning."

He looked down. "Really?"

"Really."

"Okay, well, how was that anyway? You know, before the runner interruption?"

"I still like the first one a lot, but that one was pretty good." They started walking again.

"Pretty good?"

"Yeah, pretty good. Okay, then, so who was your first kiss?"

He rubbed his chin, pretending to think. "A girl named Shay. She was my neighbor. Eighth grade dance."

"Not even surprising. Well, I guess now I know why my mom never let me go to those. Dens of iniquity."

"Precisely."

This time they heard the runner coming up behind them. They stepped politely to the side, waving and saying, "Pardon us. Excuse us," as the runner passed.

"Your mom didn't let you go to dances?" Anthony asked.

"No. I couldn't go to school dances until I was sixteen."

"Seems strict. You could go to church dances at fourteen like a normal teenager, right? I mean, your parents don't seem like the type of people to keep their daughter all locked up until she turned dating age."

At their slow pace, Ty hadn't worked up any kind of sweat, so she shivered with cold and nestled into Anthony's side. "No, they let me go to church dances. Plenty of chaperones there."

"Of course."

Another runner interrupted.

"So what was it like to be Ty Daws growing up? A lot of football, I presume." Anthony asked.

"A lot of football." Ty nodded. "A lot of family time that involved football. Practicing with Walsh and later Stevie. Going to Walsh's games. Watching BYU. You know the drill. Walsh wanted to do everything football and be on every team he could, and my parents insisted if he was going to do that, we'd all do it together."

"And that was okay? Spending your time watching football?"

"Would I answer otherwise to Rocket Rogers?" she teased. "Really, though, I loved it. He's my best friend."

They spent the next while walking in silence. The runners nodded at Ty and Anthony on their way down, some of them doing double takes and adding, "Hey, Rocket," when they recognized him.

Sooner than she was ready, the giant Y appeared before them. After choosing a spot, Anthony let go of Ty's hand to slip off the backpack and rummage in it. He pulled out a blanket, laid it out, plopped down, and beckoned for her to join him.

"This is your big plan?" she asked with her head against his shoulder, looking out at the lights in the valley below. "Hang out by the Y at six in the morning?"

Anthony dug around more in the backpack and began spreading wrapped packages and plastic containers before them. "Yes. It also includes breakfast and the sunrise."

Ty pursed her lips together to prevent a laugh. "The sunrise that will come up from behind us?"

He turned around, eyeing the faint pink spreading behind the mountain, and nodded his head. "Well. Yes."

"I'm sure it will be spectacular." She kissed him on the cheek. He turned to catch her lips, both of them forgetting about the food.

Until Anthony cleared his throat. "Uh, hi. Good morning."

A girl, clad in blue sweatpants and a pink hoodie waved and smirked. "Morning." She paused, her hands on her hips, and breathed deeply. With an awkward glance their way she headed back down the trail.

"What a fabulously romantic spot." Ty couldn't help the laughter now.

"Quiet, you. Eat your breakfast." With a bemused grin, Anthony handed her a delicious-smelling burrito, half-unwrapped.

"Why, thank you." She took the burrito and began eating, eyeing the other food around her. Muffins, juice, granola bars. "From the looks of all this food, it seems you expected the runners."

Anthony chuckled. "That burrito is for you. The rest is for me."

"Oh yeah. That's right. Growing football player." But the sweet scent of honey-cured bacon mingled with the sting of green bell peppers kept her from teasing him more. They sat close together—the morning chill even more prevalent now they weren't walking. When the sun did rise, the view was spectacular as the light twinkled across the lake little by little. The neighborhood below came to life. Street lights faded; tiny, matchbox-looking cars pulled out of little garages.

"See," she whispered. "Spectacular."

They sat and admired the view and sometimes kissed. Ty thought every day with him would be the best. For the first time since he posted about their relationship, she suppressed an urge to tell him how she felt. It might be fine to tell him he planned another perfect date, like the night at Juanita's. She didn't want to leave and have all the magic disappear. But if she said anything, she might accidentally add she wanted this to keep going on forever. Besides, speaking could ruin the moment.

Eventually they gathered their things and stuffed them back into the backpack. Ty tried not to feel discouraged, since they still had a leisurely hike ahead of them. She hardly cared about the classes she'd miss by taking her time. The tide of runners seemed to ebb as they started back down, and breaking the silence still felt wrong—until something rustling nearby made Ty jump into Anthony.

"What was that?" she asked.

He snapped to attention. "Hmm? What?"

A distinctive shake of leaves and crack of twigs seemed to echo around them. "That. What was that?"

"More runners?"

They paused and waited for one to round the corner in front of them. Nothing. Anthony's mocking smile dipped and disappeared when the twig-cracking repeated in the trees near them.

"That was definitely in the trees. Runners in the trees?" Ty gripped his hand and peered into the foliage. "Do you think it might be a bear?" she whispered.

He choked back a laugh. "A bear? Here? I doubt it."

"You never know." She glued herself to his side. He moved to step into the trees, but she hung back, keeping the death grip on his hand. "What are you doing?"

"Going to see what it is." He tugged on her hand.

"Go in there? And get eaten?"

"Go in there and prove it's not a bear." He pulled again.

Another big crash. She screamed and wrapped her arms around Anthony's waist in time to see a deer hop from the trees and bound across the trail into the bushes on the other side.

"That was the strangest looking bear I've ever seen . . . ," he said into her hair.

Taking a few deep breaths to calm her fast heart rate, Ty pulled away—slightly. "Funny. Very funny."

"For a second there, I thought it might devour us."

"Anthony Rogers—" She pointed at him, only to be stopped by more crashing in the trees. She leaped behind him. "Something will devour us now that the deer got away!" she cried. She gripped the back of his sweatshirt with her fingers and squeezed her eyes shut.

"Oh. Uh. Hi." A human voice caused her to peer around Anthony. A couple holding hands picked their way through the branches back to the trail. Anthony laughed, trying to keep silent and ruining it by sucking in deep breaths.

"Oh!" the guy repeated when they emerged. "Hey . . . Rocket."

"Hey." Anthony's voice shook. "Great day for a hike."

"Yeah." The guy nodded enthusiastically. The girl stood beside him, her mouth open in a small *o*.

"Did you catch the sunrise?" Anthony asked. His casual, conversational tone and the awe-struck way the couple reacted to him had Ty on the brink of laughter too.

"Us? Uh. No. Not really. Hard to see through the trees. Thought it might be a good place for breakfast—to picnic up there." Both their faces were bright pink now.

Anthony nodded. "Ahhh. Yeah. Good idea."

The girl started to pull the guy down the trail. "So. See you," the guy said, waving and staring at Anthony over his shoulder.

"Later." Anthony waved back. He turned to Ty, waiting until the couple disappeared around the corner—the guy leaning back until the last second, trying to keep Anthony in sight. "Clearly, I'm not the only romantic genius in Provo."

Her laughter escaped. "I beg to differ."

"At least he had the brains to find some place out of the way of the runners," Anthony pointed out.

Ty put her arms around Anthony's waist. "They sacrificed a great view for their privacy." She gazed out over the bushes and then turned back to Anthony.

Anthony pretended to look contemplative. "Yes. There's that. I probably served you a better breakfast too."

"Probably."

"Though I can't help but envy them . . ."

"Well, life isn't perfect." Ty looked at him and made a decision to at least let him know how she felt right now, how great he made her feel. "Although, this date and you . . . my life is pretty dang close."

Anthony kissed her forehead—another runner approached fast. "Now don't get all mushy on me, Daws. You led me to believe you're some tough football-playing wannabe."

"To heck with my reputation."

Chapter Seventeen

ANTHONY LOOKED AT HIS WATCH, picked up the pace, and chuckled to himself. As David and the others had pointed out numerous times, Ty had him whipped. He laughed again. That was okay. He was already late for lunch with her—it'd become a daily habit since they couldn't see each other every night with football and all—and he didn't like missing even a few minutes a day. Besides, she mentioned something about lasagna leftovers. Man, that girl could cook.

He swung open the door to his house, finding Ty already sitting at the kitchen table with David.

Anthony gritted his teeth. It was stupid to work up any kind of jealousy over David's ridiculous crush on his girlfriend. Countless dates had proven Ty was in love—he was pretty sure it was love—with Anthony. The fact that he didn't think David would hesitate to ask Ty out, should anything go south between her and Anthony, didn't help matters. David had said more than once that there was something special about Ty and the normal, best-friend dating rules didn't apply.

Ty laughed and shook her head at something David said. Anthony breathed. They were friends. Just because Keesha—he wouldn't even go there. There was no reason to compare them. Besides, Ty looked up, and Anthony couldn't miss that her expression busted with happiness. He grinned and wondered if he looked like that when he saw her.

"Hey, where's my lasagna?" He pulled out the chair next to her.

"Hello to you too." She winked and slid a plastic container toward him.

Anthony noted, with annoyance, she had brought some for David. "What did I tell you about sharing my food with him?" He narrowed his eyes at David, who laughed.

When Anthony turned back to Ty, she bit her lip and shrugged. "He's eating mine."

Anthony sat in his chair and shoved his backpack under the table with unnecessary roughness. "That's not acceptable at all. Beast, you're not allowed to steal Ty's lunch."

"She had some last night," David said.

"What are you eating?" Anthony asked Ty.

"The breadsticks. Don't worry. They're amazing too. I brought plenty, and I didn't share them with him." She handed Anthony one.

He couldn't eat it despite the smell of garlic and Italian spices wafting off it. "I'm not going to steal your lunch. I'm more of a gentleman than that."

"Take it. You're drooling." She swiped a thumb across his lips.

Mindlessly he took it. "Okay. But I'm making you a sandwich or something to make up for it." She held another one toward David. Anthony slapped at his friend's hand. "He doesn't need one."

Ty turned to him, a smile on her lips but not reaching her eyes. "Look at him. It's the exact face Harly pulls on me, and I can't say no!"

Anthony's stomach flopped a couple times. Couldn't say no? So what if David turned on the charm to try and win her over?

Stop it, he told himself. He was an idiot. She loved him. She had for a long time.

He *thought* she loved him.

"You're not allowed to give David that breadstick." His clipped tone seemed to surprise her. The smile disappeared, and she pulled the breadstick back.

Nice. Now he looked like a lunatic.

He tried to lighten his ridiculous outburst. "Eat your food like a good girl." He shoveled food into his mouth to keep himself from freaking out again.

She nodded, a nervous smile returning. "Yes, sir. So . . . when do you guys leave for Salt Lake?" She didn't even glance at David when she spoke, though she presumably meant the question for both of them.

Anthony had to swallow an enormous mouthful to answer. "Three."

Ty laughed at his manners and reached for a book from her backpack. "I'll just let you eat."

Anthony pushed it away. "Nope. No reading. Tell me your game plan."

She blinked. "Game plan? What game plan?"

"For beating Utah."

"Oh . . ." She forced a laugh. "Don't be ridiculous. I think Rocket knows how to beat Utah—with a little help from your coach. And you'd better beat them. If you guys lose, and I have to face Uncle Lee—"

"I assure you, we will not lose. It hasn't happened once since I came to BYU."

"It was awfully close last year—"

He put a finger on her lips. "Don't. You might jinx me."

She shook her head. "Even if I did, you're too talented for it to work."

"Now you're kissing up."

"Hmm. I wish."

"I don't," David interrupted, speaking for the first time since Anthony almost blew up.

Anthony looked up, trying to tame his irrational contempt for his best friend. So he flirted with Ty sometimes. And finagled her lunch (the lasagna tasted fantastic; Anthony couldn't blame him). He'd known Beast since elementary school. In middle school, he'd helped Anthony beat up anyone who made fun of Nikki.

"Since when do you care about me flirting with girls in front of you?" Anthony asked, folding his arms.

"Since it's Ty. Find me someone like her, and you can make out with her all you want."

"I'll make out with her all I want anyway," Anthony pointed out, his temper rising again. *Sheesh, get a grip, Rocket. He's joking.* But these jokes hit too close to home, and David should know that. Ty was different. Ty. Was. Different.

"Hey, can you eat and walk?" she asked.

"Sure. Why?" Anthony lifted his backpack from the ground while still holding his lasagna.

"You can walk me home. I've got a ton of homework, and we can be alone." She wiggled her eyebrows, trying to make light of the situation.

"Okay." He nodded at David as they headed out. "See you later."

David nodded back but didn't say anything.

"I'm sorry," Ty mumbled when they walked out of the house. "I shouldn't . . ."

She got it. She knew what his remarks were all about. It sent jolts of shame through Anthony. How could he think she'd pass him over so easily? Because she gave David food? Of course, now that they'd left his charming best friend behind, Anthony could think without a fog of jealousy swaying him.

"Shouldn't what?" he asked and jabbed a big bite of food into his mouth. The sooner he finished the sooner he could hold Ty's hand.

"David can be kind of flirty sometimes. I shouldn't encourage him. I'm sorry."

Encourage him? Anthony would take another deep breath but he'd choke on the lasagna. That would be a big waste of great food. "He doesn't need to be encouraged. He just does it," he answered.

She put her arm around his back, walking close. "Yeah. And really, it's flattering that you care. It means you're serious about me."

He laughed at the pink spreading across her cheeks. "Wait. You're just now figuring that out? I thought telling everyone on Facebook would clench it for you. In fact, I kind of counted on it."

"Of course I know." The pink color deepened to red. "And I am too. Of course."

"Of course." He shoved more food in, his mood lightened—though he didn't know why he let it darken in the first place. "I can tell by the food you feed me. You're a wonder."

"Rosie helped."

"So you're saying I should date both of you?"

Ty looked frightened for a second. "Oh, please no. She'd like that way too much."

He handed her back the empty plastic container and waited while she stuffed it into her backpack. Then he snatched her hand. "What girl wouldn't?"

"You're so full of it."

He rubbed his stomach. "Actually, no. Not quite enough. Next time, if you're going to give away your half of the food, save it for me."

"Half?" She laughed. "Okay. Next time I'll bring the whole pan for you. Hope that hearty sauce doesn't weigh you down tonight."

"Never." Her apartment was empty, so they cuddled on the couch and did homework. The time for him to leave came too soon.

She walked him to the door. "Good luck tonight."

"You'll be there, right? I'll have all the luck I need." He kept his fingers laced through hers.

"And how do you explain winning all those games before you started dating me?"

He laughed mischievously. "You were at all those games too, and we both know it."

"Not all of them."

"But you've watched all of them."

"It's possible."

"Name the last time you missed one of my games." Anthony couldn't help that he enjoyed hearing how obsessed she was.

"I refuse." She scrunched her nose at him. "And before you embarrass me further, I'm kicking you out. I might even stay home tonight." She started to shut the door.

Anthony jerked her back toward him, staring down hard at her. "Don't you dare stay away tonight. You've already jinxed me. Now you need to show up for luck to make up for it."

And then he insisted on a good-luck kiss before he left her apartment with a big grin on his face and not a smidge of jealousy (or hearty sauce) weighing him down.

Chapter Eighteen

"THESE ARE AWESOME SEATS, TY." Walsh stared wide-eyed at the field.

"Anthony helped me get them."

"Of course." Walsh's smile stretched from ear to ear. "I brought my binoculars, but sheesh, I could make the ref's calls from here. I'm gonna take a picture and send it to Dad. It'll kill him."

Ty tried to take his phone. "Don't rub it in, Walsh."

Walsh laughed and jerked the phone out of Ty's reach. "Yeah, right. I'm so rubbing it in. He got his chance at good seats. Too bad he wasted it on a game other than Utah."

"You're a snot."

Walsh snapped the picture.

"Ty? Is that you?" Suddenly a voice on the other side of her made her freeze. Dylan walked into her aisle with another guy and sat next to her.

"Hi, Dylan," she said flatly.

"What a coincidence. Is this where you're sitting?" He looked at his ticket again, like he had to check it, but she'd already seen the confidence in his face.

"Yes. Are these your seats?" She waved mechanically at the seats next to her. She didn't think it could be a coincidence, but how could it be otherwise? How would Dylan even find out where she was sitting to get his tickets?

"Yeah." He laughed, not catching her cold vibe. Not surprising. Had he ever? "Had to pay an arm and a leg, but it's the Utah game, you know. Have you met my roommate, Rob?"

"Hey." The tall, skinny guy reached across Dylan to shake Ty's hand. Did he look uncomfortable, or had she imagined it?

"Hi." She shook it briefly before dropping it.

"Ty, look. There's Anthony." Walsh elbowed her and pointed onto the field before waving frantically. Anthony rewarded him by waving back and giving Ty a thumbs up. She glanced at Dylan. Would Anthony recognize him? She hoped not. Anthony went right back to practicing, and she breathed a sigh of relief. How stupid of her to think he'd do something. Like he would charge the stands right before a football game. He had other things on his mind, other than her even. The brief acknowledgment more than thrilled her.

"What? He's not going to blow you kisses or something?" Walsh teased.

"Funny, Walsh. I bet if you blow kisses to us in your next game, he'll do it too."

"It's on," Walsh said. He looked at Dylan and then bent closer to Ty. "Is that the creep you told me about? The one Anthony told to stay away from you?" he whispered.

Obviously Walsh had noticed her attitude toward the newcomers. She nodded.

"What's he doing here, sitting next to you?"

"Coincidence, I guess. I don't know how else he'd be there."

Walsh pressed his lips together and clenched his jaw but didn't reply. An arm snaking around her shoulders turned her attention away from her brother.

"So," Dylan said, stretching his legs out in front of him as much as he could. "You think our Cougs are going to win this thing?"

Ty remained stiff as a board, wondering how to get out of Dylan's grasp. Her heart thumped unsteadily. Would Anthony blame her if she ditched these tickets for something far away from Dylan? Like outside-the-stadium far away? Walsh would sure blame her.

"Of course," she answered. She bent forward; it was the best she could do to get away under the circumstances.

"Dude," Walsh cut across her, glaring at Dylan. "You know my sister's boyfriend is like three times your size, right?"

Dylan jerked his arm back and scowled. "What's your problem?"

Ty bit her lip to hide laughter as Walsh leaned forward. Even sitting, it was easy to tell he was also like three times Dylan's size.

"Nothing . . . yet," Walsh said.

Turning her back on Dylan, Ty grinned at Walsh. "You are the best brother ever," she said under her breath.

"Maybe we should switch seats," Walsh suggested.

She hesitated. It wasn't nice, but Dylan scared her. "Okay." She stood and let Walsh scoot behind her into the seat. She braved a peek at Dylan's face. The scary look from their date was nothing compared to the glare now. She turned away.

With Walsh in between them, Dylan didn't say anything to her during the entire first half. Ty wasn't paying attention anyway. Anthony was having a great game. He ran so much that Beast and the other receivers would be lucky to get fifty yards. Anthony found every tiny hole in the Utah defense. Plus, she got a kick out of Walsh's wild cheering for Anthony. He was probably the only one in the stadium calling the star quarterback by his given name when he cheered. So endearing.

She escaped to the bathroom during halftime, and it didn't surprise her that Dylan walked out behind her. She ignored him on the way up the stairs toward the crowded concourse that held the restrooms.

"Worried your boyfriend will see you with me and get jealous?" Dylan asked, catching up and taking her by the elbow.

She pulled away. "No. He's got better things to worry about right now; although, the way the game is going, he's probably not too worried." She forced a smile and quickened her step.

"If it was me, every thought would be about you, Detmer."

She rolled her eyes. "Hmmm," she said, unsure how to answer.

"I'm headed to the concessions. Can I get you anything?" He forced her to pause by grabbing her upper-arm.

She winced and narrowed her eyes. "Not hungry." She tried to pull away.

"I'll get you a hot dog. I know you can't resist that at a football game." He dropped her arm and stepped into the crowd before she could answer.

Like in the restaurant, when he knew her favorite meal, his words froze her in her tracks. *Probably from Facebook or something*, she thought with a shaky breath. She turned and hurried toward the bathroom with a half a mind to text Walsh and tell him she was going home early.

When she arrived back in her seat, Dylan put the hot dog in her lap. She ignored the paper plate and stared at the field, wishing the game would end. It irritated her. Anthony helped her get great seats, and he was having an awesome game. Walsh was having fun. She should enjoy every second. Instead, she couldn't wait to bolt. But leaving early would also mean admitting later to Anthony that she didn't stay for the whole game and telling him why.

Why shouldn't she tell him about Dylan? Maybe if Anthony gave him a more forceful warning, Dylan would leave her alone. Sure, his protectiveness made her worry Anthony might be too forceful, but she'd insist he use words only. She didn't want him getting into trouble. She'd tell him the next time she got a chance.

"What's with this kid?" Walsh interrupted Ty's thoughts. He didn't even try to keep his voice down. Ty shrugged. "You going to eat that hot dog?" Walsh asked.

Ty moved to hand it to her brother. Dylan glared at her in such a menacing way that she pulled it back. "Yeah. I think so. Did you want something to eat? I can go get you something."

Walsh looked at Dylan and shook his head. "No. I'm good." He reached over, grabbed the plate, then shoved half the hot dog in his mouth, all the while glaring at Dylan. Dylan clenched his jaw. Fire practically jumped from his eyes, but he didn't say anything. Walsh finished the hot dog at his leisure, without another look in Dylan's direction and didn't talk to Ty about him the rest of the game.

BYU was up by three touchdowns in the fourth quarter and Anthony was on the sidelines, so convincing herself to stay was that much harder. Knowing Walsh wouldn't want to leave but would go in a heartbeat if Ty told him why, she kept her seat. She forced her cheers, and her mind strayed far from football, which unnerved her. She usually focused better during the games, but she couldn't help wondering how Dylan ended up next to her and why he was so obsessed with her.

That brought back uncomfortable thoughts about the way she felt about Anthony before they started dating. She took a class she didn't need to see him every day.

But she never forced herself on him. Never. Besides, her infatuation was long gone. She had real feelings for him now. And he wanted her around.

Dylan and his roommate walked Ty and Walsh to their car. Even though nothing she'd said so far had gotten through to him, she tried again. "Dylan, I thought I made it clear before that I'm not interested in you. I'm dating someone seriously."

Dylan shrugged. "For now, anyway. No offense, Ty, but we all know about Rocket and his dating habits."

She clenched her fists, determined to make him get it. "I'm serious. Please leave me alone." She opened the car door before he could say anything else.

"That guy is weird, Ty. Super weird," Walsh said when he climbed in. "I'm going to have Anthony talk to him. Again."

"Good idea."

* * *

Anthony threw himself on the couch, a grin plastered across his face. Almost two hundred yards. He was the best quarterback ever.

"Sure, sure. Sit there and grin." David sat in the chair opposite Anthony and rested his head back, closing his eyes. "After stealing all the glory."

"Can't help if it was my night." Anthony sat up. "Hey, was it just me or did I see Dylan sitting next to Ty at the game?"

David lifted his head. "Didn't notice. Wouldn't be surprised. Kid's got a problem."

"I thought he was leaving her alone." Anthony scowled. "What do you mean you wouldn't be surprised?"

"She mentioned she'd seen him a few times on campus." David's voice slid up in pitch, and he sounded awkward. He put his head back against the chair and closed his eyes—too tight.

"Why would she mention that?"

Keeping his eyes shut, David responded with a terrible attempt at nonchalance, "He doesn't go to BYU. Didn't you know?"

Anthony stood. "So he's been stalking her. And she didn't tell me."

"She doesn't think it's stalking."

Anthony wanted to lean over and poke his fingers in David's closed eyes. "How would you know that? She's been confiding in you." He struggled with the monster in his stomach, threatening to rise up and force his fist into David's face.

"Not exactly." Still wouldn't open his eyes. At least Matt had the guts to face him after Anthony found out about Keesha.

"What's going on?" Anthony demanded.

David sighed and sat up. "Listen. It's not that big of a deal. She didn't want you to get mad about it."

Anthony was out the door and stomping down the front steps, toward the street, before David even finished his sentence. He'd heard enough. If seeing Dylan around scared her, why did she always go to David first?

"Anthony!" David shouted from the doorway.

Anthony waved him off and continued stalking down the sidewalk.

"It's not like that, dude. Seriously!"

Not yet, Anthony thought. He shook his head. He shouldn't jump to conclusions. Maybe he'd call Ty. He yanked his phone out of his pocket. Almost one a.m. And besides, if he called, it'd end up like lunch the other day—he'd talk himself out of thinking anything was wrong seconds after hearing her voice.

So what was it? Was he ignoring the obvious or making something out of nothing? He sighed with frustration. He never saw it coming with Matt and Keesha. So was he missing something now?

Did he miss then what seemed to be staring him in the face right now? Ty had confided in David about Dylan since the beginning. Like how, when the kid had showed up uninvited at her house to watch a movie, she'd asked David to take care of it and never mentioned it to Anthony. And she had lunch with David a lot. Stuff stacked up in favor of her liking David.

But what about all of Anthony's perfect dates with her?

Sure, he and Ty had some good dates. What if . . . what if Anthony was a dream for her but David was real? From the beginning, David presented himself as the back-up for when—not if—things didn't work out, and who would've believed they'd work out considering Anthony's past?

"This is stupid," he said to the darkness.

He tried to remember being with Keesha, looking over his memories for evidence he should have picked up on, something to compare this too. But he'd blocked all that out. He could only remember the shock of seeing them together. Standing on the sidewalk ten feet from her door. Not moving even when she said, "Anthony. Listen. I wanted to talk to you about this first—I didn't mean to hurt you." Then he hauled back his fist and laid a satisfying punch right on Matt's nose.

Sophie Pope's face materialized in front of him—hers and a dozen other girls he flirted with, dated, then walked away from. What did Sophie ask him at that party? What did Ty have that Sophie didn't? He had a new answer now. Sophie couldn't hurt him. Ty could assassinate him. Worse than Keesha.

If I let her.

The thought startled him. He'd have to break up with her. A sick feeling pooled in the pit of his stomach. But it would be better than getting in deeper. Proposal deeper. Like with Keesha.

He couldn't do that again. He couldn't watch Ty fall for Beast. He wouldn't have the luxury of standing by clueless this time.

Anthony's feet dragged as he walked home, the euphoria of his awesome game gone.

Chapter Nineteen

Ty hoped she saw Anthony before she saw Dylan at church. She didn't know what Dylan would say. It could get awkward. Or worse. She scanned the students milling around and didn't see Anthony. Her heart sank.

Well, he would've had a late night. No one could blame him if he ran a little late for church. So she opted for heading straight for the classroom where the ward met and bypass any chance of encountering Dylan. Once inside she settled into the row she usually sat in with Anthony and his roommates. None of them were there yet. She smiled to herself, wondering how late they stayed up celebrating their win and Anthony's awesome game.

"Well, good morning. You got to church early for being up so late at the game."

She looked up into Dylan's face. What did he not understand about *leave me alone*? Hadn't she been clear? She hoped Anthony showed up soon. It would give her the perfect excuse to fill him in on all the weird stuff Dylan had done.

"You left pretty fast. We didn't get a chance to talk." Dylan went on like she'd answered him. She narrowed her eyes. For heaven's sake, of course they didn't talk at the game. She switched seats with her brother so she wouldn't have to sit next to him. How about her telling Dylan she didn't like him? That didn't count as getting a chance to talk? What did Dylan want?

"I needed to get my brother home," she answered shortly. She looked around, hoping her boyfriend—or even one of his muscled roommates—would walk in. Most of the students had sat down, prepared for church to start. Still no Anthony though.

"Listen," Dylan continued, bending over closer to her. "I'm in charge of this year's Halloween activity, and I could sure use some help with planning and stuff. Can I count you in?"

"I'm not in this ward."

"Oh, come on, Detmer. Just because you're dating Rocket doesn't mean you can't be around other guys. Surely he'll let you have friends, right?" Dylan laughed and shook his head condescendingly.

This was a nightmare. Where was Anthony? She looked around again. Two minutes until the meeting started, and he still hadn't shown up. Who would come to her rescue?

"Of course I can have other friends." She fumbled for more words.

He chuckled, and she resisted an outright shiver of disgust. How did he take everything in stride? She said outright rude things, and he steamrolled forward like she was flirting with him.

"Don't think you're getting off that easy. I'll keep at it." With a final laugh and a shake of his head, he walked away.

Ty breathed a sigh of relief. Half relief. He'd keep at it? Yeah, she needed to sick Anthony on him and make sure Dylan got the point. Part of her didn't even care if Anthony took a few swings at Dylan's face.

Just on time, Sean, DJ, and David slid into the row of seats from the other side. The bishop stood to open the meeting before Ty could ask where Anthony was. Besides, any attempt to catch David's eye seemed futile. He stared forward with unnerving concentration. What was up with him? Tired from the night before? Except, his unwavering gaze forward didn't strike her as sleep-deprived. More like uncomfortable.

Anthony showed up during the last verse of the opening hymn. He slid past her and sat in the seat next to her. He *did* look sleep-deprived.

"How late were you guys up celebrating?" she teased after the opening prayer, laying her hand on his knee. After the encounter with Dylan, she wanted him to wrap an arm around her and pull her close.

Anthony stared at her hand, looking perplexed by it. "Late." He turned forward.

She laughed softly. He was out of it. She leaned against his side. "Really great game last night," she whispered.

He nodded. "Thanks."

Poor kid. He needed a good nap. Hopefully the speakers wouldn't be too annoyed if they caught him snoozing. They'd cut him slack, she thought with a smile. Everybody watched last night's game. Rocket Rogers had almost two hundred yards running. Against Utah. He'd earned a late-night celebration.

Ty turned her full attention to the front. She'd try to make up for any lack of attention that might come from her row. She surveyed the others. All four guys stared forward. Well, if no one looked too close, they might mistake them for being interested. She stifled a giggle and grabbed a hymnbook for the sacrament hymn.

* * *

Anthony gazed listlessly at the Sunday School teacher, watching his lips move but not comprehending one word of the lesson. His mind was wrapped up in Ty, and not in a good way. Since his uncomfortable realizations the night before, he'd argued with himself over what course of action to take. The argument to get out now—and fast—was loud. And strong. He had good reasons to cut his ties now.

But thinking about losing Ty made his insides twist painfully. That was proof she already had her claws in him. He needed to break up with her, or it would be a thousand times worse.

She was oblivious to anything going on with him. Every time he looked her way, she smiled and squeezed his hand, his shoulder, or his knee. He'd give anything to know what was going on in her head. This would be easier if she saw it coming. She hadn't commented on his mood at all. He figured she would pick up on his distance right away, but she went with it all through sacrament meeting. He didn't want to blindside her.

Maybe he could just tell her they needed to cool it . . . Yeah. Right. He knew it wouldn't be long before he ended up right back here—in so deep he couldn't think straight. He closed his eyes. He'd made the decision to break up with her at least twenty times since last night, and he kept talking himself out of it. Was he masochistic?

He knew from the start David was better for her. Real relationships didn't scare David. He could marry her without freaking out about it. Anthony knew he would take months before even thinking about that kind of commitment. She probably knew that. He couldn't even take her to meet his sister without making a big deal. How long before she gave up on Anthony and headed for David's arms?

He couldn't stand by and watch it come to that.

A tiny voice begged him to think logically. To sit down with Ty and talk to her. Tell her he loved her—

He stopped his thoughts right there. Another excuse to get out of it.

He clenched his jaw. Enough.

* * *

Anthony was tempted to skip out of priesthood five minutes early and head home, avoiding Ty altogether. He couldn't put it off forever though. He had to be fair to her. He could get away with dodging her the rest of the day by claiming he needed sleep or something, but that would mean he'd have to face her tomorrow in class. Better to rip the Band-Aid off now, get it over with before he talked himself out of it another dozen times.

She walked next to him without forcing conversation as they headed home together, a habit they fell into since she started coming to church with him. Once they rounded the corner and were out of sight of the JSB and onlookers, he paused on the sidewalk.

"What's up?" she asked, turning to face him.

He let her hand slip out of his. "There's something I need to talk to you about."

Ty blinked then squinted her eyes "About what?"

"The thing is . . ." He swallowed. Man, the words were a lot harder to say than he imagined. He pictured himself blurting it out and walking away. Possibly sprinting. "Things are getting pretty serious."

Ty's face froze. Of course now she must know where this was going. "Oh?" She seemed to have to force the word out.

"I mean, you know I'm not looking for a wife right now."

She stared, standing motionless on the sidewalk. He thought she might cry. *Please, please, don't cry.* He didn't know if he could resist that. Tears might make him forget his resolve. Then she blinked, and the deer-in-the-headlights reaction disappeared along with any hint she might break down.

She laughed. (She laughed?) It didn't sound right. Too much air behind it, but she managed an easy expression. So what? Was he right? Was she waiting for this, for him to break up so she could move on without guilt?

"Of course not," she said. "Rocket Rogers looking for a wife!"

The way she said his nickname stung. "Right," he agreed, his voice raspy.

"But, uh—" She paused. Her smile trembled so slightly that if he didn't know every line of those lips, he wouldn't have caught it. She took a deep breath and seemed to power up her charming smile. Her expression relaxed, 100 percent, the corners of her lips even turned up. Like she could care less about what Anthony said to her. "But this was fun. Really. Thanks." She backed away, which was wrong. Wasn't that his move? Getting out quickly.

He hadn't seen this Ty for a few weeks, the one concerned about winning him over and keeping things shallow. He found himself wanting to see a little regret, something to show she cared about their relationship.

"Why are you doing that?" he blurted.

Caution replaced the lightness in her expression, and her smile slipped. "Doing what?"

He shrugged, already annoyed he'd dragged this thing out. He could be gone by now. She already gave him the opening to walk away.

"The charm. Like sometimes you're the real Ty who doesn't care what I think, and sometimes you're someone different, someone who only says and does the right thing."

She turned toward the street, away from him, and closed her eyes. When she looked back, the "other girl" vanished. She sighed and shook her head. "Guess I wanted to be the girl you want."

Her answer hit him like a three-hundred-pound linebacker. Yep. Those first few weeks they dated, and now, she acted like all those other girls. The ones that weren't concerned with *keeping him*. He shouldn't have asked.

He didn't know what to say. "Oh. Well . . ."

She shook her head, and in a flash that serious expression disappeared. She smiled, maybe it looked a little sad, but this one looked like she meant it at least. "No, really. This was fun. Thanks, Anthony."

And with a whirl of a long, brown ponytail, she disappeared.

Chapter Twenty

"TY!"

"Huh. What?" Ty looked around and realized she stood in her kitchen, already back at her apartment even though she walked several blocks out of the way. She didn't remember telling her feet to come here. She wanted to walk more. Not face this yet.

"Ty? What's wrong?" Rosie asked. She wiped her hands on a dish towel and came forward.

Ty noticed the warm, vanilla-chocolate smell of Rosie's cookies had filled the apartment. Rosie made fantastic cookies. She'd charmed a lot of guys that way. Maybe Ty should've made Anthony more cookies. A hysterical laugh rose up, but she swallowed and forced it down, burning her chest with the pain of it.

"Ty. You're worrying me. What's going on?" Rosie grabbed her arm, snapping her out of her reverie.

"He broke up with me," she said. She pulled her arm away and walked past her roommate. She didn't want to talk about this with anyone, least of all Rosie.

"What?" she gasped.

Ty didn't stop. "You heard me."

"How? Why?" Unfortunately, Rosie followed.

"Even if I knew, is that any of your business?" Ty's control broke.

Affronted, Rosie halted at first but then charged on as Ty tried to escape. "I thought we were in this together. I thought you asked me to help you date him."

"I asked you to help me get his attention, and you kept on helping even when I didn't need it," Ty shouted.

Why did Rosie have to act so calm? Her arms folded, and her French-tipped, manicured nails tapping against her elbows—like she was staring down a two-year-old throwing a tantrum, waiting for it to end so they could speak rationally.

"You've needed me from the beginning. You stumbled over everything in this relationship, Ty. Tell me what happened. We'll make a plan."

"No. We. Won't." Ty shook with anger. "I am in *love* with him, Rosie. This wasn't some fun exercise or dating makeover or whatever you thought you were doing. It was real. I am hurting, and all you can think about is what's the next step. How do you get back in the game? I don't think you want to get Anthony back for me. I think all along you've wanted to get him back for yourself. Well, lucky for you, he's single again. Go for it. Just get out of my face."

She didn't wait for a reply. She slammed her door with as much force as she could muster and collapsed onto her bed, where she stared at the dingy white wall six inches from her nose. What would her game plan say about this? *Don't let a loss affect the next game?*

She didn't know how long she laid there. She felt bad for how she'd treated Rosie, but she forgot about it when she started thinking about Anthony again.

"I knew this could happen," she whispered. *I knew it.* From the beginning. She said she would give it her all and walk away having done everything she could.

That didn't work though. One thought ran through her mind now: *What did I do wrong?*

Everything seemed fine. Great. More than great. They had that perfect date hiking the Y. There was that thing at lunch the other day, but it was like a hiccup, not anything serious.

"Did I miss something?" she asked the wall. *What?* She wracked her brain. This felt more like shock than post-break-up, not that she knew a lot about post-break-ups.

She took a deep breath. It surprised her when it shuddered, like something scary rising up in her chest. She lowered herself to her pillow, turning to face the other wall. For a minute she thought she might lose control, and she prepared to fight against it.

Thankfully, only quiet tears trailed down her cheeks. Oh, it was so perfect. More perfect than she thought it could be. She got her chance. And to say she fell in love with Anthony Rogers—that was something.

She smiled to herself. "That's something." She closed her eyes, trying to squeeze off the tears. She mustered up more courage to face this with optimism. "Heavenly Father, thank you," she whispered. It sounded pathetic, but she charged on, continuing in her mind so she couldn't hear her voice shaking. *Thank you for the chance. That's what I asked for. I got more than a chance . . . so, maybe . . . maybe this is how it's supposed to be. I can be okay with that. Just . . . just please* help *me be okay with that.* She spouted off a few more thankfuls and closed her prayer, the words "thank you for the chance" bouncing around in her brain.

* * *

Later that evening, Kayla rapped on Ty's door and said shortly, "Your mom's here."

"Thanks," Ty said. Kayla didn't answer. She disappeared into her room and shut the door. Frowning and knowing this treatment was probably because she overdid it with Rosie, Ty headed for the living room.

"Why didn't you tell me?" Mom asked and chewed on her bottom lip.

"Let's go outside." Ty could use the air. She led her mom out onto the landing and shut the door behind them. "How did you even know?"

"I got on Facebook to check his relationship status."

Ty wanted to laugh. It gurgled up in her chest and felt good. "I told you he changed it last Sunday."

"I'm sorry. I barely sat down to look at it." Mom smiled, but it didn't crinkle around her eyes.

"What did it say? I didn't even get a notification." So he'd already cleared her out, swept her away like one of the other girls.

"Says he's single." Mom reached for Ty's arm, squeezing it. "What happened?"

Ty shook her head and sighed, still not sure. The tears had felt good, and the shock had worn off, but it left her drained and feeling void of emotions.

"I don't know. One minute things were perfect and awesome and the next he told me he wasn't looking for a wife and things were too serious."

Mom rested against the railing outside the apartment door. "So he got scared."

"Probably. It's not like I said anything to make him think I wanted to get married or something." Ty folded her arms, feeling bitter for the first time. "Except one stupid joke. But it was a joke, and he knew that."

"You both knew that's where it was going." Mom reached up and stroked her upper arm.

"I guess."

"Well . . ." Mom hesitated. Ty could tell she wanted to say something like, *Maybe he'll come back,* or, *Everything will be fine*, but she couldn't. It might not be true.

"It's okay, Mom. Really. It may take a while, but I'll get over it. Like I said before, I wanted the chance. Just to see. And I did." She rested her head against Mom's shoulder.

Mom wrapped her arms around her. "It stinks that it was so good and then ended, doesn't it?" she whispered.

"Yeah. Totally." Ty actually chuckled at her mom's wording. "Stinks bad."

"It'll be okay."

"I know." Eventually.

* * *

Sunday evening Anthony got sick of hiding in his room. None of his roommates had tried talking about it with him, but he saw the pity in their eyes. He headed in the direction of his sister's house, calling on his way there. Nikki's phone went to voice mail three times without her picking up. Was she still mad at him?

Or was something wrong?

He dialed Joe's number. He picked up after two rings. "Hello?"

"Hey. Nikki isn't answering her phone." Anthony hoped he sounded casual. After the day he'd had, he doubted it.

"She's sleeping. I turned her phone off."

Sleeping. Nikki did that a lot when she got overwhelmed or depressed. "Is she okay?" He pressed the gas pedal before he realized how far over the speed limit he was going and switched to the brake.

"She's . . . fine."

"What's wrong?"

"Anthony, it's not a big deal. She's a little down."

Anthony ground his teeth together. "Nikki doesn't get 'down,' Joe. She's sick. She gets depressed. She gets panic attacks. Not down."

"Listen," Joe snapped, "I've been married to your sister for five years and knew her for three before that. I know her better than you give me credit for, and I've seen her through some pretty bad 'downs.' Don't lecture me like I just showed up in her life."

Anthony swallowed. "Sorry," he said genuinely. "I'm on my way over. What can I do to help?"

"Today's not a good day to come over. But if I was honest with you, I think if you brought Ty over sometime this week, it would help. It would show Nikki you trust her, and I think it would go a long way to cheer her up."

"Too late." Anthony sighed. "We broke up today."

"Really?" Joe paused. "Over this?"

"No. Something else. Have Nikki call me sometime, okay?"

"Yeah, sure. Sorry about Ty."

Anthony knew awkward silence would follow this. So he said, thanks, quickly, hung up, and turned the car around. Not back to his house and all that pity. He turned off University Avenue and kept driving.

* * *

One glance in the mirror and Anthony was prepared to skip coaching football on Monday. His eyelids drooped, proving he hadn't slept well for two nights now. She'd know breaking up with her ate at him, that he wanted to call her and take it all back, to heck with hurting later.

But if he skipped, she'd know too. He'd have to go.

Wishing he had more to study, he settled for flipping aimlessly through the textbook he didn't need. He watched her chair out of the corner of his eye. But she didn't show up. Was *she* skipping?

When Brian got up to start class, he caught Anthony's eye and then looked to the back corner by the door. Without thinking Anthony followed his gaze. Ty sat there, nose stuck in a history book. She mouthed the words to herself and ran her finger under them. He knew that meant she was having a hard time concentrating. She did that whenever she'd studied around him.

Anthony jerked his head back to face Brian, not bothering to scowl at the questioning look Brian shot him.

Ty darted out ahead of everyone when class ended. Anthony took his time gathering things and left at the back of the crowd. He pushed aside annoyed feelings that he was having to work to avoid Ty. That didn't happen with Keesha. They broke up and never saw each other again. Oh well. After a week or so, it wouldn't matter anymore. He just had to get past this awkward part.

"Great game, Rocket."

He looked around him, surprised to see High-Heel Girl standing next to him. "Uh, thanks."

"Sometimes the homework in this class is way over my head. Think you could help me out sometime?"

He stared at her. He had to get back in the game sometime, but not now. Not yet. "Uh, I don't know. Bye." He escaped before she could press him further.

At lunch Anthony sat silently next to David. His roommate hadn't said anything about Ty beyond, "I'd never date her now, you know." To which Anthony grunted an unintelligible answer. At football practice that afternoon, he took a deep breath of the sweaty smell of his teammates and breathed out all thoughts of Ty. Football took over.

They had Oregon State this weekend. He grimaced good-naturedly. No two-hundred yards this Saturday. David was going to get to shine. Oregon State had a good defense against the run. He'd have to pass.

"Trajectory passes! Two direct line, two intermediate, and two high," the offensive coach shouted after they'd warmed up.

Anthony gripped the first football, watched David run forward, and nailed a perfect short pass. He grinned.

"Back up five yards," the coach said when he completed the first set.

By the time Anthony had backed up thirty yards, he itched to let some balls loose. His coach noticed. With a grin, he nodded.

"Go long," Anthony joked with David.

David sprinted out on a long passing route. Anthony bided his time, waiting for the perfect moment. He shifted his arm back. Lined up his shoulders. Let the ball fly.

David looked back only once. The ball dropped into his outstretched arms. A pleased smile split Anthony's face. Perfect.

They moved through more drills. Nothing interrupted his concentration. By the time they got to a controlled scrimmage at the end of practice, his excitement almost rivaled that of the Utah game. No one could deny Rocket loved to run—maybe he was a little selfish—but he got a lot of satisfaction out of good passes too.

The feeling lingered as he and David walked from the locker room to David's car. Football. That was all he needed. He could get past Ty if he had football. His first thought of her in a couple hours didn't even hurt. He smiled to himself.

Chapter Twenty-One

Ty kicked at a rock on the sidewalk and watched it skid down the steps, stopping at the bottom of the stairs. She lifted the hood of her sweatshirt over her ears and followed the rock down the stairs. The chill in the air today bit at her fingers and the tips of her ears. She hadn't thought to bring a coat. Early October and she was already thinking of riding the bus to campus. It would be a long winter. She shifted back and forth as she waited at the crosswalk, her hands stuffed into the pocket of her sweatshirt. She should at least stick a hat in her backpack for days like these.

She wanted to get through this week so she could escape to her parents' and clear her mind. Like Rosie had done Monday morning—skipped her classes and headed to Logan. She'd ignored every text Ty sent. She knew she shouldn't have been so harsh, and now she couldn't even apologize.

This week ranked right up there as the worst of Ty's life.

A car pulled into the no-parking zone in front of the crosswalk. When the window rolled down, David leaned over the console. "You look cold."

"Thank you, Captain Obvious." She allowed him to see a tiny smile. Sympathy flashed across his face, embarrassing her.

"Get in."

She shook her head. "It's only four blocks. I'll walk."

"I'm going to stay here until you get in. You want me to get a ticket?" he asked. Still she hesitated. "You're telling me that because Dreamy was stupid enough to let you go, we're not friends anymore."

Sighing, she got in. "I won't go out with you, you know."

With his eyes on the road and a humorless smile on his lips, he answered, "I wouldn't ask, you know."

She stared out the window. "You said you would before."

"Stuff changes."

"Like my desirability since Anthony dropped me?" She didn't mean it. She knew tears shone in her eyes, but she didn't care with David. If Anthony had been sitting there, she wouldn't have cared with him. She would have told him she loved him, just so she could say it. So she could be sure he knew. Now it was too late.

David reached over to squeeze her shoulder. "Let's talk about something else, okay?"

She nodded and looked away. His phone rang anyway, keeping either of them from having to talk.

"Speak of the devil," he murmured. Ty knew it was Anthony on the phone. She sniffed and cursed herself for getting into David's car in the first place.

"Yeah, sure. No problem. On my way. Yup. Later." He hung up after a short conversation.

"You missed 300 East." She pointed.

"I know. I have to go do something for Anthony first."

"Please tell me you're not trying to hook me back up with him. That would be awkward and painful."

"Nope. His sister, Nikki, needs some help, and he has to go take a test he put off till the last minute. It won't take very long." He pulled up to the light at University Avenue.

Ty put her hand on the handle. "I'll get out here."

"Yeah, that would make me a real gentleman, dropping you off three blocks farther away from your place than where I picked you up. Besides I need help, and since you're already in the car, it might as well be you."

"Help?"

"We're picking up some groceries at Sam's Club for Nikki."

Ty eyed him before giving up and sitting back in her seat. "Okay, but the last time I didn't get out of a car when I thought I should, I ended up on the worst date of my life."

David chuckled. "It won't be that bad, I promise. If we stop to eat, I'll let you get what you want." He turned and grinned at her, which made her laugh. And it felt good. They rode in silence the rest of the way to Sam's Club.

"I'll be right back," he said after he parked.

"I thought you said you needed my help."

"I will when we get to Nikki's."

"O-kay . . ." She watched him hurry inside.

He returned in under ten minutes, pushing a cart filled with groceries. She hopped out to help him unload.

"That was quick."

He opened the trunk and started putting the boxes inside. "Nikki orders everything online, and Joe or Anthony picks the stuff up for her. She, uh, hates crowds."

Ty watched David as she picked up a box and put it inside. "I see."

David put another box in before pausing and rubbing his chin. "Dreamy's going to kill me for telling you, but I need to warn you," he said, a nervous hitch in his voice. "Nikki has OCD. She's not just a neat freak, she was really sick when we were in middle school and high school, but she's been fine for a while. I mean, she's still different from most people and . . ." He sighed. "I'll let him tell you if he wants to, but he worries about her, and he's pretty protective."

That explained why he never introduced her to Ty. He was waiting for her to prove she was worth it first. Protective. Yeah. A hiccup—a cross between a laugh and what might have been the beginning of a sob, escaped. Protective. That was Anthony all right. "Okay," she said quietly, picking up another box.

* * *

She was glad David had warned her; otherwise, the pristine yard they pulled up in front of ten minutes later would have intimidated her.

The door opened before they made it halfway up the sidewalk. "What's Anthony's excuse?" Nikki asked. She stopped when she saw Ty, glancing at David before turning back. "We haven't met. I'm Nikki."

Ty's heart immediately went out to the nerves she saw in Nikki's expression. "I'm Ty."

The nerves turned into surprise. "Oh. It's really great to meet you."

"You too," Ty said, immediately at ease with the warmth that replaced Nikki's initial uneasiness. "I'd shake hands, but they're full."

Nikki laughed, which seemed to jar against the dark circles heavy under her eyes. She headed for the car. "No problem. Thanks for helping out. Joe usually picks it up, but he got stuck at work. Where's Bum Face?"

Ty halted on the steps. "Bum Face?"

"Anthony," David said, walking past her into the house. "He had a test he couldn't put off."

For the second time that day, Ty laughed genuinely again. "Of all the nicknames, why didn't anyone tell me about that one?"

Nikki joined her on the steps. "I trust now you know, you'll make me proud by using it as often as possible."

For a moment, Ty had forgotten about breaking up with Anthony. She colored. "Not sure I'll have the chance now." She followed Nikki inside.

"We'll see," Nikki said.

Ty paused inside the doorway. She hadn't known what to expect of Nikki's house. Nothing out of place, but Ty liked it. Pretty baskets lined the bookshelves, and the precise way Nikki hung the pictures made the room look like a magazine.

"How pretty," Ty said, leaning forward.

Nikki came out of the kitchen. "Thank you." She folded one arm across her stomach and bit her lip. "I know it's really clean." She shrugged, and her smile returned. "I can't help it."

Ty laughed. "Where did you get the baskets? I like them."

"Online somewhere, of course."

David had neglected to mention how cool Anthony's sister was. *Anthony* had totally neglected to mention it. "Of course."

When they'd transferred all the groceries from the car, Ty asked, "Can I help you put them away?"

Nikki opened the pantry, and the rows of cans, lined up according to height and all the labels facing the same way, didn't actually surprise Ty.

"I should probably do it," Nikki said. "I'm kind of . . . precise."

Ty grinned at her and started taking food out of the boxes anyway. "Will you come do that to my pantry?"

Nikki's eyes lit up the same way Anthony's did. "Sure. Anytime."

Holding a case of kidney beans, Ty came forward. "Teach me."

Nikki pointed to a row on the second to the bottom shelf. "There are already four there, so put three more in the back and tell David to take the rest to the storage room downstairs."

Ty ripped open the package and took out three cans. As she handed them to Nikki, Ty noticed her tight expression. "I should have cut it, huh? That looks messy."

Nikki's face relaxed, and she let out a sigh. "Don't worry about it."

"David!" Ty called. "Hurry!"

He appeared in the doorway in a blink. "Take this case downstairs so Nikki doesn't have to look at it any longer."

"Okay." David lifted the box and eyed the two as he left the room with a small smile. "Just so you know," he said over his shoulder, "Nikki will probably come downstairs and cut away the messy part of the plastic as soon as you leave."

Ty turned back to Nikki, wondering how she'd take the lighthearted teasing about her habits. She shrugged. "Yeah. Probably."

"Should I go do that now so you don't worry about it?" Ty asked.

Nikki waved her off. "Let's pretend like I'm normal for a few minutes. It's fun hanging out with a girl again."

"I'll do better next time," Ty promised.

Nikki smiled again, more genuine than before. "You're a quick learner."

"I try." Ty placed the cans, lining each of them up so they were in a straight line, and admired how each shelf was at the perfect height for what sat on it. "How did you get the shelves like this?"

"My husband Joe goes above and beyond on the little things." Nikki took a box of cereal in her hands and squinted at the highest shelf. "He knows I'll be okay if I'm as comfortable as I can be. That's why he doesn't sweat about there being seven of everything up here. Anthony always thinks it means I'm on the brink of another breakdown."

"Seven?" Ty repeated. She rested against the wall next to the pantry. "That's Anthony's jersey number. It has been since—"

"High school," Nikki finished, heading back to the table. "It was his way of saying he had my back."

"I can tell you're important to him." Ty frowned at the package of almonds in her hands. Why hadn't Anthony just told her? She would have understood if he'd said something like, *I'm not ready for you to meet her yet.*

"Anthony has seen me at my worst, and it makes him overprotective. He's a good brother."

Ty looked up to watch a soft smile cross Nikki's face. She had to admit, Nikki was a lot happier than Ty expected. It made the quiet way she counted everything endearing.

"You're really strong." Ty brushed Nikki's shoulder before making a return trip to the table for more of the food. "I think Anthony knows that."

When she turned, her arms full of three boxes of Pop-tarts, Nikki stared at her, her smile growing bigger. "I'm blessed," she said. "Blessed that my medications are working and that the impulses are manageable right now. I've been worse, and I've seen people worse. For now, I'm good, and I'll take that."

Ty grinned in return, surprisingly thankful David brought her. "And I bet you've got your year's supply of food, right?" she said.

"Close. I'm close."

"Hey, Nik, I'm here to do my part. Why's David still here?" Anthony's voice sounded from the front door.

Ty froze. Then, in an effort not to appear so affected, she hurried across the room, tripping over the leg of a chair David had pulled out to hold groceries. She sprawled on the floor. The boxes of Pop-tarts flew into the air and landed with a crash on the counter before tumbling off.

"Nik, what's going on in—"

Ty lifted her head to see Anthony glaring at her. "Hi."

"What are you doing here?"

She got to her feet, wincing at the pang in her knees. "Helping Nikki put away her groceries."

"Is that the next part of your strategy?" he asked. Her face drained of color, but he didn't notice. He kept going. "Getting all chummy with my sister?"

"Anthony!" Nikki gasped at him. Ty had to admit it sounded like a perfect mom voice.

Ty shook her head and looked at her hands. She didn't like seeing Anthony angry with her. She'd rather remember him in a lot of other ways instead. "No. David was giving me a ride home when you called. He asked me to help. There were a lot of groceries."

David came into the kitchen with two little boys in his arms—one that looked a few years younger than Harly and another just out of the baby stage. Both were giggling.

"Anthony," David said, surprised. His gaze darted between his best friend and Ty.

"You were with David, huh." Anthony nodded in a jerking motion. "Getting a ride home."

Ty blinked at him. Comprehension dawned. "*That's* why?" she said, wishing tears weren't stinging her eyes, wishing she hadn't said it at all. She liked the break-up better. She'd been calm. She'd kept it together. But finding out he broke up with her, not because he'd gotten scared, but because he hadn't trusted her—whole different ballgame. "You broke up with me because you thought I'd do the same thing as *her*."

Anthony swallowed, some of the anger died, but not all. "I was right, wasn't I?"

"Anthony!" Nikki cried again. She looked shocked something like that would come out of his mouth.

Ty held up her hand. Anthony didn't need to fight with his sister over a relationship that had already ended. "No. I'm sorry. I shouldn't be here. This is your private life, and I'm just a fan."

She walked deliberately across the room and bent to pick up the Pop-tart boxes. She didn't want to leave them there. And if she concentrated on picking them up, she wouldn't start crying all out. When she turned, Nikki stood behind her.

"I'll get those." Nikki took the boxes. "David, you should take Ty home."

Ty nodded good-bye and left the kitchen. The empty way she felt told her something. She had—deep, deep down—thought Anthony might change his mind. And now she knew he wouldn't.

* * *

Anthony didn't know what expression David would choose. It looked like a battle between confusion, surprise, and guilt. He ended up frowning and turning away, disappointed. "It was cold, and she didn't have a coat." He didn't say anything else before he put the boys down, both of them quiet and staring at the adults. "See you later." He left the kitchen, and a moment later Anthony heard the front door close.

"Mommy? Rocky? What's wrong?" Porter asked.

Nikki set the boxes of Pop-tarts on the counter. She took a deep breath and avoided Anthony's gaze. "Porter, can you take Eli upstairs to the toy room? I'll be up in a minute."

Porter nodded solemnly, taking his little brother's hand and leading him out.

Anthony rubbed his forehead. "I'll put the groceries away while you help the boys. Don't worry. I've helped you enough; I think I can get it right." He hoped the lightness would lift the mood of the room. What had David been thinking bringing *Ty* to come and help? Why not Sean or DJ?

"I think you should go home," Nikki said, startling him out of his thoughts. Her voice was flat.

He stared at her. "What?"

"Whatever she did to you, whatever you thought she *might* do, was no excuse for the way you treated Ty. Mom raised you a lot better than that. She'd be ashamed. I'm disappointed. You should go home."

It took several seconds for Anthony to pull together a response. "Nikki—"

"She was perfect, Anthony. You have—had—nothing to worry about."

He'd known his sister a long time. She was the queen of using as few words as possible to get her point across. He supposed it came from choosing her interactions carefully over the years. She blinked away some tears—man, why did she have to cry too?—and left the kitchen. Anthony had no choice but to do as she told him.

Chapter Twenty-Two

He didn't talk about it with David that night. When he got home, David was studying. He acted normal, if not a bit subdued, but he didn't allude to the scene at Nikki's at all. Anthony wished he'd forgotten it, but he knew that wasn't the case. Anthony went to bed fifteen minutes later with his headphones blasting into his ears. Noise. Anything to keep from thinking about what a jerk he'd been.

Whichever of his roommates organized the party the next night, Anthony had a feeling they'd done it in an effort to get things back to normal. He couldn't blame them. He hated the mood in the house too.

He wondered how many people at the party found it odd that he parked himself in front of the Xbox with Sean and a couple of the defensive linemen. More noise; no thinking—Anthony's theme for the last day and a half. They took up so much of the space in front of the TV that only a handful of girls could crowd around and vie for Anthony's attention. Flirting might distract him, but he was smart enough to know they'd disappoint him right now.

"Hill!" Voices near the door pulled him from the video game. He looked up to see Brian coming through the door, high-fiving and shaking hands with a few of the players before he headed over to Anthony.

"Hey, Brian." Anthony reached through a couple girls sitting on the back of the couch to knock knuckles with his mentor. "Been a while since you darkened that door. Does Angie know you're at a party?"

Brian chuckled. "Yeah. She knows I'm here."

David muscled his way through the throng of people, a bag of chips in his hand. "Welcome back, Hill. What brings you our way? Some lame coaching responsibility? Did Anthony fail a test?" He still acted like nothing had happened. Anthony couldn't decide how he felt about that. Relief or wariness?

Brian's eyes flickered to Anthony, but he shook his head. "Nope. Thought I might deliver some news in person."

Anthony dropped his game controller on the table in front of the couch and moved around it to give Brian his full attention. "What news would that be?"

"Angie's pregnant." Brian beamed. "Just found out."

"Nice!" David pounded Brian on the back, and Anthony gave him a high five. He shouted over the crowd. "Break out the good root beer, Kaiser! Hill's gonna be a dad."

The room erupted into cheers. Anthony slung an arm around Brian's shoulder and chuckled as DJ pushed through the crowd with the A&W and handed the two-liter bottle to Brian. Anthony could use a genuine reason to smile right now.

With exaggerated pomp, Brian took the lid off the soda and chugged at least a quarter of it. The group around Brian, which was growing, laughed. More congratulations, knuckle-knocking, high-fiving, and back-pounding ensued.

"What are you going to do if it's a girl?" DJ asked after taking a swig from the root beer bottle.

Brian shrugged and this time held Anthony's gaze. "I've known a few girls that could hold their own when it comes to football."

Awkward silence filled the air around Brian and the four roommates. Anthony had thought Brian would give him a few minutes peace from thoughts about Ty. No matter how much he kept trying to push her away, he couldn't.

"It's going to be great," Sean finally said.

"Yeah." Brian nodded, his grin stretching so wide it threatened to spill out over his cheeks. "I can't describe what it feels like, knowing I'm going to be a dad. It's scary, but I know it's going to be worth it." He looked into Anthony's eyes. Anthony turned away. He didn't want a lecture on what he wasn't brave enough to do. "You guys would be lucky to find girls like Angie."

David and Sean groaned and shook their heads.

"So wise, so wise," DJ nodded and mockingly rubbed his chin.

Brian laughed. "I'm serious," he insisted. Anthony kept his gaze on the carpet in front of him, not even chancing a glimpse of his roommates.

"I've gotta go," Brian said, laying a hand on Anthony's shoulder. "Told Angie I'd only take twenty minutes to tell you, and I promised her a celebratory milkshake."

"Congratulations." Anthony managed a whole-hearted grin. "It's pretty awesome. Tell Angie too."

"I will." Brian waved in general at the party and made his way back to the door, slowed by more congratulatory gestures from those who hadn't been close enough before.

"Come on. I was about to win. Back to the game." Sean pushed Anthony toward the couch, not giving him a chance to think too much about what Brian said.

Not that the thoughts didn't hover, unwelcome, on the edge of his brain the rest of the night. It was like not trying to run against Oregon State. He knew, because of their ability to defend against running plays, he'd get stuffed up. He knew running would be useless and would only hurt the team. Like he knew Ty could do serious damage to him if he continued the relationship, so why go there? Why put himself up against that? He didn't take stupid chances on the football field. That got him to where he was now. Making smart choices.

But where had his choices with girls led him? Was he top of the game there? Sure, he'd dated some hot girls, but as he admitted to Ty, that didn't make him good at relationships.

* * *

Late that night, when the house emptied and Sean and DJ had gone to bed, Anthony and David stayed on the couch, and Anthony asked what he had to know.

"Did I miss something with Keesha and Matt?"

David looked up, startled. He hesitated before answering. "I don't think so. I never saw anything happening between them. Guess I wasn't looking for it though."

"And I was with Ty." Anthony sighed. "That's how it's supposed to go, right? You get flattened, so you get smart and keep an eye out so it doesn't happen again."

"Maybe." David cleared his throat and ran his fingers along the top of the coffee table. "Or maybe you start looking over your shoulder and playing tight, seeing stuff that isn't there and making bad decisions."

Truth. "Yeah," Anthony muttered.

Both sat there for a while, listening to the creaks the house made and the fan in the fridge turning off and on, before David spoke again. "Listen, Anthony. I thought you knew, but—" He sighed and shook his head. "After you went out with Ty a couple times, I knew you liked her a lot. I never would have gone after her, but I guess I kept saying stuff because I didn't want to scare you. She's special."

After everything, Anthony didn't know what to say. He leaned forward and put his elbows on his knees. "Matt and Keesha are probably really happy. I would have never wanted to take that away from them just to save myself the heartache."

"Exactly," David said. "And I would have never wanted to take happiness away from you." David left it at that and went to bed.

Anthony spent another hour on the couch contemplating. His mind turned to his mission. He'd come to BYU his freshman year as one of the top recruits in the nation and redshirted that year before his mission. He'd gone down to Guatemala with a big head and a cocky attitude.

He learned fast nobody cared that he could throw seventy-yard passes with precision or slip through a defensive line like a greasy pork chop. Nobody had a clue who he was, not even his American companions, more often than not. And to top it off, he couldn't understand a thing anybody said.

He started spending a lot more time on his knees. He figured out that if he forgot about himself, stuff fell into place. By the time his mission wound down, he'd looked back on those first few months with embarrassment at the arrogant kid he'd been.

That same kid showed up at Nikki's when he walked in and saw Ty there, sure she could only be there as a way to get back to him. And like it had Nikki, it embarrassed him.

How long had he been *that* Anthony, the cocky guy who had it all? Since last night? Or since Keesha? Dating right after he and Keesha broke up had been a relief, something to take his mind off his broken heart. Then it became a challenge not to get hurt again. Then he did it because he could.

He wanted to go back to being the guy fresh home from his mission with a love of Latin Saints and the ability to fall for a girl without second-guessing her. So he did what he'd done two-and-a-half years ago in Guatemala.

He got on his knees, and he didn't get up for a long time.

* * *

After the bell rang and Mrs. Frazier's senior American government class left, Ty stood and brought the worksheets to the front of the room. She took a deep breath as she laid them on Mrs. Frazier's desk. If she had the courage to stand up to Dylan and Rosie—and even Anthony—she could tell Mrs. Frazier how she felt about all the grunt work she had to do. Time to take Walsh's advice and learn to say no.

"Mrs. Frazier?" she asked to get the teacher's attention.

She looked up from her cell phone and raised an eyebrow at Ty. The five minutes in between classes was precious time to her. Her look said Ty better make this good.

"I think it would be best if I started interning for a different teacher. I'm going to talk to the principal about it this afternoon."

Mrs. Frazier gaped at her. "What? Why?"

Trying to summon all her courage, Ty squeezed her fists together. "I'd like to intern with someone I can gain some actual hands-on experience with. There doesn't seem to be time in this class."

"Honey, you need to let go of your illusions about teaching. You're going to spend most of your time grading papers and lecturing to fulfill objectives so these kids can pass all the tests required of them."

Ty pressed her lips together and nodded, holding her gaze on Mrs. Frazier. "Maybe. But I need more teaching experience all the same. I thought I should let you know."

Mrs. Frazier shrugged. "Fine." She went back to her cell phone.

Nodding her head more at herself than anything else, Ty left the classroom with a smile and went to find the principal.

* * *

One more day of coaching football this week, Ty said to herself. At some point the awkwardness would fade away. And maybe soon it would be like it never happened. Which was sad.

She tugged her hat over her ears and trudged down the sidewalk, knowing it would be a long winter—and the cold wouldn't have anything to do with it.

"Have you given any more thought to helping me out with the Halloween activity?"

Ty jumped so bad at the sound of the voice next to her, she nearly tripped. Dylan caught her by the upper arm, keeping her upright. "Huh?" she asked, shaking her arm free.

Dylan smiled. "Well, now that you don't have a boyfriend, you must have more time on your hands."

Ty didn't bother wondering how Dylan knew. Facebook? Word of mouth? *Watched* them break up? Who knew? It could be anything with him.

"Way to put it bluntly," she muttered, annoyed, especially since she couldn't text Anthony for a swoop-in-and-save-me-now rescue. Dylan's answering chuckle sent icy shivers down her back. Why her? Why couldn't he obsess over some other girl?

"So? Will you help me out?" he asked.

She would rather do a lot of things than spend time with him. "I'm not in your ward. I crashed it to hang out with Anthony. I won't be coming anymore, so no, I won't be on your Halloween party committee."

"Well, you still have friends in the ward," he bumped her shoulder, "so you're welcome to stick around."

"No, thanks," she said dryly. Go see Anthony every Sunday and torture herself some more? Yeah, right.

"I could still use your help. I'm sure you've got some great ideas."

"Sorry. I can't." Her downcast mood made it that much easier to say no. She picked up her pace, but he still followed her up to the base of the stairs on 800 North.

"What are you doing on campus?" she asked.

He didn't hesitate, but something flickered through his eyes. Suspicion? "Why not?"

"Don't you go to UVU?" Ty took the steps two at a time even though she knew she'd regret it at the top.

Dylan shrugged. "I'm meeting friends."

Sure. "Oh." Running up the steps might kill her, but it accomplished one thing. It left them both too out of breath to talk. When they reached the top, Ty didn't cut her pace. "See you around."

Dylan looked at his watch. "I'm early. I'll walk you to class."

She gritted her teeth. So because she wasn't dating Anthony anymore, would it be impossible to get rid of Dylan? How would she solve this? She contemplated how to take care of his unwanted attention. She could tell him—again—that she wasn't interested and to leave her alone, but that hadn't worked yet.

She couldn't go to David for help. Her last encounter with Anthony proved he broke up with her over him. She wouldn't confirm his misconceptions, even if it didn't make a difference to Anthony anymore. Maybe Sean or DJ?

Dylan put his hand on her back, guiding her through the students. She flinched and stepped away. He didn't notice. *Ugh. Ugh.* She shook her shoulders as though she could somehow shake him away.

"I'll still be around at lunchtime," Dylan broke the silence. "I'll meet you over at the Wilk."

Why did he assume she'd agree to anything he suggested? "I don't know what time I'll be able to eat."

Dylan folded his arms and smirked. "You eat at the same time every day. Noon. Between your coaching football class and your history teaching–methods course. Except on Wednesdays, of course, when you go to help out at your brother's school during your lunch hour."

Ty gaped at him. Her voice shook when she answered. "How could you possibly know that?"

"Why do you think your life is so private, Ty?" Dylan laughed and rolled his eyes. "You were dating Rocket Rogers. People talk about him. People see him at the Wilk everyday with the same girl." He shook his head as though it was nothing.

Her entire body went cold. She swallowed and saw her statistics classroom, looking like a haven. "There's my class," she said in a hoarse voice, hurrying toward the door. *But you already know that.* She didn't look back or wait for him to reply.

When she dropped into her chair, she took several deep breaths. Dylan came to campus looking for her. He knew her schedule. He knew where she went. He knew her classes. He knew when she ate lunch.

She should tell Anthony. Ask him for help.

No. He made it clear at Nikki's he didn't even want to be friends with her. She had to figure out how to take care of this on her own.

Two excruciating classes later, she headed to coaching football early. She had sprinted from one class to another so she wouldn't chance running into Dylan. Considering how often she looked over her shoulder for him, it was a wonder she didn't run into anyone.

"Detmer! Glad I caught you."

Ty turned around to see Dylan stepping into the empty hallway behind her. "What do you want?" she asked, keeping her voice crisp and cold.

"There's something I want to show you." He laced his fingers through hers and gripped hard so she couldn't extract herself.

"What are you doing? Let go." She tried to yank away. Why was this happening to her? Hadn't she done everything she could to get him the message she didn't like him? Why wouldn't he listen?

He ignored her and dragged her down the hall, stopping when he came to an empty classroom. He pulled her inside. In a few steps, they stood in one of the back corners, Dylan placing himself between her and the door.

"What are you doing?" The situation had gone from scary but solvable to downright horrifying. He looked down on her, his eyes shining with excitement so intense it pierced her. What would he do?

"I've been waiting for this chance for weeks, the chance to show you how I feel." He ran a hand over Ty's cheek and cupped her chin with it.

He'd watched way too many romantic movies. She gulped down the panicked lump in her throat, forcing herself to sound confident and in control. "I already know how you feel, Dylan. I told you before that I don't like you, and I asked you to leave me alone."

Dylan shook his head. "No. No, you need to give this a chance." He slid his hands down to grip hers—vice-like, claustrophobic, painful. He brought them up to hold against his chest in a pleading gesture. "I know we're meant to be together, Detmer. I know it."

She wanted to scream at him, but she knew she needed to remain calm. Deal with this rationally. The painful way he held her left little doubt that he would hurt her to get his way. *This can't be real*, kept running through her mind. *This can't be real.*

"I do not feel that way about you."

"You're just saying that."

"I'm not." She counted to five as she breathed in, then counted off another five seconds as she breathed out. She worked at keeping her voice steady.

His eyes glimmered now with something that looked like fanaticism. Ty'd seen it before but usually on the faces of over-the-top fans at the stadium. "Let me show you how I can love you so much better than Rocket. He didn't deserve you. I do."

Before she could respond, his lips assaulted hers. She wanted to gag. She wanted to laugh. She wanted to cry. The situation was ludicrous and frightening at the same time. It felt more like Dylan was trying to eat her than kiss her.

His body pinned hers against the wall. His hands were still locked in a death grip over her fingers, holding them against her sides. He had one of his legs pressed against hers. It left only one of her legs free. With all the force she could muster from her position—it wasn't much—she drilled her knee into his thigh.

Dylan gasped, his heated breath washing over her face. She gagged but didn't waste time. She used the same leg to sweep his legs out from under him. He had to let go of her hands to catch himself against the wall, trapping her still by placing them on either side of her shoulders. She pushed against his chest, moving him enough to get away and bolt for the door.

He snagged her hand. "Detmer," he gasped, "wait. Let me show you."

She yanked down, dislodging his grip, and threw herself at the classroom door. She ripped it open, praying she could stay one step ahead of him as she rushed down the hall. If he caught her again, how far would he go to show her his "love?"

"Detmer!"

She burst through the door, wiping at her mouth with the sleeve of her shirt over and over again until it rubbed raw at her cheeks. Sunlight filtered through the door at the end of the hall, leading outside. She sprinted to it.

Dylan's footsteps caught up with her as she reached the door. She felt his hand grab at her shirt, trying to pull her back to him. Once she had the door open, though, she saw Anthony, and she knew she'd be safe.

She just had to get to him.

Chapter Twenty-Three

"ANTHONY!"

Only one girl called him that, so the shrill voice made his head snap up. Ty sprinted down the sidewalk toward him from the RB. Where was she going? Why was she running *away* from class?

Why was she running at him?

"What's going on?" David asked from beside him.

Before Anthony even processed what he was doing, he moved toward her, holding out his arm for her.

Then he spotted the figure hurtling after her: Dylan, face red, arms extended. Ty was leaving him in the dust. Why was he chasing her?

She reached Anthony. With a sweep of his arm, he placed her protectively behind him. He registered that David had stepped up next to him. Anthony heard her breathless gasp from behind him.

"Help me."

Dylan didn't seem to notice the obstacles now between him and Ty. He still barreled toward them, full tilt. Anthony reacted as he did to any oncoming threat. He lowered his shoulder.

Dylan hadn't even slowed when he hit Anthony. The force knocked Dylan flat on the ground, where he lay, shocked and gasping for breath. Fury kicked up from Anthony's chest.

"What happened?" he shouted, looking between Ty and Dylan, forgetting he'd broken up with her five days ago, forgetting he'd accused her of using his sister, needing to protect her.

Students had started to form a circle around the group. Ty's face was pasty-white, except her lips, which glowed bright red. But she tipped her head back and closed her eyes. A long, relieved breath rushed out. "He kissed me," she said.

Anthony had to press his fists against his sides to stop the anger that erupted. David put a hand on his shoulder. Anthony nodded at him, taking several breaths in an effort to calm down.

How dare Dylan touch her? Whether or not Anthony was ready to take the risk of loving Ty, no one could touch her without her permission. He wouldn't allow it.

As calmly as he could manage, he crouched next to Dylan's still-prone figure. "Do not ever come near Ty again. Ever. Or I will personally make sure you can't. By whatever means necessary."

Dylan stared at him, defiance draining away from his expression, leaving an ashen face and trembling chin.

"I'm taking Ty to the campus police later, so coming near her again will most likely get you arrested. You better take it seriously."

Dylan nodded.

"Are you sure you understand?" Anthony used a low, rasping voice that worked for Coach.

Dylan nodded and coughed.

"Don't even look at her."

He nodded again.

Anthony leaned even closer, lowering his voice more. "If I even see you on this campus, I won't stop to ask questions."

Dylan looked terrified. He nodded.

"Good."

Anthony stood back up and looked at Ty.

She stepped toward him. "Thank you, Anthony," she whispered. "That was . . ." She looked at Dylan. "Nice." She rested her hand against his face and gave him a peck on the cheek. For a brief moment, she let her fingers linger. "Let's go to class."

* * *

After class they walked to the Wilk to have lunch together so Ty could give him a full rundown of everything that happened. They'd only had a few minutes before coaching football started for Ty to explain.

They got their lunches and sat at their corner table. Except for the awkwardness between them and the fact that she sat a good two feet away, it was like old times.

"Before we get into what happened with Dylan, I need to apologize for the way I treated you at Nikki's."

"Thanks." She brushed his arm with her hand then pulled it back with a shake of her head.

"When I took Keesha to meet Nikki, she didn't handle it well. It was obvious Nikki's habits made her uncomfortable. She bolted out of there right after dinner. I hated that someone could feel that way about my sister—that someone I loved could feel that way about another someone I loved. I never took you because I assumed you'd react like Keesha. I was wrong. And when I saw you there, I assumed you did it to prove something to me. I was wrong again."

Ty reached for his hand and squeezed it, this time leaving it there for a moment (a moment he didn't want to end) before she pulled away. "I understand. Your sister is strong and amazing. If I was in your shoes, I wouldn't want anyone hurting her either."

"I should have taken you to see her a long time ago."

She laughed. "It would have been fun. It was fun."

"Until I got there and acted like a big jerk."

"You're not the only one. I blew up at Rosie this week, and now she won't talk to me." Ty unwrapped her burger and took a bite.

"I tackled a guy on campus earlier."

"He deserved it."

"Rough week."

She sighed, her smile looking worn. "Yeah." She took another bite, then said, "Have I said thanks, for saving me, despite . . . everything?"

"Anytime. Finish your burger, and then tell me what he did and if I need to go find him later and beat him up some more."

So the whole story came out. The way Dylan knew everything. How she'd worried, but didn't realize how crazy he was until today.

"Why didn't you tell me?" he asked, more exasperated with her than anything at this point.

She studied her burger closely. "I didn't want you to get into trouble for fighting. I've seen football players get suspended for stuff like that."

He laughed. Maybe because she'd worried about him; maybe because he'd feel too guilty about misjudging her if he didn't.

"You're too good for me," he said and meant it.

She shook her head. "I'm too much of a people pleaser—my brother tells me that all the time. I downplayed everything so I didn't have to bother you and convinced David not to say anything. I just wanted to keep everyone happy, and in the end, nobody was."

"You're perfect just like you are."

Her gaze snapped up, and she swallowed hard as she stared at him. "Thanks," she whispered.

"Can we still be friends? Even after I acted like such a jerk?" He didn't deserve it. Not at all. But she still trusted him when he'd given her every reason not to. So maybe she would accept that.

It took her a long time to answer, but she eventually nodded and said, "Of course."

He walked her to her next class and then called Nikki.

"Hey, Bum Face."

He knew when she answered like that she couldn't be too mad anymore. "You were right about what I did. I was a jerk, Nik. I'm sorry."

"You're a good guy. I'm sorry if I made you feel otherwise."

"I deserved it. Honest to goodness, I didn't introduce her because I didn't want her to react bad and hurt your feelings. It scared me she wouldn't love you enough, and then what would I do?"

"Because you love her a lot?" Nikki said, her voice sounding almost teasing.

"Yeah. Maybe."

"What are you going to do about that?"

"I leveled a guy for her today. What does that count for?" He found himself telling her the story about how he'd redeemed himself.

Nikki didn't sound as impressed as she should have been. "What are you going to do about the next guy?"

Anthony frowned. "The next guy who tries to stalk her?"

"The next one who wants to date her. What are you going to do about him?"

He took a long time to answer. "Level him too." He sighed.

"Can I give you some advice?"

"Please do. I'm surprised you asked permission."

"Ha. Ha. Just love her, Anthony, and quit worrying so much about everything else. It'll fall into place. She's not Keesha. She's going to make her own mistakes with you. You're going to make them with her. That's okay."

"You're so wise. Thank heavens I have you for a sister."

"I love you too."

* * *

As Ty stood next to the seats where she and her roommates usually sat in LaVell Edwards Stadium, she couldn't explain why she felt so calm. Perhaps because she knew Anthony had taken care of the Dylan situation? But it was more. When she looked down on the field, *far* down onto the field—man, Anthony had spoiled her!—and watched him warm up, the feeling intensified.

But it's not . . . we're not . . . She couldn't finish what they weren't. It didn't matter. Of course, the way he'd laid Dylan out earlier flattered her. So did the barely controlled way he breathed and clenched his fists when she told him everything at lunch.

Things would be okay. That's what Mom said. Ty believed that. Whatever okay was. She desperately wanted okay to mean that Anthony would come back to her. *Please let "okay" be us together.*

She needed Anthony. She needed him for more than protection, for more than someone who could intimidate Dylan. He had become her best friend, and as she poured out everything to him while eating her hamburger, she wanted lunch to last forever. So bad that it ached. And yet it soothed, telling him everything.

She watched him on the field, smiling to herself. She loved that boy down there. She couldn't live without him.

"Is this my seat?" Rosie asked.

Ty turned, staring at her roommate in surprise. They hadn't seen each other that week, despite Rosie coming home on Wednesday. She'd become an expert at avoiding Ty.

"Of course. Hey. How are you?" Ty said. And then they both blurted, "I'm sorry," at the same time.

"What are you sorry for?" Ty asked, shaking her head.

"I went too far, like you said. I didn't let it go when I should have." Rosie twisted a brown and pink mitten in her hand. "I get like that—my mom pointed that out to me. I take goals and wrestle them into submission."

Ty laughed then bit her lip. "It doesn't excuse what I said to you."

"You were understandably upset."

"Still not an excuse."

Rosie smiled. "It's okay. There's been other stuff going on with me too. I think forcing my plans on you was an outlet for that."

"What other stuff?" Ty asked, feeling even guiltier. Rosie had been there for her at every step—overbearing, yes, but there for her nonetheless—and Ty didn't have a clue something was wrong.

"Guy stuff." Rosie's shoulders slumped.

"Cameron?" Ty guessed.

Rosie laughed and shook her head. "Wayne. You know, the TA from my computer class. I can't stop thinking about him. Isn't that ridiculous?"

Ty burst into laughter then bit her lip and pulled Rosie into another hug. "Tell him, Rosie. Don't let yourself regret this."

Rosie nodded and chuckled again. She turned her attention back to the glove. "Kayla said Anthony helped you out with Dylan. So do you think things might work out for you guys?" She looked up and held out a hand. "I'm asking out of pure curiosity, I swear. I won't try to advise you anymore."

Ty laughed. "I don't know. I really don't. Maybe we'll just be friends."

"You can't be his friend, Ty. I can see it in your eyes."

She sighed. "I know."

* * *

Ty sat on her bed that night after the game, trying to concentrate on her history of England paper outline. She was too buzzed. So much had happened that day, and to top it off with such an exciting win—a trick play got Anthony a fifteen-yard run into the end zone with less than a minute left—it all made her head spin. She looked at her phone. Only an hour since the game ended. Anthony probably wouldn't be home yet. She'd debated since she left the stadium whether to call and congratulate him. She needed him to know she didn't want to give him up, but how would he react? Push her farther away?

The steady thrumming of bass somewhere didn't help. She tapped her feet with the beat, wondering how someone was getting away with such loud music so late at night. It was almost midnight.

Then she realized it was coming closer to her and getting louder. Frowning, she moved to her window, staring out into the darkness. Nothing.

She went to the living room and leaned over the couch to peer through the blinds. She gasped and pressed her face closer to the window. Startled, she yanked at the blinds, pulling them up with vigor. A sea of blue uniforms with glittering gold trim greeted her.

"What is this . . . ?" She stared, uncomprehending as the mass moved up the street, closer and closer.

"What's going on?" Rosie joined her, squinting out the window. "It sounds like the marching band is playing right outside the apartment."

"They . . . are." Then Ty spotted the lone figure in the middle, still maybe a block away. He didn't hold an instrument, and he walked off beat. She must have been seeing things. She must. She hopped off the couch and rushed outside, standing on the landing outside her door.

The marching band moved in, pressing together to fill the street, the lawn, the strip of parking space between their building and the next. The band spilled onto the sidewalk and grass on the other side and filled up every available space in front of her. More arrived from farther down the block, and the band members in the street shifted north, making room. The sight was overwhelming, the sound deafening.

And Anthony stood in the middle of them, staring up at her. He held a piece of white poster board with "I Love You" scrawled in big, block letters.

She pressed a hand to her chest, thinking her heart might have stopped. He loved her?

He loved her!

Ty looked around. It was hard to believe this was real and not some dream. For the first time, she stopped to listen to the song, so familiar she didn't even think about it at first. "Hey, Baby?"

She noticed the neighbors standing on the sidewalks (where they could), taking pictures, pointing at Anthony if they could see him, and sticking their heads out of windows. Some girls in the next building leaned halfway out their window, swaying to the music.

She stood there, staring at him, the guy she loved, the guy she wanted so bad to be hers forever. Moving might wake her up. Here, on the balcony, it could last forever.

Anthony dropped the poster board and picked up a megaphone. Ty raised her eyebrows and giggles surged through her stomach, up into her chest, trying to burst out. She couldn't *giggle*. Not at an important moment like this.

"Will you come down?" he asked.

He didn't have to ask twice. The week she spent without him almost killed her. She rushed down the steps. Anthony was here. Anthony wanted her. Anthony, who wasn't looking for a wife or a serious relationship. Anthony, the guy who impressed her by changing his relationship status on Facebook, was proclaiming in the most over-the-top way possible he needed her too.

She threaded through the band, the music almost too much to bear now that she was this close. But she grinned, so wide her cheeks hurt.

Anthony appeared amidst them, much like he did the night of the party, the night he first kissed her. He held out his hand.

"Will you dance with me?"

She took it, her fingers burning at his touch, but it was a relief to hold them again. He pulled her close, so her cheek rested against his chest, and wrapped his other arm around her waist. His breath rushed past her ears.

He had to press his lips against her ears for her to hear as he sang to her in a gentle whisper.

She nodded against him, smiling and waiting for more. She had to turn and look up. She couldn't help herself from clamping both hands on the side of his face, pulling him down to her, pressing her lips to his with a relieved urgency. He held her there until they were both out of breath.

She held on to his face. "I love you."

"Don't stop," he said. "Not ever."

"I promise."

Chapter Twenty-Four

Ty watched the tall, blonde woman walk toward her, trying not to let nerves get the better of her. The woman carried Anthony's nephew Eli. A blond, even taller man followed. Ty's nervousness surged. She hugged her coat closer around her like that would explain her trembling to the fans around her.

The couple squeezed past a half a dozen people already sitting in their row. She took a deep breath. Anthony didn't get this worked up when she brought him home to meet her family. Of course, Anthony'd had Ty standing right next to him, holding his hand. Coward was down on the field now, getting ready for the game.

A line of six empty seats stood between Ty and the couple now. Her muscles twitched; she flexed her fingers. Tried to remember to breathe. Anthony said his mom was the nicest person he knew. And she raised Anthony and Nikki, so it couldn't be too bad.

Anthony's mom turned to meet Ty's gaze. "Hello!" She threw out her free hand and enveloped Ty in a hug. "Ty, right? That would be embarrassing if I got the wrong girl, but you look just like the pictures he sent—even underneath that hat. It's cute, by the way. I'll have to get one like it."

"Thanks." Breath rushed out of Ty when Anthony's mom released her.

His dad snaked an arm around his wife and reached for Ty's hand. "Good to meet you, Ty—right? Not TyAnne. He said you preferred Ty."

"I do." Little by little the tension eased out of her muscles. They were as nice as Anthony promised.

"I'm Tony, and this is my wife, Claire, but most everyone calls her Mama Rogers."

Mama Rogers pulled her into another hug. Ty's nose squished against the woman's shoulder, and Eli squirmed. "You won't blame me for thinking you might be something he made up, do you?" She laughed all out again—a laugh that made Ty sure she would love Mama Rogers, no doubt about it. "I've bugged him so much. Poor kid." She shook her head, but the mirth still encompassed her expression. "Is this your family?" She looked past Ty.

Ty pointed down the row. "Oh! Yes. My brothers Walsh and Stevie, my mom, my dad—"

"Vern Daws, right?" Tony Rogers squeezed past Ty and the others to pump her dad's hand. "Anthony told me you played with Detmer."

"Anthony's coming on the field, Tony," Mama Rogers reached over Ty to tap him. He ignored her, but Ty, Walsh, and Mama Rogers all looked toward the field.

"Is he gonna do it?" Walsh asked under his breath.

Ty laughed when she thought of their bet. "He won't let you outdo him, that's for sure." And she was right, Anthony turned toward them. Laughter welled up. Ty figured she and Walsh might be the only ones in the stadium who realized Anthony was pointing right at Walsh and not at Ty or Mama Rogers. Winking, Anthony pulled his hand to his mouth, kissed it, and blew it toward Walsh.

Ty and her brother dissolved into laughter. Mama Rogers looked confused. Joe arrived with Porter and a younger version of David. "Did Anthony just blow a kiss at Ty? From the field?" the younger boy asked.

Mama Rogers looked at Ty and then at Joe. "I might be wrong, but I'm pretty sure he blew a kiss at Ty's brother." She pointed. Walsh grinned proudly.

"A bet," Ty managed to get out. "They made a bet."

Mama Rogers and Tony both cracked identical smiles. "Nikki was right," Mama Rogers said. "She's the one."

At first Ty didn't know what to say. They'd probably already badgered Anthony about it though, so she didn't worry what he'd think if he heard them. She smiled back.

"If I can talk him into it . . . you better believe it."

About the Author

DURING HER EARLY YEARS OF reading, Ranee` S. Clark devoured fantasy books, and that continued into her adulthood—since she often believes that a well-written romance novel is a delightful fantasy. Though raising kids can sometimes hamper both romance with her own Mr. Charming and her writing, she tries to get a little of both in every day. And most of the time, she succeeds.